About the author
Colin Crang was born and educated privately in Kent and after a short term commission in the Army worked for fifteen years in the money markets in the City.

Wishing to escape the commuter rat race, he moved with his wife and young family to Devon, where he developed his interest in sailing and trout fishing.

Missing the south-east of England, after ten years the family moved back to Kent, where he became bursar of a private school for fourteen years.

Always an able sportsman, cricket is Colin's first love, but he also still sails, plays golf and skis when not devoting his time to writing. Written between 1993 and 2010, *'Heads Must Roll'* is his first novel and is set in the early 1990s.

First published in Great Britain in 2011 by Batson Books

Batson Books
c/o Touchstone Books Ltd
Highlands Lodge, Chartway Street,
Sutton Valence, Kent ME17 3HZ

Copyright © 2011 Colin Crang

The moral right of Colin Crang to be identified as the author of this work has been asserted in accordance with the Copyright Designs and Patents Act, 1988.

All rights reserved. No part of this publication may be reproduced or transmitted in any form or by any means, electronic or mechanical, including photocopying, recording, or any information storage and retrieval system, without permission in writing from the publisher.

ISBN 978-0-9568998-0-4

This book is a work of fiction. Names, characters, businesses, organizations, places and events are either the product of the author's imagination or are used fictitiously. Any resemblance to actual persons, living or dead is entirely coincidental.

Edited by Anthony John
Designed and produced by Sue Pressley

Printed and bound in England

HEADS MUST ROLL

COLIN CRANG

BATSON
BOOKS

For Elizabeth, Nicholas and Alison.

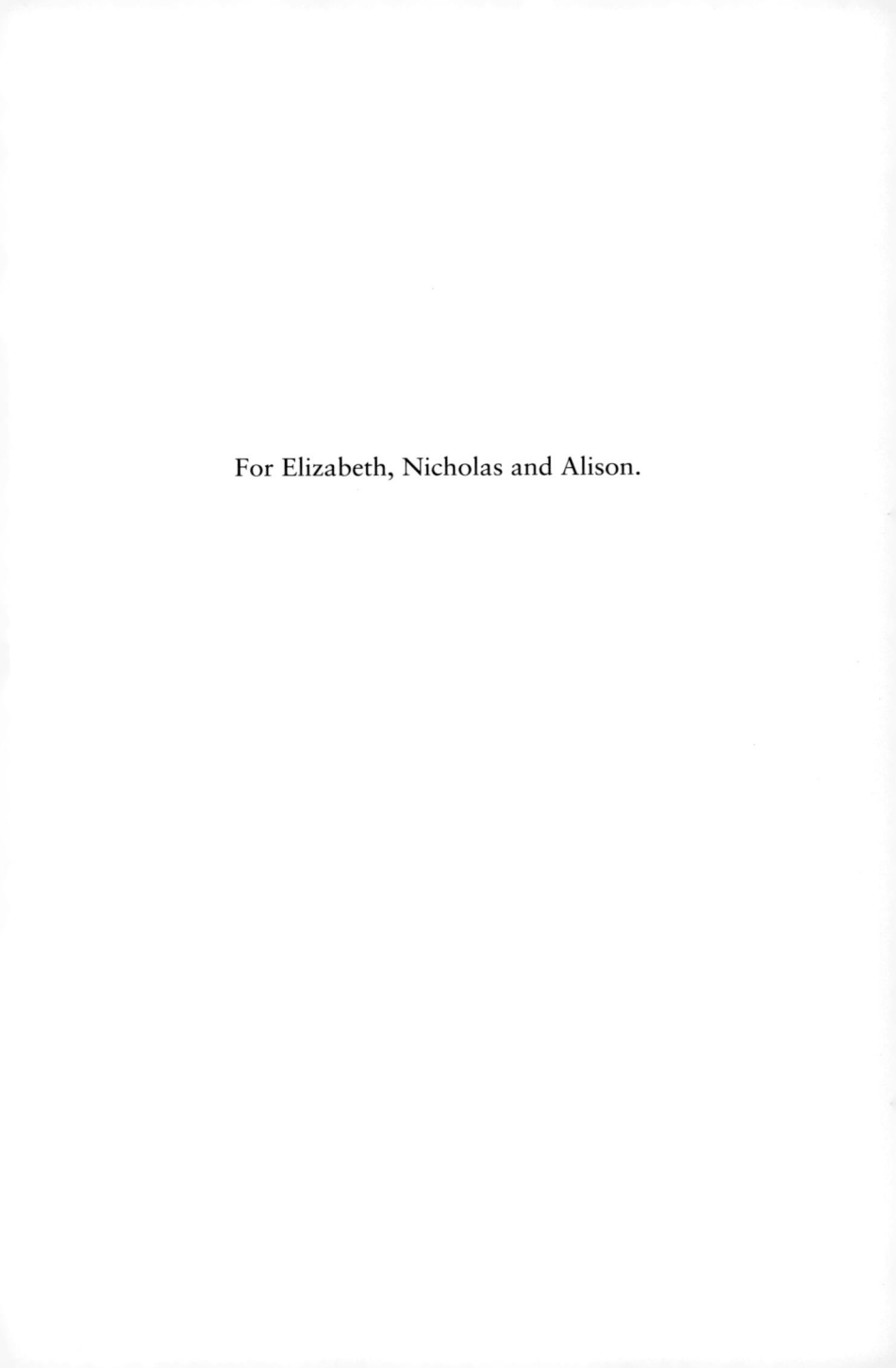

Chapter 1

It was unmistakably the Headmaster's voice. 'Well, I'm telling you, Bursar... if we can't cover the losses on those deals, then we're in serious trouble. Yes, you as well, because you're a signatory. That was the agreement... so if you don't keep your mouth shut, I'll see to it that you take the rap, and never get a job at another school. Do I make myself clear?'

The advice from the inner office sounded aggressive, and I was just raising my hand to knock on the outer door to avoid any embarrassment when I received a similarly curt suggestion.

'It says knock so why don't you bloody well knock? You're supposed to be a schoolmaster. Can't you even read?' The Headmaster express swept past, leaving me shaking and swaying like a suitcase standing too near the edge of the platform.

'Christ!' I muttered, sensing that this might be one of those moments for going to ground instead of getting involved in someone else's dramas. After all, I was only innocently obeying a summons from the Bursar to confirm my school accommodation arrangements and probational salary!

Aware that the Headmaster was highly strung and could be irritable at times, it nonetheless annoyed me that, because of this unexplained outburst, I should now spend the rest of the day fretting in case I should bump into him again.

I knocked on the Bursar's door with some exaggeration, although it was already ajar. I waited for the customary barked 'Come!', but there was no reply. Easing the door open, I poked a bit of my head round, half expecting to get it shot off.

The reason for the lack of reply was that the Bursar was unable to converse. He was speechless, his face an alarming crimson, and his overfed and gin-bloated abdomen shaking, as he attempted to stave off the approaching heart attack or stroke, which looked like being his next problem.

I had no sympathy for him. He was always bloody rude and made me feel like a lower-class irritant. I probably was, but I didn't see why this pompous, thick-headed idiot should make me feel inferior.

My immediate worry was the disruption he was about to cause my well-ordered day by being ill and by my having to pick him up or send for someone and explain myself. Fortunately, he solved the problem himself by recovering somewhat and slumping into his executive swivel chair like a grounded hippo, sweeping a pile of papers to the floor as he did so.

As I gathered some of the debris and started to replace it on his desk, he confirmed his regained state of normality by telling me to get the hell out and not to bother him with trivialities. As this latest piece of advice came in the form of a paranoiac scream, I was glad to oblige and fled to the common room, pile of papers still in hand, and keeping a wary eye open for the Headmaster en route.

As a naive and newly qualified twenty-four-year old, educated via the State system, I was in no mood to clash with the pillars of authority in this bastion of male-dominated autocracy called an English public school.

In fact I had been lucky to get this job. I had a good degree in history from London University but had had virtually no training or hands-on experience in the classroom. It was only my sporting prowess that had come to the rescue during my interview for the vacancy in the History Department.

They were short of someone to take history for sure, but at public schools sporting results meant a great deal, especially if a reputation for rugby or cricket or whatever was well established. Such reputations were hard won over many years, but easily lost, sometimes taking generations to rebuild. Many a father sent his son to a 'rugger' school, because he'd fancied himself as a fly half at his local club twenty-five years before.

Bradchester College was certainly a 'rugger' school, but had also recently broken into the jealously guarded ranks of the top cricketing public schools. I was therefore in luck. Apart from having played No 8 for the English Schools Rugby XV when I was eighteen, I'd also had a cricket trial for Middlesex after I left school six years before in 1985, having a brief spell on the ground staff at Lords, and a couple of games for the second eleven before being courteously advised to seek professional employment elsewhere.

The Headmaster had said to me, 'Carter, I can't promise you anything permanent as your teaching ability must be suspect, but I'm short in cricket and rugby so I'll see how you get on. I've lost my top sportsman John Groves with a spinal injury and he won't be fit for months. You'll help Peter Simpson with the first fifteen this term, and if your history allows it, you can take the first eleven in the summer.'

I'd jumped at the chance but hadn't forgotten his parting words: 'I want immediate results, mind... anything less and you're out.'

This had seemed perfectly reasonable, and as I hadn't heard from or had much contact with the Head for the best part of two terms and was still teaching history, I wasn't complaining.

I needed the stability this post might give me if I could succeed in holding on to it. My life had been turned upside down in my first year at university when my mother had been tragically killed in a road accident. My father and I had never been very close and it came as no surprise when he announced that he wanted a completely new start and had taken a consultancy post in America. He would support me financially through university and then I would have to make my own way. I was very upset at his decision as I had hoped we might forge a stronger relationship, but my efforts to persuade him to change his mind had failed. As I was an only child and had no relatives close enough to offer any support, my next decision was in effect an easy one. I would throw myself wholeheartedly into my time at university, it being the only form of protection I could look to during the next few years. After that, well, we would have to see.

Reaching the sanctuary of the common room, I sought out my mate Richard Pilcher. Richard had been at 'Brads,' as it was fondly known, a year longer than me, and had befriended what he'd described as a 'vulnerable individual' the minute I appeared on the scene.

I told him how I'd been bawled out of the office.

'Panic not till ordered,' he advised. It was an expression he used often, explaining it away by having a military father.

'Sit,' he continued, and I obeyed, feeling like a spaniel, while he removed the handful of papers from my shaking palm and placed them on the chair beside me.

I envied Richard his calmness, whilst being eternally grateful for it. He was one of those types who always seemed to be more than equal to the situation. Public school himself, Winchester I think I'd heard him say, he always treated impending dramas with a beautifully delivered sense of triviality. I'd often wondered whether any of it would rub off on me if I kept in his company long enough. 'No chance, old man,' he'd taunt. 'It's all in the breeding, you see.'

Mid-morning break was ending and I was due in class, so still shaking I started to make for the door.

'Don't forget your papers,' said Richard.

'Thanks,' I muttered, starting to worry again.

Realising I had under my arm the reason for another bollocking from the Bursar if I took the papers back to his office, I made a slight detour via the staff car park. Throwing the papers into the boot of my Fiesta and locking it, I made plans to return them later, when he'd gone home, thereby escaping a second dose of his wrath.

The Third Form were hurling bits of paper at each other as I entered the classroom. This was their normal method of preparing themselves for the life of pressure and responsibility that would be their lot. History droned on for forty minutes, but my mind wasn't on it. I was anxious about the papers that I knew I should return. The longer I left it, the more difficult my explanation would be.

I started to get angry again. Why the hell should I be getting in this state, when all I'd done was stumble upon a row between two people and offer to pick up some papers for one of them? Why was I the one to feel embarrassed when it was their bad manners and temper that had caused the damn things to fall on the floor in the first place?

The bell rescued me from worrying myself into a frenzy, and checking my timetable, I saw I was free until lunch. That would give me a chance to calm down a bit. Perhaps I could return the papers to the Bursar's office while he was in the dining hall.

I met Richard on my way to the common room. 'I say, old man, you must have really upset the Bursar,' he said, taking hold of my arm in a concerned manner. 'He's after your blood and no mistake. He's had the contents of your locker all over the floor, and when I questioned his right to go through a member of the teaching staff's private papers, he threatened to report me to the Head for being obstructive.'

'Christ,' I stammered. 'Don't worry, I'll take them back right away. It's just that I was so nervous of doing it in break, I thought I'd put off the evil hour for a bit. They're in my car. I'll get them.'

' What's in those papers that's making the man go bananas? Is he having a sneak preview of the A-level exam questions, do you suppose?'

'Don't know, but the Head was with him and they were having one hell of a row.'

Richard assumed his innocent expression, and I immediately knew he was plotting something. 'I think you and I ought to have a look at those papers,' he announced.

Being a well-built and extremely fit rugby No 8 means you're not easily physically persuaded to do something against your will. Richard, however, was well schooled in other methods of persuasion. He used all his wiles of psychological reasoning to overcome my protests and quickly had me agreeing that we should photocopy the evidence before I returned it.

'But there's almost certainly nothing in it anyway', I said.

'Rubbish. A man doesn't behave like that for no reason. What else did they say when they were arguing?'

'Something about covering some deals, but it could have been something to do with the school finances as that's part of his job, isn't it?'

We were at my car now and I felt powerless to argue. I opened the boot and handed over the few sheets of A4. They disappeared into the inside pocket of his jacket, and we made off in the direction of the Art Department.

'Where are we going?' I said.

'Arts. Jack's got a copier and lets me borrow it on the side sometimes. No questions asked. Come on.'

Jack Walker saw us through his large glass partition and his face took on an enquiring expression. Richard gesticulated to the end of the passage, waved the papers and gained the assent of the Art Master, who returned to the losing battle of teaching boys who did not want to paint.

'Now, let's have a look at these', said Richard, as he sorted through the half dozen sheets. 'They seem to be lists of dates and figures, with some sort of reference numbers maybe, and against them headings like copper, aluminium and other metals. Some of the other papers have similar lists, but with different headings – cocoa, sugar, coffee. Can't see much of interest here, but we might as well copy them, particularly as they seem to be the subject of such a hue and cry.'

I was beginning to feel like a criminal as I furtively glanced round to see if anyone was approaching. Richard copied away happily though. 'Bloody hell!' I thought, as he extracted the last copy, switched the machine off and whistled his way back down the passage. 'Where do you get confidence like that?' He cheerily waved the papers at the Art Master and tucked them back into his pocket. We crossed the quadrangle and headed for main school. 'Don't look so guilty, Alan,' he instructed.

'That's the way I feel.'

'For God's sake, saunter or something, there's a good fellow.'

On reaching the sanctuary of the male staff loos, Richard separated the papers into originals and copies, handed me the originals and told me to take them back to the Bursar when I felt like it.

'I'll keep the copies for the moment,' he said. 'I want to have a closer look at them.'

'I'm beginning to go off taking them back,' I said feebly.

'Nonsense. Take them back right away. The longer you hang on to them, the more you'll worry. You know what you're like.'

I did know and silently cursed myself for it. 'All right, I'll do it now,' I agreed.

I usually did what Richard told me, so on the way to my next class, I gingerly approached the main school office, with the papers burning a hole in my inside pocket. I wanted to give them back directly to the Bursar himself, as I felt the fewer people involved in handling them, the smoother their return would be. The trouble was, that to get to his office, you had to get by his secretary and a couple of accounts clerks, all of whom occupied an outer room. The secretary was bound to want to take the papers from me to give to him when he was free or when it was more convenient, and I was in the process of deliberating how I should play it, when things started to happen.

The Bursar's secretary came out of her door, and on seeing me, immediately back-pedalled and made what was obviously an internal phone call to the Headmaster's office.

I was just wondering which door to knock on when her shrill voice commanded that I go to the Headmaster's office at once. I'd barely reached the door a few yards up the passage, when the Headmaster's secretary, a thin, spinsterish soul, flung it open and ushered me in with the air of a priestess administering the last rites before my hanging.

'You're to go straight in,' she ordered with evident satisfaction, and I had the distinct impression that someone had been giving everyone in this part of the school a hard time.

She opened the inner door and knocked apologetically at the same time.

'It's Carter, Headmaster,' she announced, and I could imagine her thinking, 'And we'll all be glad to get you out of our hair, you little troublemaker.'

The door eased quietly to behind me, but to my trembling ears it sounded like the clanging steel gates of the KGB's Lubianka.

Duncan Masterton had risen from his desk and was standing in front of the window just behind and to the side of it. His hands were behind his back and he was making little swaying movements while silhouetted against the light. He had a habit of tightening and relaxing the cheek muscle on the right side of his face, making his overall expression difficult to decipher, and the fact that he didn't speak made me all the more nervous. I guessed he was doing it purposely to soften me up.

I tried not to think in such melodramatic terms and said, 'You wanted to see me, Headmaster?' There had been a little note in my 'Joining the Staff' instructions that stipulated that he should be addressed in this fashion.

Again he failed to communicate, and I started to look round his office to alleviate my embarrassment. There were the statutory photographs of wife and children, four of them, a boy and three girls, ages ranging from ten to sixteen or seventeen, a picture of himself holding up a salmon by a river – Scotland, I supposed – and a glass-fronted cupboard crammed with silver trophies, although I couldn't see what they were for. The room was full of high-quality antique furniture, of the rather ornate kind, with loads of inlay and gilt. The whole aura of the room was impressive and oozed the traditions of success that the school had inherited over the years. I couldn't help feeling that if I were a prospective parent thinking of sending my son here, I should be thinking... 'My goodness, can I keep up with this?' Perhaps it was my lower-middle class background rather than the overpowering, challenging attitude that the room emitted. 'We don't want your boy here if you're not already successful yourself,' it seemed to be saying.

The Headmaster's very being radiated success. He was an extremely confident man, in his late forties and possessing that unnerving characteristic of making you feel that he was too busy to talk to you, however serious the subject. I hadn't actually had much to do with him since my initial interview, but I'd heard that he was considered to be one of the modern breed of heads for this type of school – more of a public relations executive or managing director than a schoolmaster. The old-style headmaster who smoked a pipe, actually played in the common room cricket matches, had gone to Oxford or Cambridge, and was not afraid to be seen drinking a pint in the local pub, seemed to be a thing of the past. The competition amongst independent schools was so hot that every hour of the Headmaster's day was spent projecting the image and attracting the customers.

'Bursar tells me you've run off with some of his papers, Carter.' I was surprised he'd remembered my name and was taken aback by his sudden statement after what must have been thirty seconds of silence.

'By mistake, sir, I said, 'They fell on the floor and I picked them up and was going to give...'

'Call me Headmaster, Carter,' he interjected smoothly, 'You should know the drill by now.'

He took the folded papers and quickly glanced through them. Placing them in a folder on his desk, he motioned me to sit down in the chair in front of him. With both hands on the desk top, he levelled his gaze at me and seemed to be boring into my innermost soul as if his next comment would be life or death to me. I felt as if I was strapped to a lie detector, but his gaze was so concentrated and I was so nervous that the machine was bound to register a lie, even if it wasn't.

'Taking confidential papers from the office is a serious matter, Carter, and frankly I'm amazed that someone of your apparently dependable character should wish to do such a thing.'

'I didn't intend to take them out of the office,' I said. 'The Bursar knocked them on the floor and when I picked them up, he threw me out. I was so amazed, I left the room with the papers still in my hand.'

'That's not what he told me,' said Masterton, leaning further forward on his hands. 'He says you deliberately made off with them and what I want to know is why you should want to do that? Why should you particularly want those papers? What was so interesting to you about them, Carter?'

I was beginning to feel angry, and his intimidating attitude was encouraging me to blow my top. 'Look,' I said. 'I don't know why the Bursar should say that. It's quite untrue. I haven't the faintest idea what those papers are and I'm not interested. I've had the courtesy firstly to pick them up and secondly to bring them back to the office, despite the Bursar losing his temper with me for no reason.' I was amazed at my ability to produce such a long and eloquent reply, without my usual stammering and feelings of guilt, in the face of such provocation.

'You must have glanced at them,' Masterton persisted. 'Why was it so long before you returned them?'

I stood up and confronted him with new-found confidence. 'I have not looked at them,' I lied. 'Why should I? They're none of my business. I was so astounded by the Bursar's attitude that I didn't feel able to face his temper until things had calmed down a bit. That's why I've brought them back now and not then. I also had a history period to take.'

It suddenly dawned on me that he was interrogating me to find out if I'd read the papers or not. Why else would he persist with this line of questioning? It also meant that there was something in the papers he desperately didn't want anyone else to see.

'All right, Carter, don't get excited.' His voice held a less aggressive tone and he removed his tightly clenched hands from the desk.

And then I did a really stupid thing.

I was still angry at this uncalled-for investigation and, as I was fired up and had the feeling he might be going to back off me a bit, I felt like getting back at him and his attitude. So I asked, 'Why? What's so important in those papers that you must know if I looked at them or not?' And then I could have bitten my tongue off.

He put his face very close to mine. 'Nothing. Nothing at all, Carter. Why do you ask?'

'Shit!' I thought. 'Keep your bloody mouth shut.'

'No reason, Headmaster,' I recovered. 'Just that I resent this type of questioning when I've behaved quite correctly. I've told you the truth, and if you can't accept it, then I'm surprised, that's all.'

Masterton looked affronted. He wasn't used to being challenged by junior staff. 'I'll be the judge of that, Carter. And be sure that I'll be watching you. You'll keep your nose clean if you know what's good for you.'

The interview was at an end, but I was so furious at being threatened, I held my ground to have another go at him.

'That's all, Carter,' he said dismissively, and I thought better of it, especially as I'd gone too far the last time. I turned to leave the study, still bristling with anger and made for the door.

'Oh, Carter,' he said. 'One more thing. What were you doing in the Art Department with Pilcher? That's not on the way to your classroom, is it?'

I didn't actually stop dead in my tracks but was sure he must have noticed a slight pause in my progress towards the door.

'Christ!' I thought, 'What do I say now?'

My delay in replying seemed tantamount to pleading guilty. He waited for my reply with the hint of a smile.

'Oh, he just wanted to discuss something over there and as I had a few minutes, I went with him.' 'God!' I thought, 'That sounds pathetic.'

To my surprise, he didn't pursue it and to my relief I reached the door, to find his secretary had already opened it and was standing there, also with a slight smile of satisfaction.

I skipped lunch as I was feeling completely drained and lay on my bed in the small flat opposite the school that I shared with Richard. I needed the afternoon to think this thing through, but that wasn't possible as the first eleven were playing Haileybury and I would be expected at the match all afternoon. My job in charge of the team meant I had to write a match report and since the game had started at eleven thirty, I already had some research to do.

When Richard arrived after lunch, I relayed to him my ordeal with the Head, during which his jocular manner changed to one of uncharacteristic gravity. I was pleased in a way, because it meant he was listening to me, instead of sending me up, which was his habit. When I'd finished, he disappeared into his bedroom and re-emerged holding the copies he'd made that morning. He sat down and started to study them in detail.

'What is it?' I queried. 'You spotted something?'

He waved a hand, motioning me to be quiet. I got up and went out to make some coffee. 'I haven't got long,' I reminded him. 'I'm due at cricket.' Placing a cup in front of him, I sat down and waited patiently.

'Do you know, Alan, there could be something odd here.'

'What do you mean? Something sinister?'

'You say there was a row going on between the Head and the Bursar – something about covering some deals...'

'Mmm. The Headmaster said the Bursar'd be in trouble if they couldn't cover them or something. Why? What d'you make of it?'

Richard scanned the sheets again. 'I'm not sure, but I think I've seen these sorts of figures before. If I'm not mistaken, these are commodity deals listed by a broker, probably in the City. I remember going on a career visit when I was at school myself, and the commodity market was one of the operations we saw.' He leant back in the chair and closed his eyes.

'I don't remember it in detail,' he continued, 'but I think you can buy any number of metals or other goods rather like stocks and shares without having to pay for them at the time. Then you can sell them again before paying for the purchase. If they've increased in value, you're quids in. If the price goes down, you've only lost the difference, or something like that. I'm not too clear. It's a long time ago.'

'Is that what these lists are?' I enquired, impressed at his knowledge.

'Could be, but there's no name on them at all – no client, broker, dealer or anything.'

'Perhaps they're just for information,' I suggested. 'Like prices in the Financial Times.'

'They may well be just that,' said Richard. 'I wonder.'

That was all the wondering we had time for as duty called, and I made my way across the lawns to the cricket ground. Bradchester were batting and hadn't made a promising start. Seventy-three for four at lunch and now, with the score at a hundred and fifteen, we had just lost our opening bat, who had looked set for a big score. I sat down with the rest of the team on one of the benches in front of the pavilion.

'What's it doing?' I asked Collins, the captain, who was just out.

'Not a lot now,' he said, 'moving about all over the place before lunch though. In the air and off the seam. I guess that's why they put us in.'

'Bad toss to lose, eh?'

'Certainly was, sir,'

'Tell the rest to stay out there as long as they can,' I advised. 'No sense in giving Haileybury longer to get the runs than they need. And when they bat, keep the bowling very tight. Try to get them behind the clock and put some pressure on them.'

'Right, sir,' acknowledged the captain, and he went to deliver the instructions to his lower-order batsmen.

I strolled round the boundary as far as the line of poplar trees and found an unoccupied bench, one of those large garden ones that parents present to the school when their boys leave. This one had 'J. A. Bolton 1975-80' on a weathered brass plate. Looking at it made me feel suddenly under threat. The events of the morning seemed like an attack on my well-being, my reasonably safe job, and even my integrity.

I leant back in the sun and thought how much I should miss all this. I used to scoff at it when I was younger, cricket at a public school, the old school tie, 'old boy' and all that sort of thing. 'Them and us' it was when I was at grammar school. I didn't think like that now. It wasn't as though I were a convert, but that I'd discovered there were just as good friends to be made here as anywhere else, and that talent was really appreciated in an institution such as this. It had its bastards on the staff and amongst the pupils, like any school. The difference was they were cleverer and more devious at being bastards at this sort of place. It was the money, I supposed. If you had it, you could mix with people who were well trained at being evil sods, thereby becoming a more evil one yourself if you wished. Conversely, you could become better able to deal with them if you didn't.

'Good shot.' Enthusiastic clapping greeted a fine cover drive by Woods. I glanced at the scoreboard. 148 for 5. If we could get 220, it might be enough.

I didn't want to lose what I'd got here. Life was good. I was twenty-four. 'I had it all before me,' or so I was always being told. I wanted to make sure I kept hold of it and this morning's experiences were putting it under threat. I should talk to Christine about it.

Christine was my first what you might call serious girl friend. I'd never been confident with the opposite sex. I always seemed to get in with a group of blokes who attracted the party-going types – all going out in a group, getting tanked up, and going on to a party somewhere else. I had rather hankered after a one-to-one relationship.

I was amazed when Christine had showed an interest in me because she certainly loved a party and was in no way lacking in self-confidence. Just twenty-three, dark haired and not too tall, she had sparkling blue eyes that matched her nature, and a personality and figure that oozed femininity. It was over at the yacht club that I'd met her. Three of us had gone over by car in answer to an invitation posted on the common room notice board at the end of the autumn term.

'Laying-up party,' it had said, and not being familiar with yachting jargon, we'd decided it merited investigation.

I'd made my usual slow start to the evening, drinking pints with the lads and not having the courage to ask anyone to dance. I'd noticed Christine, however, and thought she looked incredibly sexy, but rather out of my league. I must have said as much to Richard because later on she came over to check some beer barrels behind the bar in her capacity as Club Secretary and said, 'So you're the timid Alan who won't ask me to dance. Well, I'm dancing with you, and as you're here at my invitation, you can't refuse, can you?'

'Definitely not,' I said, almost falling off my bar stool with surprise and excitement.

I suppose it was that she'd broken the ice for me. I'd never been able to chat up a really good-looking girl with any degree of confidence, always assuming she would have loads of boy friends and that the competition would be too hot.

She seemed to be reading my mind. 'Well, now I've done the difficult bit for you, did you really want to ask me to dance?' She was searching my face for any sign of hesitation. She didn't need to.

'Yes, I really did,' I vowed. 'It's just that...'

She put her hand up to my mouth to stop me. 'Don't!' she said, 'Just dance.'

Any feelings of inadequacy I had went out of the window at that moment. Here was someone who wanted to get to know me, however briefly, and I was more than willing to show how much I respected her for giving me the chance to reciprocate.

After the customary grooving about and generally offering one's hips to everyone on the floor except the person you went on there with, we found our eyes to be firmly fixed on each other – faces mostly – but I could be forgiven for occasionally dropping my gaze to her loins which she was gyrating at me in the certain knowledge that I was as randy as hell for her. Every time I looked up she was smiling and her eyes were saying, 'I'm happy you're pleased with what you see.'

Christ! It was a man's dream. This girl certainly knew how to make me her slave.

I decided to be a willing one.

After that, we danced close together and she looked at me and said, 'I hope you don't think I'm coming on too strong, Alan. It just seems a pity I shouldn't get to know you just because you're shy.' She pulled herself away a fraction as if sensing I might think she was a tart.

When the music stopped, we separated and to my amazement I reached for her hand to lead her off the floor. It was something I'd never dared do before, but with this girl it seemed natural. Her hand was ready and her eyes found mine and said, 'Thank you.'

It was then I knew I wanted Christine more than anything else.

More clapping interrupted my thoughts as our last man was run out going for an impossible single. All out for 228. The boys had done well.

Thinking of Christine had jolted me out of my morose mood and I felt sure she'd be able to convince me I was worrying unduly. I wouldn't be able to tell her about it until the evening although she sometimes came over to the school at the end of an all-day match, so at least I could say I was worried and give her the whole story later.

She worked as a trainee legal executive at a firm of solicitors in Thaxbury, the nearby market town, and it being a Wednesday she wouldn't get away until five thirty. She wouldn't get to school before six at the earliest and that would only be if she didn't go back to her flat in Thaxbury first. The fact that I was trying to calculate the exact time of her arrival confirmed to me how uptight I was about the morning's events. Even though it was only four o'clock, I found myself anxiously glancing to where her car would enter the school grounds and make its way round the long drive to the pavilion.

My attention was drawn back to the match. This was my job, I kept telling myself, so concentrate on it. If my position was to be threatened, don't let it be because of not doing the job properly. By tea, Haileybury were twenty-nine for one, and I made my way over to the pavilion and acquired a cup of tea and a sandwich. Out of the corner of my eye I saw the Headmaster coming out of the Art Department and heading towards the pavilion.

I felt myself go hot around the neck and shoulders but, as I turned to make my escape through the changing rooms and out of the rear door, my arm was held from behind.

'The team's doing well this term, I hear, Carter.'

It was Sir John Glazebrook, one of the School Governors. A kindly man, to whom I'd been introduced on the touchline at a rugby match in the autumn term. He was a keen supporter of all sport at Bradchester and his many contacts had been instrumental in the school collecting some prestige fixtures. Releasing my arm, he backed me into a corner by the tea urn.

'I'm told you're quite hard on the boys but they respect

you for it. That's rare for one so young. Groves will have to watch out when he comes back, won't he?'

'Well, I don't...'

He cut me short. 'I'm only teasing,' he said, with a mischievous grin. 'Keep up the good work.'

The Headmaster strode into the pavilion and his gaze swept the gathering of cricketers, parents and supporters like the beam of a lighthouse traversing the ocean. I moved so Sir John's frame was covering me, convinced I was the one being sought out.

Duncan Masterton, however, bathed in the glory of being a headmaster and succumbed gladly to the attentions that such a position brings. It was his job after all, and he knew he was good at it. He made polite small talk with several groups of staff and boys and captivated some mothers who had sons in the team.

'You hiding from someone, Carter?'

'No, Sir John. Sorry, I was just...'

'He shepherded me towards another group and just as we reached it, Duncan Masterton rose up, as if from the ground, barring our path.

'Ah, there you are, Carter. A word with you, if you please.' It was a command, not an invitation.

'Steady on, Headmaster.' It was Sir John who interceded. 'Can't keep a chap from his duty, y'know. Host to the customers and coach to the team, what? I say Masterton, what d'you think of Carter's effect on the eleven this term? Pretty good, eh? I was telling some of my people we're going to give Radley a bloody good hiding this year. What d'you say, Carter?'

Before I could answer, the Headmaster slapped me

heartily on the back and told him, 'Absolutely right, Sir John. There's no doubt at all we think he's doing a fine job. Results speak for themselves.'

I muttered my thanks and made my excuses in order to speak to the team before they took the field again.

'Carter.' I turned back to find Masterton's eyes fixed on me like lasers. Praise for my efforts was no longer in his mind. 'Spare me ten minutes tomorrow morning at eight forty-five, would you? My study. Sharp. I've a busy schedule.' His words were clipped and he dismissed me by turning away.

I was left staring at his back and stammered, 'Yes, Headmaster.'

I took what little solace I could from the fact that the match developed into a nail-biting situation. When stumps were drawn, we had nine of them out for 223. A drawn game and, as I shook hands with the visiting master in charge, I felt a twinge of disappointment at not having won. Nevertheless, it had been a fine day's cricket and I was proud to have contributed to such an event. I hoped I might contribute to many more.

Such thoughts sent my gaze towards where Christine might appear. There was no sign so I assumed she'd gone late shopping, been delayed at work, or gone back to her flat to have a bath before coming over. I was getting frantic for her help and quietly cursed that she was late today of all days. Half an hour later, as Haileybury's coach disappeared through the school gates, I spotted her red Escort convertible coming down the drive. 'Thank God,' I thought and ran over to meet her.

She had the hood down and the breeze caught her hair as she pulled up beside me, lifting it from the side of her face and exposing her radiant smile and excited blue eyes. 'Did you beat them?' she demanded, hoping for an affirmative.

'Draw,' I replied. 'Were you held up at the office? I hoped you might be earlier than this.'

She got out of the car, her expression changing as she sensed a problem. 'Something wrong, Alan?' She searched my face anxiously.

'I'm afraid so and, if I don't tell you about it, I'm going to be ill. I'm so wound up. Honestly, Christine, I don't know what's happening to me today. It's been one drama after another and I really think it could be serious.'

She put her hands on my shoulders and faced me. 'Come on, we'll go to a pub and you can offload it.' She had an uncanny knack of saying what I wanted to hear without making me feel foolish.

She drove in silence the twelve miles to the Fisherman's Creel, a rustic little pub by the river, not far from the yacht club. It was the perfect choice for when you had a problem and wanted to share it with one person. Despite its appealing name, it was rather run down so consequently not patronised by loads of posers from the nearby town. If you didn't mind a bit of dust and dim light, you could get a good pint and plenty of privacy. I was grateful to Christine for choosing this place and by the time we swung into the car park I was actually looking forward to pouring out my troubles.

Sensing I was strung up, she plonked me down in one of the high-backed alcove seats and made towards the bar. 'I'll get them,' I protested.

'Like hell you will. Stay where you are,' she ordered.

I obeyed and she returned with a foaming bitter for me and a half of lager for herself. Sitting herself opposite, she watched silently, staring at me with those blue, compelling eyes, as I downed half of my drink.

I told her the complete story of my day, from the moment I'd knocked on the office door in the morning, up to the time she'd driven through the school gates half an hour ago. I tried to remember every detail, including all my doubts and fears and the possible ramifications, and when I finished some twenty minutes later, Christine had not said a single word and I'd not drunk a single drop more of my beer. I sat back in the pew and drained the rest of my glass in one.

'Tell me I'm dreaming it,' I said. 'Or at least that I'm making more of it than there is.'

She still didn't say a word and picking up my glass took it over to the bar for a refill. I couldn't stand her silence. It reminded me of the way the Headmaster had subjected me to similar treatment that morning. I followed her.

'For God's sake, Christine, you've got to say something.'

She turned to me and putting her finger to her lips, collected my refill and motioned me back to the table. We sat down again and she took my hand, holding it for some time, never taking her eyes from my face.

Then she said, 'Listen, Alan, and don't interrupt. Let's paint the blackest possible picture first.'

I started to protest.

Her voice became more intense. 'I've come into this completely cold. You've given me the facts, and I'll sort them out for you, but you must let me do it my way. You're so stressed you can't see the wood from the trees, so sit quietly, drink your beer and listen.' Taking a notebook and pencil from her handbag, she fixed me with a slightly patronising look.

'Now I'm only thinking aloud,' she continued, 'but let's

assume for a moment that there is something in those papers that's so damaging to the Headmaster and the Bursar that their careers would be finished if the contents were ever leaked. What would they do? They'd have to prevent the information going any further. But before they were forced to take desperate measures, they would try to retrieve the papers without causing suspicion, and before the person taking them – that's you – took a look at them or realised they might be "hot property". That would be the time the Bursar tried to find them in your locker. Right?'

I nodded. 'That's right, and Richard said...' She held up her hand to stop me.

'If you came back to the common room after being thrown out by the Bursar, that could be when he realised the papers were missing. He spent say ten or fifteen minutes checking his desk and office for them, then put two and two together, and realised you must have gone off with them. He would have had about half an hour, while you were still in history, to check the timetable, see you were in class, and go and ransack your locker in case you'd put them there. That's when Richard fell foul of him. The incriminating evidence not being there, because you'd already put it in your car boot, he goes and tells the Headmaster, who puts out the word that you're to report to him immediately.'

She tapped the pencil against her teeth, at the same time gazing over my head for inspiration.

'Okay! So you'd both been to the Art Department to copy the papers and decided to take the originals back. It might have been during this period that the Head decided you might not actually realise what was so important about them. You said you got the impression he was trying to find out from you if you'd read them or not.'

'Yes,' I said. 'He seemed to back off me a bit at one stage, as if he realised there was no point in arousing my suspicions if I didn't have a clue what all the panic was about.'

She nodded. 'But then you say you got angry and challenged him about the contents of the papers and that made him nervous and start to pump you again.'

'Yes, and that's when he asked me why I'd been to Arts with Richard. Really threw me that did, I can tell you.'

'All right, you've told me that. Don't get excited.'

I grabbed my glass and drained it. 'I can't help it. Maybe another pint will calm me down a bit.'

I was already halfway to the bar, leaving her scribbling something on her notepad. When I returned, she was making a numbered list of headings. She again motioned me to be silent.

'So, if we're to assume the worst,' she continued, 'and those papers are dynamite, the Head would definitely have checked with Jack Walker, who may have told him that some papers were copied on his machine by you and Richard not too long after you made off with the documents from the Bursar's office. Then he comes over to the pavilion to question you about it, but can't mention it in front of all the people who are having tea, particularly Sir John. Right?'

I nodded, feeling depressed and wishing she wasn't so insistent on assuming the worst. As everything she'd related was perfectly true, I couldn't see how there could be any 'best' side to it at all. A morose feeling started to engulf me and I drank half my next pint in one, knowing it would make things worse rather than better.

'You know,' I said, 'I really wish I hadn't let Richard talk me into getting the papers copied. I knew it was a stupid thing to do, but he's so sure of himself and he's bound to bluff his way out of it in that cocksure manner of his.'

'All right, don't fret,' said Christine, scribbling on her notepad. 'It's done and you can't undo it.' Her mind was working fast, and I could tell that the atmosphere of a solicitor's office had certainly rubbed off on her. She was like counsel doing a mental sorting of the evidence while cross-examining a witness.

She tossed her hair back and took a swig of lager before returning to the problem. 'Now concentrate, Alan,' she scolded, her eyes dropping to her notes again. 'We've done the bad news. Now let's see if we can improve the situation a bit.'

I nodded pitifully.

'It seems to me you're reading more into this than you should. First of all, it's unlikely a man in Masterton's position would be stupid enough to get involved in something sinister. He's got too much to lose. Not impossible, but unlikely. Secondly, he's got no reason to think you know what's in the papers, or that you'd be able to interpret the contents anyway. As you say yourself, you haven't really a clue what the figures mean. Thirdly, if he did go and ask Jack Walker what you two were doing in the Art Department, and Jack did tell him you wanted to copy some papers, you told me Richard often went to use the copier on the quiet. If that's true, I'm sure Richard would own up and admit his guilty past, and say that this was just another of those clandestine visits. All it would mean would be a carpeting and paying for the copies he'd had previously. Surely he'd do that just to clear the matter up. The Headmaster and the Bursar have got their papers back and nobody need be any the wiser. You and

Richard will get a slap on the wrist tomorrow morning and that'll be the end of it.'

'But what about the copies Richard's got?' I reminded her.

'Just get them destroyed and tell Richard you want to forget the whole episode. He'll understand. It's your neck on the block anyway, and he knows how sensitive you are. I'll tell him if you like, but whoever tells him it'd better be tonight, so you can both spin the same yarn to the Head in the morning. I assume Richard will be on the carpet as well?'

'I don't know,' I said, 'Haven't seen him since lunch.'

'Well, one way or the other, he ought to be put in the picture tonight.' She threw her pencil on the table with a dismissive gesture, slumped back in her seat and polished off her lager. 'Now I'll have another half,' she demanded, sliding her empty glass across the table. 'And then, while we're in this cosy little alcove, you can come round this side and demonstrate how brilliant you think I am.' She stuck out her chin, looked down her nose with slightly narrowed, mischievous eyes and, assuming a wicked half smile, mentally seduced me in less than five seconds.

I felt a great deal happier now her post mortem was over and she'd contrived to make me feel slightly more innocent than guilty. I got her another lager and sat down next to her, knowing that her feminine wiles were going to compel me to pay a great deal of attention to her. That was the word for Christine. She was compelling. She could switch off a serious conversation like a light fuse going and demand that you made sexual advances to her by just looking at you.

I certainly had no problem with that, but I also greatly respected her many other talents, no least her ability to listen to and analyse a dilemma with a calmness and clarity of mind which more than made up for my own lack of skill in such matters.

I'd often wondered where she got these characteristics from and had once asked her about her parents and brothers or sisters, and was she in touch with them? That had been soon after we'd met and she'd put up a bit of a smoke screen so I hadn't pursued it. More recently, and when rather the worse for wear from too much whisky, I'd told her about my mother and father, and she, in turn, had divulged that she was also an only child and that her father was a senior diplomat. Her parents were almost permanently abroad but she'd been educated in England and gone to Oxford to read law. At the age of nineteen she'd got foolishly involved with a married lecturer, resulting in her university career being curtailed. Her parents had arranged the job with the solicitor's office in the interim and left her in no doubt that they hoped for better things for her than a liaison with a teacher. She'd given me a conspiratorial look and informed me that she didn't always see eye-to-eye with her parents' aspirations for her.

She slouched back on the alcove seat again in a provocative attitude and with a teasing smile said, 'Nobody can see us in this alcove, Alan. You may now pay me for services rendered.'

I stifled a laugh and her eyes told me she approved of my better frame of mind. 'I bought you a lager,' I said, looking at her breasts. 'What more do you want?'

'If you keep staring at my tits like that, I'll show you,' she teased, starting to undo the top button of her blouse.

'For Christ's sake, not here,' I gulped, 'You'll have us thrown out.'

'Pay me then,' she taunted, undoing the next button, and leaning back further.

'Oh God, Christine. Okay, you win.' I leant right over her and held my mouth half an inch from hers, desperately hoping no-one would want this alcove just at this moment. 'I'm in enough trouble. Don't get us chucked out of here. I really don't need that.'

'I know what we both need,' she whispered. 'All right, I'll stop if you kiss now, pay later. I feel like being a really naughty girl.' She wiggled her hips under me.

'Sexy bitch,' I said as we pulled ourselves apart.

She grabbed her handbag, brushed herself down and we made an embarrassed exit past several elderly country locals who gaped at us over the tops of their pints. Even the collies under the benches at their feet took their noses out of their paws to watch our departure.

She drove fast but precisely. We arrived at her flat and she continued to seduce me all the way up the stairs and into her living room.

Christine and I had been together now for over six months, and with the sexual appetite she had, it meant we'd spent a fair proportion of that time making love. Teasing each other had become a bit of a speciality and this moment was to be no exception... and teasing takes time.

Chapter 2

It was half past nine when I'd recovered enough to realise I was lying on the sofa without a stitch on. I could hear the shower running in the bathroom and made my way shakily over to the door. It was locked. 'Can I have a towel?' I raised my voice over the noise of the running water and one came flying out.

Eventually Christine emerged, covered in a bathrobe and crossed the room with a jaunty swing of her hips. She kissed me lightly on the lips and with a suggestive smile enquired, 'How are you feeling?'

'Knackered.'

'I should think so,' she said, looking pleased. Then her expression changed back to the concern that she'd showed earlier in the pub. 'We must ring Richard. Are you going to or shall I? Or shall we drive back to your digs?'

'I'll do it. He should be in. Probably watching the box.'

I punched the numbers and Richard's voice answered almost immediately.

'That you, Richard?' I said. 'Alan.'

'You'd better get round here, Alan,' he said with a worried edge to his voice. 'You at Christine's?'

'What's the matter? Anything wrong?'

'Yes, there is, but don't ask me anything until you get here.'

'Richard, what is it?' I persisted, raising my voice and glancing at Christine who was now beside me.

'Just get here, will you?' he repeated.

'I'm bringing Christine. If it's about those papers, she knows all about it.'

'Just stop talking and be as quick as you can – and don't talk to anyone on the way.' The line went dead and I looked at Christine.

'Something's happened', I said. 'He sounded really worried. I'm sure it's about those bloody papers.'

'Come on,' said Christine. 'Better not waste any time finding out.' We flung some clothes on and flew down the stairs.

Christine spun the wheels of her Escort as we shot out of the drive. Being early June it was still just light although there was a bit of a nip in the air. We found nothing to say to each other, both being preoccupied with what could have happened to make the normally placid and jocular Richard sound so anxious. Christine parked in a side road round the corner and we hurried into the front passage to be confronted by my dishevelled-looking friend. He was holding a half full glass of whisky and was certainly in an agitated state.

'Okay, you two, come in and grab a drink. I think you're going to need it.' He hustled us into the sitting room, and I could see he'd been at our rather meagre supply of Haig. I fetched two more glasses from the kitchen and we both sat down and waited. Christine hadn't said a word since we got into her car.

'What on earth's happened, Richard?' I said impatiently. 'For God's sake, what's going on?'

He appeared to calm down a little as he pulled over another chair, but seemed to be marshalling his thoughts with some difficulty. 'You're not going to believe this,' he began. 'These rooms have been searched sometime during the afternoon on the pretext of an inspection for a burst pipe by the Clerk of Works. Someone has been through our belongings, Alan, and I'm sorry to say has removed some copies I took of those papers you took from the Bursar's office this morning.'

There was silence as Christine and I gaped at him, trying to believe it wasn't true.

Christine was the first to recover. 'Are you absolutely certain, Richard? Perhaps you mislaid them – put them somewhere and forgot where.'

'No.' He was adamant. 'I may have had a few of these,' he said, raising his glass briefly, 'but I can tell you I've been checking everywhere for the last couple of hours and they've gone, they really have.' He got up and started to pace round the room. 'I actually put them under my mattress for safekeeping, seeing as how they were slightly illicit. You don't forget doing a thing like that. They've definitely gone.'

He looked across at Christine and then back at me, pausing as if uncertain as to whether to continue. 'I don't know how much you've told Christine but you might as well both know. A few things like beds and clothes have been disturbed. Not much, you understand, but there's no disputing it. You'll almost certainly find a few of your belongings have been moved.'

'What do you mean "some copies"?' I said. 'Did whoever it was take some and leave some behind?'

'Look! I'll explain that in a minute,' he went on. 'But

don't you realise what it means? It means that there is something in those papers important enough for someone to feel it necessary to search through private belongings twice in one day. It's unprecedented in a place like this. Such a clumsy effort too. There was no attempt by the Bursar this morning to hide the fact he was rifling your private locker. And now, in here, there's been no effort to put things back carefully.'

He paused and studied the remains of his whisky. He suddenly seemed less tense, as if our being there had brought a sense of logic to his reasoning. 'It must have been the Bursar,' he continued. 'Who else would have used the Clerk of Works to gain entry without causing suspicion?'

'Wait a minute!' It was Christine who interrupted. 'What do you mean exactly, Richard?' The question was designed to slow him down a bit, and get him to bring us into the reasoning, instead of rushing ahead and losing us in the process.

'Well, when I returned here at about... oh, I don't know, half seven, I suppose, there was a note on the table, signed by G. Stratford, Clerk of Works, which said...' He unearthed the slip of paper and read, 'Reported water leak. System checked and found satisfactory, five fifteen pm.'

'Yes, George Stratford,' I said. 'He works for the Bursar and has keys to all the staff flats and houses, just in case there's a problem when we're teaching, or during the holidays or if a meter needs reading or something.'

'Don't you see?' continued Richard, 'The Bursar could have come with him, waited until George had finished and found no leak, and then dismissed him saying he would lock up and return the key later. Then he would have had a quick search for the papers and I suppose under the bed would be a fairly obvious place to look. He clearly looked in several other places too, in your room, Alan, as well as mine.'

'I would have been at the cricket, and you were at the rowing as it's Wednesday, right?'

'Right.'

'So that means,' I said, 'that if I'd have come back here after the match instead of going to the pub with Christine... I'd have found that note and not you.' I tried to imagine what sort of a state I'd have got into if it had been me who'd discovered the place had been searched.

Christine was reading my mind. 'You might not have noticed anything was amiss though, unless you knew Richard had left the papers here.'

Richard said, 'When I saw the note, I didn't actually twig there was anything wrong until I noticed my wardrobe door open, and a couple of ties on the floor. It was then I went to where I'd put those copies and found they were missing. That's when I realised we've now got a serious problem, and I think we ought to decide what we're going to do about it. The Head wants me in his study first thing in the morning and I'm not looking forward to it.'

'Me too,' I added. 'Quarter to nine.'

'That's odd,' said Richard. 'He wants me there at eight thirty. That means he wants to see us separately. I would have thought he would carpet us both together...seems more logical.'

'Unless it's another interrogation session,' put in Christine.

'Or a sacking for both of us,' I said, reaching for what was left in the whisky bottle.

The three of us talked round the subject, trying to work out every possible angle and what might happen next, particularly in the Headmaster's study in the morning. It was obvious we were going to get no further, and it was well after midnight when Christine said she was going back to her flat and reminded me that now the papers had been taken it was not possible to destroy them as we'd agreed in the pub earlier.

'No, I suppose not,' I said. 'But hang on. Didn't you say, Richard, that only some of the copies had been taken? What did you mean? If they weren't all taken, we'd better destroy the rest or there might be another attempt to search the place.'

Christine hit the bullseye.

'You took two copies,' she said with a broad grin. 'You crafty old devil.'

'Well, errrr, yes – actually I did,' stuttered Richard, trying to pretend he was not immensely pleased with himself. 'Don't really know why. Force of habit I suppose, or just luck.' He beamed at us with one his superior expressions.

'I didn't notice you doing that,' I said, ' Well, where are they, for Christ's sake?'

'Under your mattress.'

'God Almighty,' I said, rushing into my bedroom and emerging with the second bundle of offending evidence. 'You complete prat, Richard. They might have been found as well.'

'One set's been taken and that's sufficient for whoever it was,' said Christine. 'The important thing is they don't suspect there's a second set. I'd better have those. I'll take them back to my place and tomorrow morning I'll put them in my office safe. No one will get at them there...but just in case this thing does escalate, I'll take another set of copies and keep them somewhere else. Or you can have a set back if you like.'

She grabbed the papers as I stood there gaping and trying to interpret her obvious logic.

'Good girl!' said Richard. 'Now this has gone so far, we might need to get an expert to look over those figures.'

They settled the matter between them and I was happy to go along with it. As Christine was now fully involved and seemed to be one step ahead of us both, I was glad to hand the responsibility of leaving the decisions to her quicksilver but level-headed mind.

I walked her round to her car and told her how great she was for involving herself so completely in my problems. She threw her arms around my neck, kissed me hard on the lips and replied that I was a smashing bloke for letting her help me. 'Most men,' she said, 'would think it beneath them to ask for a woman's assistance in such things.' Then she told me that ours was a wonderful relationship and she would drive home very carefully. I was to go to bed and sleep, and not start a post-mortem with Richard which would go on for hours. She then jumped into the car and disappeared into the darkness.

The next morning at ten minutes to nine, I was sacked.

If I'm honest, it shouldn't actually have come as a surprise. I'm the sort of person to go over every possible angle of a problem, good and bad, and I'd already concluded that the worst conceivable outcome would be dismissal.

Masterton told me to sit down, gave me notice for the end of term, told me why, and then rang for his secretary to show me out.

It was then I found I couldn't move. I was dumbstruck... it was as if I'd had a bad car accident and was suffering from shock. I came over cold and then started to feel sick. I knew

I should retaliate, but no words would come. I needed to put both my arms on the side of the chair to haul myself out. The secretary was ushering me towards the door. I desperately wanted to push her away, even use violence... I knew that at this moment all my dreams of a career in teaching at a school like this were leaving me, like a pebble tossed casually into a pond to sink, never to be seen again.

I turned to protest, to ask for another chance, say I was sorry, beg forgiveness even. But Duncan Masterton was an expert at anticipating awkward moments. He'd already picked up his Dictaphone and was speaking into it, with his back turned to me. I was a thing of the past, a minor inconvenience to be discarded like a rotten apple and forgotten. The appointment was at an end. Another history master would be recruited, the cricket and rugby were all over. I would move away. The friendships I'd made here would end – Richard, Christine even. God! What was happening to me? I turned to go back, but the door was firmly shut. It seemed to say, 'This part of your life is over, Carter. You've missed your chance – you've thrown away a golden opportunity and from this moment you don't belong here'.

I could feel a lump beginning to swell in my throat. Why didn't I have I the guts to make a stand, have a shouting match? Why didn't I have my arguments ready to throw at the man who'd so easily destroyed me? He would have spent more time scraping some dog mess off his shoe. I stumbled to the main door and out into the sunlight. It felt like emerging from a courtroom with a life sentence upon me.

Richard was waiting for me outside in the courtyard. He saw the glazed expression of shock on my face.

'For God's sake, Alan, what's happened?'

'I've been sacked,' I whispered.

Thank God he didn't try to tell me not to worry or anything. He just took my arm very tightly and walked me over to the cloisters and through the rose garden. He then steered me through the little side gate in the wall that led to the road and up the steps to our front door. When we were in the sitting room, he sat me down in an armchair and told me we were both going to fight this thing and that he was going to ring Christine immediately.

'No, don't do that,' I pleaded. 'I'll have to tell her. I'd rather tell her.'

He'd already rung her office number and had asked to be put through when I grabbed the handset from him.

'Hello!' It was Christine's voice. She seemed very far away.

'It's me, Christine. I've been sacked. I'm in a bit of a state. Richard's here and I'm all right. You're not to worry. It'll be okay.'

She was shouting at me down the phone, but somehow I couldn't bring myself to let her get a word in.

'That's all there is to it, believe me. There's nothing you can do. I'm fine and I'll see you later. It's best this way and there'll be no more trouble, and I'm really fine and Richard's okay.' She was screaming at me to shut up. 'It really is for the best and I'm probably not suited to this place anyway. I'll be more comfortable at another school, and you have a good day and I'll look forward to seeing you this evening, and... Oh God, Christine, I love you and I don't know what's happened to me and I need you like hell and...'

Richard wrenched the phone away from me and shoved me violently into a chair. I couldn't hear the words he was using to comfort Christine, but he obviously succeeded and after a few minutes returned the handset to its cradle and turned to me.

'Alan, it's not over. We're going to fight this thing starting from now.' His voice and manner brooked no argument.

It was then I remembered he would have already seen Masterton himself, and here was I, with probably less to lose than him, thinking of nobody but myself. 'I'm sorry, Richard,' I blurted, feeling a selfish bastard. 'Not you as well?'

'Well, no, I've haven't been sacked. I've been severely disciplined, and a report to that effect is to be placed on my file. It seems most unfair on you though, Alan, and it's all the more reason why I'm going to help you move heaven and earth to be reinstated. The most I expected you to get was an official bollocking like me.'

I looked at him thoughtfully. 'Masterton had the copies there in his study,' I said. 'He told me I was the one responsible, as it was me who'd removed them from the office and got you to copy them.'

Richard looked me in the eye. 'It's my fault, Alan. We both know it's my fault, so let's not have any more of that sort of talk. I forced you into letting me copy them, and you will never know how sorry I feel for that. But I tell you... and you just listen and take this on board. There's more to this than meets the eye, and we're now going to start finding out what's going on in that evil little brain of Masterton's.' He turned away, satisfied that I'd calmed down sufficiently to think logically about the next step to be taken.

I was indeed feeling calmer but worried about Christine. 'What did you say to her?' I said.

'Don't worry, it's all right. I just told her to leave it to me and I would ring her back shortly.' He glanced at his watch. 'Look! I don't know about you, but I'm overdue in class. The best thing you can do is not to ring her, but go and teach and continue as if nothing had happened. We don't want to give that sod the chance to find further fault with us today. You can bet there's nothing he'd like better than the chance to put another entry in our files for slack attendance in the classroom.'

I could see the logic of that, so gathering my things together I followed him out of the flat and hurried over to my waiting history class.

I departed from my usual Thursday morning habit of setting a short appraisal of a historical event. I was desperate to avoid sitting in silence or doing some marking, so I lectured away about the Bolshevik uprising and rambled on about Lenin and Trotsky and provisional governments and their failures, quite forgetting myself, and even holding the form's interest for more than a few minutes. When the bell went, I resolved to do this more often – if the syllabus would allow it.

I had a full teaching schedule up to break and managed to keep calm with the belief that Richard would know the best way to get me back in the Head's study as soon as possible, and tell me how to plead my case.

Talk about kicking a man when he's down.

When I breezed into the common room trying to look normal and matter of fact, I felt as if I'd been shot in the stomach. My attention was drawn to a notice on the Headmaster's board. It informed the staff that 'Due to matters of a confidential nature, Alan Carter will be leaving the teaching staff at the end of this term.' That was it – curt and terminal.

It meant Richard's idea of 'fighting this thing' seemed rather pointless now. There was no way a man like Masterton would withdraw his dismissal of me now he'd posted it on the notice board. The whole teaching staff would know in about ten minutes and that would be final. He certainly wouldn't put himself in the position of having to eat his words by backing down. He'd got that notice up so quickly it crossed my mind that he meant the rest of the staff to see it before I had a chance to ask him to change his mind.

My dismissal became the subject of much speculation. It was not every day a member of staff was actually sacked. It was quite obvious it was a sacking, because normally, if a teacher was leaving to take up another post, the explanation would be mentioned, usually with the statutory good wishes. The problem with this notice was that it left the way open for all sorts of scurrilous theories to be put about as to the reason for my sudden departure. Questioning looks were already apparent. Most of the comments were of a sympathetic nature. Some, from the more senior members of staff took the form of a simple 'Never mind, Carter. These things happen. You'll get over it.'

Nobody asked me what I'd done that was of such a confidential nature for me to be dismissed for it. I found this disquieting. Perhaps they thought my transgression was of a sexual nature and it would be discourteous to mention it. Rather, they gave me furtive glances and quickly turned away to scan the timetable or games programme. I wondered what the result would be if I were to write under the Head's notice in huge letters, 'You're all wrong. I've actually been dismissed for uncovering a financial fraud which is being perpetrated by the Headmaster. Signed Alan Carter.' That would give them something to think about.

I was just pondering this move when Richard came into the room with a pile of books under his arm and looking anxious. He saw me and came straight over.

'I've seen it,' he said in a whisper. 'You haven't discussed it with anyone, I hope?'

'I may have got the sack,' I said, 'but I'm not that stupid.'

He looked at me as if pleased I could offer a rebuke. 'Okay, I'm sorry. But for God's sake don't breathe a word of what's happened. If anyone else gets wind of those papers, it'll make it impossible for us to find out what's really behind those figures. So let's play dumb and say nothing. You'd better remind Christine too.'

'Did you ring her back?'

'Yes, of course, and I did tell her not to talk about this. She's quite calm about it, and also extremely relieved that you're okay, Alan.' He looked at me sternly, and I knew a lecture was coming.

'You know, for a bloke who's just lost his job, I can think of no finer person to sort you out than Christine. You really are an incredibly lucky bastard. Most of the chaps here would give their right arms and their jobs to have her.'

'Yes, I know,' I said. 'Believe me, I know it.'

The next two or three days passed me by as if I were in a dream. It was not until the Sunday night that I began to take serious stock of what I could do about my plight. I taught history as if in a trance, and if the Head had wanted a justified reason for sacking me, I was offering the opportunity there and then. I was currently the worst teacher of history that Bradchester had ever had and deserved to be dismissed for that alone.

It was when we were in the Fisherman's Creel later, just the three of us, that it dawned on me how active Richard and Christine had been on my behalf.

'Right,' said Richard. 'Here's what we do. I've arranged a meeting for all three of us with this commodity broker in the City. He's a good friend of my uncle, who as I think you know is a merchant banker and has his office in Gracechurch Street. I've told him all about what's happened and believe me, you can trust him. He's put me in touch with the Chairman of one of the leading brokers in this field. All my uncle has told him is that you're in trouble, and that it would be better if the reason were not known. I'm told this fellow will respect that confidence and give us all the help he can. I had to explain to my uncle that we would want to know the ins and outs of commodity dealing, and particularly how someone would go about covering deals, whatever that means. I've explained the difficult position you're in and that no names can be mentioned. When I fixed up the meeting with this Chairman, whose name is Robert Donaldson, he seemed most sensitive and diplomatic, and assured me that he could give us all the facts we needed without requiring to be put in the picture further.'

'Where's all this going to get us?' I asked. 'It's not going to get me my job back.' I glanced across at Christine. We were sitting in the same alcove as last Wednesday evening. Half a lifetime seemed to have passed by since then.

'Maybe not,' she said. 'But it could lead us to some facts that will enable us to put some pressure on Masterton to reconsider.'

Richard went on. 'The other thing I've done is to get Norman Willett, that maths bloke who's always trying to flog the Teachers' Union to us, to give me the name of the local Branch Secretary and his number. I've since rung him and there's a letter in the post advising you what to do next. Something about unfair dismissal, he said.'

'I'm a member,' I said, rather sheepishly. I knew some of the senior staff were not paid-up union members and I hadn't yet found out whether it was controversial for junior teachers to join or not. I assumed that common rooms of public schools were not fertile recruiting grounds for such organisations. I had, however, seen the logic of it as far as I was concerned, being as it were, without family contacts or strings to pull. There were definite advantages I'd been led to understand, with regard to social security difficulties and redundancy problems, things like that. I had nevertheless not liked to broadcast the fact and had kept a low profile about the matter.

'Norman persuaded me to join when I started here last autumn.'

'That might come in very handy,' said Richard in a surprisingly approving manner. 'You never told me.'

'Nor me,' put in Christine.

'No. Well, you never know whether people approve of unions or not these days.'

'Well, as you know,' said Richard, 'I'm not a member. Not because I don't believe in the principle of unions. Everyone has the right to have an organisation behind them to fight their corner. It's just that unless I can be sure there's no political motivation or brainwashing involved, I'd rather stand up for myself.'

Christine leapt into the conversation. She was a radical at heart and a bit of a rebel to boot. 'It's all right for you, Richard,' she said. 'You've got friends in high places and contacts. If you have a problem, you can bring pressure to bear via the old boy network. That doesn't work for people like Alan or for the vast majority of us. Political brainwashing and playing party politics goes on in every single influential and powerful organisation in the land, whichever side of the political fence you sit on. There's no need to dismiss totally the good a union can do simply on the basis of a small amount of harm it might do. In any case unions don't have the political muscle they used to. Maggie Thatcher saw to that.'

Richard retreated to the corner of the alcove with his hands up in surrender and grinning broadly. 'Okay, okay, I give in.' There was no getting the better of Christine in this mood.

She sat back with a satisfied expression and allowed Richard a gracious smile. 'Right then,' she said. 'But if the union are to be brought in to help Alan in any way with this, it must be with the wholehearted support of all three of us. No smirking or mickey-taking. It's my belief they could help a great deal. There are a lot of redundancy and unfair dismissal cases coming through my firm right now, and I know that the unions are particularly involved with making sure employers follow the correct procedures in the former, and when they get involved in the latter employers really sit up and take notice, I can tell you.'

'That's fine,' said Richard. 'We're agreed then. We'll use the services of the union to try to get an unfair dismissal case against the Head.'

'And then,' continued Christine, fixing me with a intensive look so severe I felt distinctly uncomfortable, 'if that doesn't look as if it will get us anywhere, the only way to get you off the hook will be to obtain proof that Masterton and the

Bursar, or at any rate the school, are involved in a fraudulent financial operation somewhere. We'll meet Robert Donaldson with the intention of finding out firstly what these commodity figures are likely to be and then try to establish how someone would go about using them for ill-gotten gains. We have the copies of the transactions and hopefully will have acquired the knowledge from him to enable us to interpret them to our advantage.'

Richard was nodding in agreement. 'I've fixed up this meeting with Donaldson for Tuesday evening, nine o'clock. He wanted us to go to his office in the City, but when I explained that during term time that would be impossible for us as teachers, he suggested we meet at his home. It's about thirty-five miles from Thaxbury, and as I thought it was generous of him to suggest it, I agreed. I hope that's possible. What about you, Christine?'

'Yes, of course.'

'Alan?'

'No problem,' I replied. 'I think we should act straight away, just in case. And I want you to know,' I added, 'I can't thank you enough for helping me in this. There's no way I could handle this on my own, and I just hope we're not all getting a bit out of our depth.'

'Nonsense,' they said, almost in unison. Richard added, 'You can't just lie down and let yourself be trampled all over. Anyway, I've a feeling that it all may be settled sooner than we think when the union's legal people go into action. When Masterton realises what he's up against, he'll probably decide that the bad publicity he'll get, and the flack he'll take from his Board of Governors, will not make pursuing his course of action worthwhile.

'Do you think the union will advise us to bring an unfair dismissal case?' I said. 'After all, we did actually copy confidential documents, didn't we?'

Richard pondered for a bit. 'Hmm. I take your point. Maybe they'll advise that we go down the road of unfair dismissal, in the hope that Masterton will back down when he realises the contents of the papers may be revealed. I believe there would be a tribunal, similar to a hearing, where evidence can be presented rather like in a court case. And then if he doesn't reconsider, we'll have to decide whether to continue or not. But it would be best, I'm sure, to test his resolve to start with.'

Christine said, 'All this is conjecture at this stage, you know. Don't forget you haven't even got your dismissal in writing yet, so you can't do anything until it's actually official.'

Richard seemed to want to bring this little meeting to an end as he got up and said, 'So, we'll wait for Alan's letter of dismissal from the Head and then see what the union advise in their letter, which is already in the post. If we get those two bits of information by Tuesday, so much the better, as we'll then have a better idea how to use any information we can get about commodity dealing from Robert Donaldson.

We all seemed in agreement about the course of action, so we left it at that and decided to try to concentrate on our jobs for the next two days.

* * *

Norman Willett had been absolutely delighted that somebody had actually consulted him about a matter that might have to involve the union. As this did not happen often, it made him feel important and justified his patience in putting up with the good-natured but irritating ribbing he got from most of the staff. He had managed to recruit only five members during his three years at Bradchester, and was the object of some vindictive oral abuse from some of the older and more traditional members of the common room. He was a good maths teacher though and knew it. He also knew that a teacher has the perfect right to belong to a trade union, no matter what school he taught in, and, as long as he could not be accused of unreasonable behaviour in upsetting other staff by his methods of recruiting, or be seen to be harassing them in any way, he had an equal right to act as their representative. The Employment Act was quite clear on that, and he had been well advised by his Branch Secretary as to what he could and could not do in connection with union matters within his place of work. It was not that he was a very successful union representative. Indeed, his recruiting record made sure that he would never be a shining star in this field. He was, however, happy to think that he had at least made small inroads into one of the most difficult areas for union representation and took every opportunity to tell his branch so whenever he attended meetings.

Alan Carter had been his latest signing. He therefore felt a special responsibility for his well-being. If he could show the rest of the staff that belonging to the union really did have enormous benefits, it would indeed be a feather in his cap. An unfair dismissal case would be a golden opportunity to increase his stock. If the case was brought to tribunal, there would be a quite dramatic increase in membership in this common room. He'd been told also that the union didn't bring a case unless they were sure of winning it and their legal people had a very high percentage of successes. He was hopeful therefore that the union would advise for a case, and he himself would make it his business to see that Alan agreed to go along with its advice.

Norman Willett didn't like Alan much. He was too successful at everything. He'd got the top cricket job in the school almost straight away, and was popular with pupils and staff alike. He related well to his history pupils and the word was that he would be destined for higher things when he'd been at Bradchester a few years. House tutor had been mentioned more than once, which riled Willett as down that road lay a housemaster post. As union representative, he preferred his younger members to be passed over to start with, to carry a small chip on their shoulder and to consider themselves underprivileged. That way they were more receptive to his political views and he felt he had some allies in the camp.

It had been Richard Pilcher who'd approached him about some assistance for Alan. Norman had adopted his most patronising manner and had asked Richard to come to his office. Actually his office was a table in the far corner of the common room, which he shared with two other members of staff. He had invited Richard to sit down and commenced to treat the conversation as if it were an interview for a job.

'Name?' he had enquired with an air of importance that made Richard smile.

'Don't be bloody stupid, Norman. It's Richard Pilcher, you idiot.'

Norman adjusted his ill-fitting tie and reached inside his slightly frayed jacket pocket for a biro. He could begin to feel himself becoming rattled. He paused and looked up at his interviewee. 'Of course... so it is,' he smiled. The manual had said that if someone patronises you, smile at them and go very slowly. 'You wish to see me about a union matter? I don't recollect you being a member, I must say.' He pretended to look thoughtful. He must be careful with this one. Too clever by half.

'Norman!' Richard had said. 'For God's sake, cut the crap. It's for Alan Carter. You know, history.

'Well, what sort of a problem is it, and why can't he come and see me himself?'

Richard paused. It would be as well to go easy on Norman Willett, as they really did need his cooperation. Silly to put his back up at this stage.

'He's really cut up, poor chap, as you can imagine and he feels he's being badly treated. He thinks your people would help him. He says he's been dismissed unfairly.'

Norman's eyes had widened and his fingers tightened round the ballpoint he held poised in front of him. 'Unfair dismissal, you say. Serious charge, that. Unfair dismissal, or wrongful dismissal would you say? Important difference, you know.' He'd looked down his nose at Richard and positively glowed in the knowledge that Richard would not have known.

'Oh, I don't know. No idea. He'd rather leave it to you experts to sort it out. Just tell me the procedure, will you, there's a good fellow.'

'What did he actually do to get dismissed?' said Willett, trying to maintain a matter-of-fact tone in his voice.

'Can't tell you at this stage,' was the short reply.

'Well, I'd sooner speak to him personally as it is he who will be calling upon the union's services.'

'No time,' said Richard. 'He's ill anyway. Look! Are you going to give me the procedure or do I have to ring up the union myself and tell them you aren't able to help?'

Norman was rattled. 'No need for that, I'm sure,' he said sharply. 'Here's the procedure to follow and the branch details. I'll ring them and notify them of your enquiry and get back to you.' He handed over a photocopied leaflet, and Richard had grabbed it, disappearing in the direction of the telephone.

He had immediately arranged for details from the union head office to be put in the post. Better than that. By saying it was a staff member at Bradchester who was involved, he'd got put through to the person he was told would most likely be the liaison between the union and the member, a fellow called Maurice Tyler.

Branch Secretary Maurice Tyler had been most interested to speak to someone from Bradchester School calling on behalf of a friend who thought he had been unfairly dismissed. Any chance to join battle with an institution that stood for the wealthy and privileged few would not be passed by if he had anything to do with it. Even if this enquiry was only a dismissal case, win or lose, there would be the opportunity to perhaps dig a little deeper. Carry out a little muckraking. See if there was some dirty linen that might benefit from being washed in public. It was Maurice Tyler's speciality.

* * *

It was Tuesday morning when I received the letter I'd been dreading but expecting. As usual it was short and to the point. It was, however, unexpected in that 'the Headmaster regretted etc, etc, that due to your failure to attain the standards necessary to be confirmed as a regular full-time teacher of history during your probationary period at Bradchester... Yours etc.'

And that was it! Nothing about wilfully copying confidential papers and hiding them in the flat. Not a mention of that. Just basically incompetence.

I was flabbergasted and when I told Richard and Christine about it separately, they were certainly puzzled, but not for long. Both of them were quick to work out the thinking behind the change of reason by the Head, and their conclusion was identical. He couldn't use the copied papers as a reason for firing me as, despite the fact that he thought he had retrieved the copies, he couldn't risk me challenging the dismissal in case the contents of them were called for during any hearing. He also could not be sure we had only taken one copy. In addition, it meant that there was something really incriminating in those papers that made it essential for him to cite incompetence as a safer reason for getting rid of me.

When we were back in the flat together, Richard said, 'You know, I think you might be able to wriggle out of this quite easily, Alan.'

'How do you mean?'

'Well! The whole staff knows you're a good enough teacher, and I'm sure enough of them would support that fact. And if that is the case, then a tribunal would surely find in your favour. Masterton would then have no option but to reinstate you.'

'Hmm! I bet it won't be as simple as that,' I said. 'Masterton will have thought of every angle. He's a clever bugger. And I have to say that the thought of going through a tribunal with the Headmaster in opposition to me fills me with horror. I'm not sure I could handle it, Richard.'

'Yes, you can and you will because Christine and I will be doing all the thinking for you and taking a lot of the hassle as well. All you'd have to do would be to act as your normal pleasant and efficiently quiet self, and together the three of us will crack it.'

Richard was back to his confidence-oozing self again and I found it infectious.

'We'll lobby some of the staff and then you'll see how many of them think you're a damn good teacher.'

'But will they all actually say it in a tribunal?' I said. 'You know what people are like. They'll say one thing to your face, but when it comes to the crunch, will they speak against the Head? He is their employer after all, and not many people would want to cross Masterton. They'll be only too aware of where it got me.'

'I think you're worrying unduly,' he said. 'Anyway, the evidence of your track record and results will speak for themselves.'

I remained unconvinced but wanted to hear what Christine had to say, so I grunted a form of agreement and turned in for the night.

Next morning various leaflets and forms to do with the procedure to be followed for grievances arrived, and there was quite a bit of paperwork involved, so I put it to one side, deciding I would run through it with Christine at a later date. There was also a short separate letter from a chap called

Maurice Tyler, recommending that I go and see him as soon as possible. He explained that it would be prudent to discuss the matter while it was fresh in the mind, and in order to short-circuit most of the paperwork and the time it would take to pass all the red tape through the correct channels, he would be at my service to smooth the way for me. The letter bore all the official stamps of the union's headquarters and to me it seemed very supportive.

When I had shown it to both Richard and Christine, we agreed that there was nothing to be lost by at least going to meet this fellow Tyler.

In fact we wouldn't be able to fix a meeting with Tyler until after we'd met Robert Donaldson. It was now Monday and our scheduled visit to the prominent commodity broker was the next evening. It wouldn't make any difference, however, and the sooner we had all the information and advice we might need in our possession, the clearer our position would be.

Chapter 3

Robert Donaldson was not at all what I'd expected. I thought all successful city types who were chairmen or directors of financial firms were overweight, had fat lips, and wore dark blue, made-to-measure, pinstriped suits that hid their three o'clock lunchtime paunches. I was wrong.

He was standing at the front door of his beautifully restored period farmhouse as we drove up the post and rail-fenced drive. A small, well-preserved man of about sixty, he was clad in a paint-splattered, blue, lightweight boiler suit, and, although his hair was all grey, he had an awful lot of it. It fell all over his face and stuck out over his ears, and I thought that if he ever did wear a jacket, it should be a dinner jacket and he should have a baton in his hand and be throwing himself all over the podium at the Albert Hall at the Last Night of the Proms. He was, however, a quiet man in speech and movement, and when you could see his eyes through his hair they were sincere and welcoming.

'Good of you to come over,' he said. 'Do forgive me if I don't shake hands. Just putting another coat on that fence. Come on in round the back if you don't mind. The memsahib will be after me if I take you in the front in this garb.' He wiped his hands down the sides of his legs and led us guiltily round to the back and through the porch stable door.

'Now I'll just get these boots off. Don't want creosote all over the carpet, do we?' He eased them off by standing one heel on the other toe in turn, and slid them into a corner by a couple of folded stable rugs. 'There now, I'll have this boiler suit off and we can start. I assumed you wouldn't have too much time, so I thought we'd go into the study and we can get right down to it. My wife actually has had to pop out this evening and will be sorry to miss you. I thought you'd probably have eaten but I expect you could use a drink.'

He ushered us through a beautifully carpeted hallway and into a beamed room which he called a study but in fact was first and foremost a library. The walls were lined with pine shelving and books stood from floor to ceiling. There was an antique writing desk to one side of the inglenook fireplace and an enormous vase of cut summer flowers stood in front of the empty fire basket. He motioned us to sit down in easy chairs and then busied himself getting us some drinks. When he was sure we were comfortable, he pulled up another chair into the little circle and looked at Richard.

'Well, now,' he began, cupping his small hands as far as they would go round an enormous brandy glass. 'Your Uncle Peter told me you were in some sort of trouble and that I might be able to assist you in some way.'

I said, 'It's me, I'm afraid, Mr Donaldson, and I'm very grateful to you for giving us your time.'

He held up a hand. 'Please call me Bob, and if I may, I should consider it a privilege to call you Christine, Alan and Richard.' The three names rolled off his tongue as if he had known us all our lives. No hesitation. Ladies first too. This man had a kind of charming humility that you couldn't help admiring. He was what I thought of as a gentleman, and his manners and the way he put you at your ease put him in that category known as 'well bred.'

'To save you the trouble of a full explanation,' he went on, leaning forward and embracing us all in the conversation, 'I should perhaps tell you that I know Alan has been given notice and that all of you consider there may be grounds for suspecting foul play. Richard's uncle and I are close friends, and I would like to say that I feel you have paid me a compliment by asking me to help you. I fully understand that you would be nervous about giving away confidential information to a complete stranger, information that perhaps you'd be happier not to possess in the first place.

'I do think, however, that I can serve you best by knowing a little of the background, and I am happy that what I have been told so far will suffice. There should be no need to elaborate further.'

I looked up at Richard and received an approving nod. Christine too, I could see, was impressed.

Richard pulled out the little bundle of papers and handed them to the commodity broker. He scanned each one in turn and then leant back in his chair. 'Statements of transactions you would get from any broker dealing in these particular commodities,' he said. 'Thousands of these go out to clients every day.'

'Could you tell us, Bob,' said Richard, 'whether there's anything in those figures which would make it undesirable for them to fall into the wrong hands?'

'Well! Let's see.' He fell silent for a moment and inspected each sheet in turn. 'No,' he said, 'I couldn't say that at all. All the transactions listed here look perfectly normal to me.

Some of the later ones are open-ended, but there's nothing unusual in that. The prices of the various commodities seem about right for the dates they were made. Of course, without checking each one individually, I couldn't vouch for that absolutely, but they're near enough. I could get them checked for complete accuracy if you wish.'

'No, that's all right,' said Richard, unable to hide the disappointment in his voice. 'I'm sure there's no need for that.'

I glanced at Christine for some small measure of encouragement, but she was absolutely poker-faced, showing nothing but complete concentration.

'Of course,' said Donaldson, leaning back in his chair and inspecting his glass with a conniving expression. 'It would depend on whose hands were considered to be the wrong ones.'

Christine leant forward towards him with a smile that indicated acknowledgement of a superior mind and said, 'Mr Donaldson...' She hesitated. 'Bob... I think you're ahead of us. What do you mean?'

He laughed out loud and then said, 'I'm sorry, my dear. I didn't mean to tease.' He assumed a serious pose once again and went on. 'No. You see there's absolutely nothing here that can possibly indicate any form of illegality. Thousands of deals like this are done all round the financial centres of the world every minute of the day. Some smaller than these. The vast majority ever so much bigger. The fact that the information on these papers indicates that the client of this particular broker is showing a trading loss of some thirty thousand pounds is certainly not uncommon and is certainly not illegal.' He swilled the remainder of his brandy round in his glass. 'I remember the one commodity showing a loss here, copper in fact, to be a bit of a speculative star, at or around these dates. Price soared, then fell away even faster. A few fingers burnt there, I believe. A few fortunes made as well, I shouldn't wonder. The fact though, that some of these deals are left open-ended is also not illegal. Unwise perhaps in that particular commodity, but there's nothing unlawful about it.'

Richard was on his feet. 'I knew it,' he said. 'I knew it would be something like this.'

'Knew what?' I offered, limply.

'That that bastard Masterton is up to no good.' His hand went to his mouth. We all looked at him in astonishment. 'Oh God!' he said, 'I've let the cat out of the bag. Damn!'

'No, you haven't,' said Donaldson. 'I know you didn't mention to me on the telephone that you suspected this Masterton fellow but I think you'll have to credit me with a little more guile than that, Richard.' He smiled benignly.

'Being in the City naturally means that one is surrounded by bankers, and some of them will become one's friends, sometimes close friends. When you told me the other day that Alan here had picked up these papers in the Bursar's office and made me aware of your suspicions, together with some of the facts, it was quite obvious that you wished to find out whether or not there was any 'misconduct' financially speaking going on.

'A simple call to one of my banker friends, and I was soon in possession of the information I required. For transactions of the kind we have here, if a cheque is to be made out for payment to cash or to a broker or anyone for that matter, for these kind of amounts, any bank would expect the governing body of a large school to stipulate that more than one signature should be on the cheque. Indeed, I'm informed that for very substantial amounts it is usual for the signature of the chairman of the governors to be needed. Normally, however, the bursar will sign, and in his absence the headmaster. Occasionally both would sign if the amount were large but not abnormally so. It therefore follows that if you told me the Bursar was implicated, it doesn't need the mind of a genius to tell me that the Headmaster might also be implicated, even though you took care not to mention his name to me. As the Headmaster was the one to dismiss you, in your opinion I assume, he must be implicated.'

Richard looked suitably humbled and reached down to the table to pick up his glass.

'So you see,' went on Donaldson. 'It is apparent to me that the 'wrong hands' that these papers might fall into as far as this Bursar fellow and your Mr Masterton are concerned, assuming they are up to no good in the first place, are your hands, Alan.' He looked at me sympathetically. 'As well as anyone else's with whom you associate closely. That of course means Richard and Christine. But I have to emphasise again that there is no proof from these figures that there is anything amiss. They could have the authorisation of the governing body to deal in commodities on behalf of the school. In my opinion it is most unlikely, but you could not rule it out.'

He rose from the table and went to a small cabinet to replenish our drinks. When he was satisfied that we had everything we required, he continued.

'Let me tell you what it is I think you wish to know. But please! Stop me if I am on the wrong track.'

I didn't think he would be on the wrong track. In fact, he was telling us not only what we wanted to know, but also what we ought to know. He was miles ahead of me, and I suspected a fair way ahead of Richard and Christine. As I was vaguely wondering which of us was going to drive home tonight, he went on.

'Somebody who wishes to speculate in the commodity markets has only to instruct his bank to deal on his behalf. He may also contact a commodity broker like myself and make known his wishes. If he has little experience of such markets, he may authorise such a broker to deal to his best advantage and use his discretion on the client's behalf. This is very common and much money is often to be made in this way. The broker will use his own experience and that of his contacts, to utilise the client's investment to show some profit by shrewd manipulation of that investment. It's common knowledge, however, that much money can just as easily be lost in this way if speculation and the temptation of a quick profit take the place of sound judgement.'

Christine cut in. 'Look! We all know that we're talking about Masterton and the Bursar as our prime suspects for sacking Alan to cover up their misdemeanours. We may be mistaken, but we have to find out if it's true or not, in case we have to use that knowledge to pressure them into reinstating him. Could you tell us, Bob, from a broker's point of view how those two would be likely to go about commodity dealing?'

'Well, first of all,' he said, 'if it were my firm who were approached, I would be most surprised to have a school wishing to deal in such markets in the first place. Much commodity dealing is speculative by nature and not the sort of business an institution with charitable status, which is almost certainly what Bradchester is, would be wise to get involved in. In any case, there are all sorts of rules and regulations, many of them introduced in the recent Financial Services Act, which are particularly designed to make it difficult for anyone, and particularly private individuals or non-financial institutions, to be misled or encouraged to invest under anything but the most scrupulously honourable circumstances. The onus is laid squarely upon such people as us brokers, to be responsible for following those regulations to the letter. An organisation found not to be doing so could expect its licence to be withdrawn immediately. Any reputable broking firm would certainly think twice about its responsibilities in this direction and even if it did decide to undertake the school's instructions, it would definitely wish to have the authorization of the board of governors before proceeding.'

He picked up the papers again and shuffled through them as if making sure of his ground.

'What I was going to tell you, and this is perhaps the only thing that might arouse one's suspicion, is that whoever the broker is who transacted the deals, he has not put his name or the name of his firm to the statements. This in itself is not illegal but is certainly most unusual. It may be, of course, that these particular lists have been supplied to the client in this form by request. There is also no mention of the client's name, which you obviously assume is the school or those acting on its behalf. It is only, I hasten to add, an assumption.'

All three of us jumped to the same conclusion. It was Christine who got the first word in. 'Doesn't that mean then that they're playing the commodity markets and don't want anyone to be able to link them with the transactions because they're using the school's money to do it?'

'Also,' said Richard, his manner getting more excited, 'there's no broker's name through which the deals could be traced back to them.'

Donaldson held up one hand. 'Hold on a minute,' he said. 'You're assuming an awful lot. The deals could be private ones, and the lists just happened to be on the Bursar's desk. Nothing wrong in that.'

'Then why,' said Richard, 'has Alan been sacked for copying them? Doesn't make sense.'

'Don't forget,' I said 'that the official, written reason is that I'm incompetent at my job suddenly, or words to that effect.'

Donaldson interrupted. 'I feel we're getting slightly sidetracked,' he said. 'If you'll allow me to answer your question, which was "How would the transactions be made through a broker?", I think the answer must be "with difficulty". Assuming that a broker of a lesser reputation was chosen, and there are plenty of those still around, I regret to say, such a broker would deal despite any misgivings he might have about the risks involved to the school. In any event, I suppose he would not question too closely the reasons behind the deals. This broker would need money upfront to open an account on which he would trade. He would certainly not start dealing without a cash input. Looking at these figures it would seem that a hundred thousand pounds was the initial amount involved. The broker would then utilise this amount to buy or sell commodities in whichever way he felt would benefit his client the most.'

'Good Lord!' exclaimed Christine. 'A hundred thousand. How could they get their hands on that sort of money, even from the school?'

'Well, maybe they wouldn't have to. Not in the way you

think,' said Donaldson. 'Forget about how they got the money in the first place just for the moment. I'll come back to that in a minute. Let's say the broker is happy to deal for this client and therefore starts trading on his behalf. In simple form, he might, for instance, buy one hundred thousand pounds worth of copper at tomorrow's date and sell it a week from tomorrow, all in the same phone call. If the price of copper rose ten per cent during the week, then the value is one hundred and ten thousand pounds. No need to sell it in a week's time because it was sold the day it was bought.

'When settlement time comes around, which may for instance be in three weeks' time, the client's profit is ten thousand pounds, less dealing charges, commission etc. If, however, the price falls ten per cent, then he's lost ten thousand pounds. Large financial institutions would not be expected to pay in advance for every deal. They would simply be sent a statement, and every so often they would either receive their profit, or, if a loss had been incurred, they would settle the loss with the broker.'

'Does that mean then,' said Richard, 'that Masterton would have to start by giving the broker, what was it, a hundred thousand pounds?'

'I don't know,' said Donaldson. 'I think any broker, however dubious, would insist on it. It's possible, however, that he might risk it. It has been known to happen. A small investor as in this case would normally have to deposit the amount of his trading investment before dealing on his behalf would be commenced. In that case, if a loss were incurred, the client would receive ten per cent less than his original investment if he decided to cease trading. Unfortunately, what happens so often is that private clients try to recover their losses by continuing to trade with the residue, often against the broker's advice, hoping for that lucky break.'

'That's what could have happened then,' said Christine. 'Masterton and the Bursar could have made a loss, using the school's funds. The sheets Alan picked up show such a loss as you've told us, and they're panicking like hell, not only because they've lost a lot of money, but also because those sheets can prove it, and they've been copied.'

'That's why Masterton was having a row with the Bursar about getting the deals covered,' said Richard.

He and Christine were looking thoughtful, but it was Bob Donaldson who spoke. 'Look,' he said. 'I'm not sure I can help you much more, but it's obvious that all three of you have a lot of thinking to do. But let me advise you to concentrate on two points particularly. Firstly, this is all conjecture. You would have great difficulty proving any of your suspicions even if they are well founded. So don't go accusing anybody of anything in public with the flimsy evidence you have at present. I would also suggest that the fewer people that know about your suspicions the better. You know how rumours can be misinterpreted. Furthermore...' He smiled at us in a slightly conspiratorial manner. 'I know that Richard, if he's anything like his uncle, will definitely be persuading you two to follow this thing through to the bitter end. So if I were you, I would consider this.

'Any organisation like your school, having charitable status or not, will have to produce accounts, and such accounts must be audited. This would be done by a firm of chartered accountants appointed by the board of governors. Now such a firm would have access to the school's bank accounts and financial investment records, and I am told that many schools have accounts produced every four months to coincide approximately with termly periods. It means that any cheques written on any of the school's bank accounts would be subject to the scrutiny of those appointed accountants at regular intervals. It would be most unlikely in my opinion that your suspects would be using school funds by this method, if indeed they are at all. In addition – and here is your problem – I consider it really unlikely that any commodity broker, whoever it is, would deal for a senior school official, whether acting on behalf of the school or not, without insisting that the initial trading amount be deposited before dealing began.'

Donaldson stood up and pushed his slim fingers through his mop of grey hair. He looked like a very mature schoolboy who wanted to join in this rather secretive game, but perhaps felt he was too senior. 'That leaves you with one or two unanswered questions,' he said. 'So now's the time to sleep on it for a bit. Chew it over during the next day or two. You're welcome to ring me here or at the office any time. If I'm busy, just ask my secretary when I'm likely to be free and try to get back to me. I know it'll be difficult for you during a teaching day, but whatever you do, don't just leave it. If you need to know anything further about the commodity business, or want to go over anything again, contact me.'

We had taken nearly two hours of his time, so we expressed our gratitude and departed. I left with the feeling that he was a man who was genuinely on our side. I felt I could trust him. I supposed that because he was a friend of Richard's uncle, it went without saying he would be honest. Even though I had begun to doubt my rather naive judgement of people, I still felt that our secret would be safe with him and I said as much to Richard and Christine.

'Of course we can trust him,' said Richard.

'Sooner or later we've got to trust somebody in this,' said Christine. 'We'll never be able to get to the bottom of it on our own. There's too much we don't know. Too much advice we need.'

Chapter 4

Maurice Tyler had been keeping a low profile for the last few years. His real name was Stephen Winch. He had been forced to change it when things got so hot for him with the police that he couldn't continue to operate as a political activist. That was when he was in his element, as part of a small group of extreme-left, post-graduate students who dealt in the business of 'Extra-Parliamentary Activity,' as it was known. This was a general term for breaking the law, and saying the law was wrong anyway. The slight difference, however, was that Stephen's happy little band was one of many in those days who used to do it with bombs, thus attracting rather intensive police attention.

His sister Maureen was still inside for it. She'd been the complete fanatical tearaway. Used to get high first and then hang around to see the results of her work. Was bound to be caught sooner or later. 'Serve her bloody well right,' the rest of them had said. 'Putting us all at risk.' Stephen was cleverer. He was never within two hundred miles of an explosion. Always made sure the detonating device was of a different type each time. Never left a 'Told you so' note, and never walked at the head of any rally or protest march. Even when he was pulled in for questioning, the police had no file on him, no photographs, never enough to hold him.

When the group split up after Maureen had been taken, he went to Glasgow and got a job teaching English. He laid low politically and then formed a group much smaller even than the previous one. They never allied themselves to any political party, or even any extreme group within a party. But they were as militant as hell and sordid with it.

One of their delights was to target a certain pillar of society for whom they felt a particular disapproval and then get hold of the family dog, cat or rabbit or something. Any animal that would be a pet of the children in the household. They would then kill it, usually by cutting its throat, and have it delivered by parcel post to the front door marked with 'Animal Welfare Club', or some such acceptable organisation's stamp. A threat against the offending parent would be enclosed. They also became experts with the exploding package through the post. Stephen had the top of the little finger of his right hand missing, owing to a mishap before they had become experts.

He had been dedicated to toppling the establishment ever since he could remember. He was a clever individual with a great deal of outward charm. He looked what he was, an intellectual, and he had that exceptional skill of being able to argue both sides of a case equally effectively. He used to do it on purpose. He would wind people up by arguing against them and then exasperate them by telling them how they should have presented their case in the first place.

He would wear a slightly faded sports jacket, with patches at the elbows, and a woollen tie with the top button of his shirt undone. He had curly, mouse-coloured hair, and on the tight-skinned bridge of his nose sat a pair of steel-rimmed spectacles. He had a slight squint in his left eye which unbalanced his gaze. This was as a result of his parents' similar problems of identification with society. They had this little boy with a squint, but his father was so intent on castigating the National Health Service as a political objective that the child was used as a test case in the left-wing press. He was made to miss his appointments with the orthoptists and ophthalmic surgeons, the blame firmly laid at the Health Minister's door for a delay of two years before the boy was properly treated. By that time it was too late for any standard form of cure without resorting to an operation, which he had, to this day, never undergone. A lot of political capital was made out of that, and the boy had lost the effective use of one eye.

Stephen's other valuable talent was in collecting around him people of the same militant leanings who had ordered and tidy minds but no inclination for leadership. This meant that with his brilliant brain he could define his ingenious plans to the group and also inspire its members, safe in the knowledge that there would be no challenge to his position as leader. This was important when dealing with intelligent people with unpleasant social habits.

He looked through the notes he had made when talking on the phone to this chap Pilcher. Sounded a public school type. Sort who wouldn't be a union member but wanted their help when the going got rough. Typical. Was speaking on behalf of a friend, he'd said. Why couldn't the friend ring up then? It usually meant there wasn't a friend and it was the caller who needed the advice. Have to watch that. 'Hmm, Bradchester. Love to stir a few things up there.'

He would have to be careful though. In the last few years,

since the miners' strike, things had not been too comfortable in the unions for the likes of Maurice Tyler. Suddenly they didn't want extremists any more. They were being voted off committees all over the country. Bad publicity. The rank and file member felt his job security threatened with too many of them at the helm. When unemployment had gone to four million, it wasn't the well-off, snotty middle classes who were out of a job. It was the card holders on the shop floor who never even used to vote at all who suffered. Now they were waking up and laying the blame squarely at the feet of the left. Thick idiots. Didn't they realise that if they'd stuck with it for a few more weeks, the Government would have cracked? Serve 'em right if they were out of a job. Why should Maurice Tyler care? Stupid buggers.

He'd always found it easy to use other people. They trusted him. He could persuade them that their best interests lay with his ideas and plans. He was very persuasive. He made people feel persecuted, downtrodden, underprivileged. 'You bloody well deserve better,' he would say. It was a language they could understand.

At Branch Headquarters where he'd got his job he'd managed to draw a veil over his distant past. That was a long time ago. He wasn't one for looking back. He hadn't even written to his sister for five years. A teachers' union wouldn't want his kind if they knew what his kind was. He had smoothed his way into the post with good references from his Glasgow job and a genuine approach to the current problems teachers were facing. New curriculum, assessment, extracurricular activities, bottom of the league table in real terms in pay, the new Children's Act. Maurice understood them all and was articulate with the press and other media.

The perfect branch secretary and maybe he could go all the way. Who knows? He'd been well behaved, courteous, and above all, dedicated to the teachers' cause.

Actually, he couldn't give a shit about them. As long as he had them as a respectable cover, he would wait until the right opportunity came along, when he could satisfy his yearning to go back underground and have a go at the establishment and its rotten corruption. His position at the moment suited him very well, and he was building up a fine reputation for a hard but meaningful approach to teachers' disputes with employers. The fact that he despised them and most of their other representatives for the weaklings they were didn't worry him as much as it would have done some years ago. Maybe he was maturing.

He hadn't neglected to make available to himself a few of the dubious characters he might need were he to see the opportunity of getting back to his old habits. Just a few, mind. Like-minded characters who just could not stand anyone who bore the stamp of 'Establishment'. The group were not active at the moment, as Maurice had seen to it that its small number of members understood fully that there was no future these days of being active just for the sake of it. You had to wait for the opportunity that would really make an impact. 'Wait for the big one', he would say. 'No bombs, no sickening parcels through the post, but good, honest sleuthing to undermine somebody in a really powerful position. If they happened to have leanings towards the Conservative Party, so much the better.'

The meeting with Carter and Pilcher from Bradchester had not been a great success. He'd had to travel to a place called Thaxbury, some forty miles away, to meet the two teachers in a small hotel as they couldn't get to his office until the school holidays. Since he'd needed to ascertain quickly whether there was going to be any mileage in this case, he'd agreed to their suggestion. Carter was a union member all right and was the injured party, but the other one, Pilcher, seemed to be the more astute and did most of the talking. Maurice took an instant dislike to him. Conceited, self-assured, silver-spoon type and rather patronising. Nevertheless, Maurice went out of his way to be civil to him.

He knew straight away that Carter had a reasonable case for unfair dismissal as he did not appear to have been warned at all for it, which he should have been under the Employment Act. It was quite obvious also that if Maurice were to really look into the circumstances, he would almost certainly find some other departure from the statutory procedures for dismissal. He was not, however, interested in a run-of-the-mill, unfair-dismissal tribunal case but preferred to see if there was anything rather more meaty he could uncover.

He had told them that in his opinion there would be no future in going for unfair dismissal, and they had seemed surprised and disappointed. He'd misled them with one of his smoother performances but unfortunately hadn't been able to get them to divulge any other possible misdeeds by the school authorities. He felt that if he'd been talking to Carter on his own, he'd have got more. He was convinced the history teacher had been on the point of divulging some sort of additional information. Pilcher, however, had put his oar in to shut him up and quickly changed the subject. Maurice had made a note to try to get Carter on his own sometime.

The meeting had broken up with neither side hearing

what they wanted to, but that was because Tyler had been lying, and the two teachers had only been telling half the story. Richard and Alan had gone away feeling surprised at Tyler's attitude, and the union man was damn sure there was something being held back.

Norman Willett received a note two days later asking him to ring the union branch office and ask for Tyler. The Branch Secretary had wanted to know if he thought there was anything else behind the sacking of Carter. Willett couldn't throw any further light on the matter but assured Tyler importantly that if there was anything, he would find out. Tyler told him he probably wouldn't and that he was not to try. He put the phone down and wrote 'prat' against Willett's name in his notes.

He then rang a member of his little group of social misfits, one Ernest Diggens, and told him he had a job for him of an investigative nature.

Diggens had a fondness for the devious but had been trained to leave that side of things to Maurice, whose talent in that direction was in a much higher league. Diggens was intelligent enough to acknowledge the fact and thus was a useful and subservient means of obtaining information by patient watching and waiting. He was put to work patiently watching Richard Pilcher and Alan Carter and waiting.

The address he was given, obtained from the union membership details, was just across the road from Bradchester School main buildings, and he found a convenient spot at the end of an adjacent side street from which he could watch the front door of the flat from his parked car. His instructions were to make a note of the physical description and time of anyone who entered the building. Being one of the nation's unemployed by choice, he didn't actually mind sitting in his car most of the day. It was boring for sure, but he had learnt by experience that whenever Maurice asked him to do anything, there was invariably a worthwhile end product. Maurice's hunches were a hell of a lot better than anyone else's. Also his payment for services rendered was more reliable than most although he would only pay up if the information supplied was beneficial to the cause on which Maurice had decided to embark. All in all, working for Maurice was usually profitable, and he had indicated this little exercise would only be for a few days.

The Branch Secretary was only mildly interested, however, when Diggens rang him at his home after a week and said that two males were regular users of the flat in question, and that a dark-haired girl in her early twenties often accompanied one of them in and out, and had stayed the night on one occasion. Diggens had then been told that he might as well give the Headmaster's house a few days' and nights' surveillance and he was to phone in a week's time for further instructions.

Tyler had been much more interested when he had received a call at his office from Alan Carter saying that some information had come to light which put a totally different complexion on the matter. This information would be made available to the union if Maurice would meet him again at the same hotel as before. He'd quickly agreed a mutually convenient time and, as he replaced the receiver, he awarded himself the luxury of a satisfied smile. At last, he thought to himself, maybe we are to be given something to work on. I wonder what this 'new information' can be.

He was already formulating in his thoughts to what good use he would put it, should it turn out to be damaging enough for what he had in mind.

* * *

I suppose it was after receiving the Headmaster's letter of dismissal that I started to grow up where the ways of the world are concerned. That letter had shaken me out of my naive belief that the world in which I would like to earn my living was a nice safe ride to retirement and that everybody to do with the education of our children couldn't be anything else but basically honest. Well, bollocks to all that!

I had just come from a real eye-opening experience with the school's Director of Studies. He set out for me the exact opposite of what I thought, and of what everyone in the common room had seemed to be saying. My opinion, and apparently that of my colleagues, was that I was a more than adequate teacher of history at the level for which I was employed, and my prospects for being kept on to do that job alone would be considered to be almost a foregone conclusion.

The Director of Studies had delivered a well-prepared lecture to me about it not being enough just to appear to be popular with the boys and other staff. One's relationships with pupils had to be translated into hard evidence that the right results were likely to be achieved, not only for boys but also, of course, for the school. 'This was not happening in my case,' he'd said. 'There was evidence of complacency in letters the school had received from some parents.' No! I would not be permitted to see these letters, as they were confidential admissions of concern and had been addressed to the Headmaster. Yes, the Headmaster had consulted him on several occasions spanning the last few weeks and, yes, the concern had been justified – most regrettably, of course, but up until now the school had followed its policy of allowing a new teacher time to settle before raising issues such as inadequacy.

My interview with the Head of the History Department had been no more successful. 'I'm very sorry Carter, but when the Head calls for an appraisal of a teacher's performance, which is quite common, especially when there have been complaints about commitment and dedication, a department head such as myself really has to take a responsible attitude and relate the facts as he sees them. In your case, I really am very sorry to say that I had no alternative but to report that I've had doubts about you measuring up for some weeks now. Most of this term, in fact. Possibly you have some problem outside school which you have been bringing into the classroom. Or perhaps the cricket coaching has been taking too much time from your preparation of the history curriculum.

'You see, Carter, it's the long-term view that we have to think about. You've only been here less than two terms admittedly, but it's time enough for us to see that as a long-term prospect, your future does not – most regrettably I have to say – lie with us. Believe me, Carter, we have a great deal of experience in these matters. Many young teachers like you pass through our hands, and we would actually be doing you a disservice, you know, if we were to allow you to go on thinking that your future lay with us. I'm really sorry.'

I suppose two weeks ago I would have believed every word they were saying. I would have nodded thoughtfully, tried to hide my disappointment and probably even said thank you for the advice. I would then have decided to abandon my career as a teacher on the assumption that such wise and venerable educationalists had my best interests at heart and really were giving me their wisest counsel.

Now I thought they were two lying creeps who had been got at by the Headmaster to manufacture an almost identical story, which it would be very hard for anyone to disprove. Both of them were in the later stages of their teaching careers, with the greater part of their superannuation contributions intact. They would find it very difficult to obtain a similar position in another school at a comparable salary so why should they take the risk of crossing the Head? No, they weren't going to be taking any chances on my account. 'Most regrettable,' my arse!

I felt quite pleased that I'd come to this aggressive conclusion about two senior teachers for whom, until just now, I'd had nothing but respect. I was quite surprised at myself, but still felt the tiniest bit of doubt as to the wisdom of casting their smoothly delivered conclusions aside without considering them further. I knew, however, that Christine and Richard would agree with my new-found description of them and would countenance no going back. I decided I needed Christine and Richard's support in preference to anyone else's. It also appeared that I had little to lose now by antagonising senior members of the common room.

The three of us had talked long and hard since my interviews with the Director of Studies and my Head of Department, and I could see no alternative but to throw myself on Masterton's mercy and plead for a second chance.

Richard had disagreed. 'No, no, Alan!' He was on his feet,

almost attacking me. 'If you do that, he'll manipulate you. He'll wring out of you what it is we're thinking of doing. The best thing we can do is try to work out how we can prove there's something incriminating in those papers and use that evidence as a threat to get him to reinstate you.'

'But that will take ages,' I said. 'Even if we do manage it.'

'Well, he'll certainly not change his mind unless we force him to. Look at the trouble he's been to getting old Dawkins and Edmonds to doctor their reports about you. I've never heard anything so bent in my life. No, it's better if you appear for the moment to be accepting the situation. At least that way he won't be on his guard so much, and it might give us the chance to come up with something.'

I looked at Christine for support.

She had been thinking through a different line of approach. 'I think he'll have considered that we might consult the union,' she said. She was staring hard at the table in front of her as if trying to wrest a logical train of thought from it. 'If so, what would his next move be? Maybe to question Norman Willet. That wouldn't get him very far, I shouldn't think. In any case, Norman doesn't really know anything, and he certainly wouldn't get anything out of the union branch office. They never divulge a thing about a member's affairs until they're good and ready. If this Branch Secretary chap Maurice Tyler is not enthusiastic about an unfair dismissal case, then I don't think there's much point in our trying to change his mind, especially as the two people to whom we should have to look to for support have been nobbled already.

'The Headmaster has obviously been way ahead of us all the time. The moment he thought the union might be brought in for unfair dismissal for inadvertently taking away and then copying papers, he changed his approach and decided on an incompetence charge against Alan. He then immediately saw to it that, who was it, those two, Edmonds and Dawkins, were put under enough pressure to report about you exactly what he wanted to hear. I'll bet he's got it in writing from them as well.'

I was beginning to feel frustrated by the way things were turning out. I looked to Richard and Christine to come up with something positive, but despite their sharp minds, they were shooting all the possible options down in flames.

'Look!' I said. 'I really can't wait around for something to happen because it won't unless we make it.' I put on my pleading expression. 'If I go and see Masterton and ask for another chance, at least I'll be keeping in contact with the problem. As it is, I feel it'll all go away quietly and me with it.'

Neither of them spoke.

'All right,' I said. 'Your silence settles the matter. If no-one's got a better suggestion, that's what I'm going to do.'

'Just suppose,' said Christine, 'that Masterton says "No way", or words to that effect. What would you do then?'

'I don't know,' I said. 'I'll just have to think of something on the spur of the moment. Maybe I'll say we've got another copy of the papers.'

'For Christ's sake,' said Richard. 'Don't do that. You'll blow the whole thing.'

'Well, what do you suggest?'

Once again the normally effusive Richard was at a loss for words.

Christine said, 'You know, I can't really see any harm in whatever you were to say. The only thing that'll happen if we do nothing will be that you will remain dismissed.' She glanced at Richard for approval but received a blank look of mild confusion. That was also the way I was feeling, so we left it there and I went to bed rather encouraged by my show of decision making, even if it was born of a state of perplexity.

Of course I should have realised I wouldn't get anywhere near the Headmaster. His skinny beanpole of a secretary soon made that clear. She was well trained, I'll say that for her. 'I'm sorry, Mr Carter, the Head can't possibly see you until the middle of next week. His schedule is very full with meetings and conferences. I could leave a message, of course.' I thought that if she had a bigger plum in her mouth, she might choke.

That settled it. I would write a letter saying that if he didn't see me within forty-eight hours, as was my right after being dismissed, I would inform the union. I didn't know if it was my right or not. Probably wasn't. I didn't seem to have any rights these days. It sounded good though.

Not only did it sound good, it was good. I was in Masterton's study the next day. The secretary informed me that she'd had to rearrange his programme to fit me in and 'would you not take too long, please'. A 'please' no less. I must have hit the right nerve.

I tried the pleading tactics first.

He was actually quite charming. 'I appreciate you coming to see me, Carter, and I also respect you for it. But you see, I have to think of the long-term view.' He turned away and moved around the room with very measured steps, his gaze angled at about forty-five degrees above the horizontal. He seemed to be inspecting the tops of the pictures on the walls.

He thrust his hands deep into his pockets. I wondered if he'd been practising this speech.

He rabbited on for a bit and I seemed to be hearing nothing but a slur of words. To my surprise it didn't concern me greatly what they were, but I did hear them. 'So, of course, you must see that we all really have your best interests at heart, and will do our very best to ensure you are able to further your career at an establishment more suited to your particular talents and level of experience, Carter. I'm sure you understand.'

I didn't understand. I said, 'Well, if you won't consider my request to be reinstated, Headmaster...'. I was now beyond the point of no return. '...I have no alternative but to instruct my union to proceed with a case for unfair dismissal.'

'Suit yourself, Carter,' he said, without turning a hair. 'You'll get no reference from me if that's the stand you wish to take. But it's your decision.' He stopped pacing and leant over me with a benevolent expression. 'I can help you if you'll let me, but my patience is limited and I'm a very busy man. It may interest you to know that we've handled quite a few tribunals here, if that is what you're referring to, and since I've been Headmaster, we've won them all. Also,' he went on, 'you would be placing your friend Pilcher in an awkward position.'

'What do you mean?' I said.

'Well, he's already had a formal warning, and I don't think it would look too good for him if he were to be seen in sympathy with a teacher who lost a tribunal case against the school.'

Bastard, I thought. And then I said, 'What was the warning for, Headmaster?'

'Now look, Carter. I really can't discuss it. It's a confidential matter and I shall tell you for the last time. Either you accept your dismissal and a reference from me or you make trouble from which I shall certainly not lift a finger to extract you. Now kindly leave my office and make your decision. I've given you more time than your situation deserves.' He rang for the beanpole and I was dispatched like something unpleasant that had got stuck to the carpet.

I decided I would get the papers and take them to Maurice Tyler. I knew Richard would be against it, so I told Christine. Funnily enough, she wasn't totally opposed to the idea. When I described how Masterton had thrown me out after I asked him what Richard had been warned for, she nodded as if in agreement.

'I suppose he would have guessed Richard would have told you anyway,' she said, 'and throwing you out was the only thing he could think of to avoid the ticklish subject of the copied papers.'

'Yes,' I said. 'And I honestly think that settles it. I'll have to get Tyler and the union to take it from here.'

'It's going to be a bit difficult to prove there's enough in the papers to make Masterton back down, you know.' Christine's forehead was furrowed over her dark eyebrows. 'He may just deny there's anything untoward in them and, to tell the truth, we don't actually know for a fact that there is, do we?'

'I know that. But as I've said before, if we do nothing, I'm dead. If we give it a try, at least I'm still in the game. I've got nothing to lose and it'll be the last card I've got to play.'

I broke the news to Richard of the decision Christine and I had reached, after I had described in detail my abortive pleading session with the Headmaster, and the apparent reason for my swift exit.

He started to protest, but without much conviction, and so we were all agreed that the copies of the papers should go to the union. I felt relieved that I had the support of both of them, as this was the sort of thing I didn't fancy tackling alone.

Next day I phoned Tyler and told him why I thought we should meet again. He had no hesitation in agreeing to come over again the next evening. I thought it was uncommonly good of him to do so at such short notice.

Chapter 5

'No, I'm bloody well not discussing it on the telephone,' said Masterton. The first half of the sentence was delivered at maximum volume but the second almost under his breath as he realised the need for care. Somebody in the outer office might just be interested in a raised voice. Better to be cautious. He cupped his hand round the mouthpiece. 'And there's no way I'm coming anywhere near your office. That would be really stupid. You'll have to come here. It would be quite natural for the father of a boy at the school to visit the headmaster. You've been here before? Oh, I suppose that's all right... yes, yes... this evening at ten then.'

He slammed the receiver down and turned to the Bursar, who was sitting bolt upright in one of the easy chairs. 'That was that damn fool broker. Says he must see us urgently. Apparently there's a problem.'

The Bursar, Colonel Bradley William Trent (retired), had not been looking forward to hearing this particular piece of news. In fact, ever since they'd got involved in this commodity-dealing business things had gone from bad to worse. The trouble was that the Colonel – actually he had not made it past Lieutenant Colonel and felt he'd been passed over – was a proud man. He was proud of his title and his position at Bradchester. Rather prouder as it happened of his own achievements, which were not too spectacular, than the institutions he served. He was, therefore, one of those men who never quite held the respect of those around him, and, although thick-skinned enough not to realise it, was always the object of a certain amount of ridicule. Mind you, as a Bursar, one was not expected to be popular, particularly amongst the teaching staff. Constant monitoring of departmental expenditure was part of the job, so one was always looking over other people's shoulders, which tended to upset them. Just lately, however, he'd been feeling the pressures of the job. He'd never been comfortable with the banks of computers, word processors, answerphones and various state-of-the-art machines that now were the norm in large schools such as this.

His assistant handled all that sort of thing, but he had noticed that a large proportion of other bursars he met at district meetings and association gatherings were younger, better qualified, and well versed in the language of modern office technology. He could hold his own at things like drains and building regulations, and he fancied that the clerk of works department, the domestic bursar and all the catering and cleaning staff respected him for his man-management qualities. He was, however, mindful of the fact that he was having to delegate more and more decisions to the staff under him, who seemed entirely capable of handling things. So much so that they'd begun not to refer to him at all where a quick and decisive answer was required. He was, therefore, not unexpectedly under more stress than he would wish.

This latest business of the commodities was altogether more than he could cope with. He had really been blackmailed into it by the Head, by whom, if he were honest, he was overawed. The man was so capable, had such a quick brain and actually understood more of the Colonel's job than he did himself. It had been about a year ago when Masterton had basically told him that he would have to make way for a younger, more qualified, man.

The Head had been clever. He knew full well that the Bursar was no longer up to the job. It had been painfully obvious for some time. But he also understood how essential a position like that was to a man like Trent. Ethos and pecking order were what kept him going. The bursar holds a very senior position in a public school. He is considered to be on a par with, and very often senior to, the deputy head and is usually the only employee of the school, apart from the headmaster, who is appointed by the board of governors. Everyone else is either employed by the head or bursar themselves on behalf of the board, or council, as it is sometimes called.

Masterton needed the Colonel in the job, as he was vulnerable. He could also be manipulated. A more apt word than 'bribed' in this case. Trent was hard up. There was no doubt about that. He had a very sick wife, who had been in and out of mental institutions, but he'd managed to persuade a residential home to keep her, by agreeing to the condition that an extra full-time nurse was employed to attend to her special needs and to keep her out of the way of the other residents. This was costing him far more than his Army pension and school salary would cover, especially as he had taken to playing the horses in a desperate attempt to make ends meet. He was not the type of man who could face the reality of having his wife in a mental establishment. He had, therefore, agreed to Masterton's proposal that the board could be persuaded to keep him on, providing he delegated more of his duties to his subordinates and also assisted the Head on those very rare occasions when the odd financial discrepancy became necessary.

Masterton's idea of an odd discrepancy was not the same as Trent's and consequently the Bursar was now way out of his depth. He was also drinking a lot more than usual, which meant a hell of a lot.

'What does he want?' enquired Trent.

'If I knew that, he wouldn't be coming round here, would he?' snapped Masterton.

The Headmaster had a good idea though, and it was already making his brain work overtime. The phone call had been the logical follow up to the ones he'd been receiving regularly up to a week ago and which had sparked off the row between the two of them. That had ended in the unfortunate occurrence when a junior master had taken the commodity statements away and copied them. The previous calls had been to confirm that their dealing position was vulnerable, and that if the deals were not covered quickly, a substantial loss was likely. The next part of Masterton's defensive plan would not be so easy as it involved the putting of pressure on another of his slightly unwilling allies.

He ejected the Bursar from his office with a wave of his hand as if dismissing a waiter from the table. He then sat down to think.

He had, until about two minutes ago, judged himself to be in a reasonably invulnerable position. The school was flourishing and, apart from having a slight shortage of boarders in common with the national trend, was virtually full. He had achieved what the Governors had asked of him in both improving the academic standard and promoting the school into the same league as some of its more illustrious competitors. The fixture list now included Winchester, Radley, Tonbridge and most recently Harrow, and he had received the encouragement of his employers as a result of the way things were shaping.

On the way to this indisputable success, however, he had unfortunately created one or two skeletons, which he'd rather were not occupying his cupboard. Masterton never did anything by halves and consequently, on his way up, he had deemed it necessary to remove obstacles that might hinder his progress. He felt justified in so doing as he reasoned that, in his case, to impede a talented man's progress was a greater sin than the removal of such impediments.

He had decided much earlier in his career that, in order to influence those with influence, you needed money – and quite lot of it. He considered that the likelihood of him ever having enough for what he had in mind was nil. Being penniless was consequently an obstacle that had to be removed.

He therefore married money. It hadn't been too difficult. He had the charm, the confidence, and to his own great surprise, the patience in those days to make himself play a little hard to get with a very well-heeled lady who was not quite good-looking enough to be snapped up before she began to get worried. He remembered having to decide whether an impoverished good-looking wife would be more useful to him than a plain but wealthy one. As there didn't seem to be any wealthy good-looking ones available, he found the compromise a simple one to accept.

Unfortunately the lady had turned out to be determined

and rather intelligent. She had presented him along the way with four fine children and provided him with the trappings of affluence sufficient to keep him on course for success. He had made the right contacts, moved into higher social strata and had begun to impress some extremely influential people in the educational hierarchy. A pity it was then when, on meeting one of the previously absent females possessed of both wealth and good looks, his head had been turned.

His wife had punished him by making him totally reliant upon her for the financial wherewithal necessary to maintain the little luxuries to which he had been pleased to become accustomed. Nothing too drastic – just pocket money, really.

Her inheritance included a substantial lodge in the Highlands of Scotland with ten miles of salmon fishing, a fourteen-bedroomed house in Hampshire standing in three hundred acres and what most experts agreed was the finest trout fishing on the river Test. Both these estates formed part of a property company set up by her father many years before, shortly after his wife died. Her brother had inherited similar assets, mostly in Scotland, and he looked after the management of all the properties, through an estate management company of which she was an equal director. Brother and sister got on well enough, so the operation was, in fact, most harmonious.

A generous part of the income she received from the fishing and the house, part of which had been turned into an extremely exclusive and lucrative country hotel had, initially, been made available to Masterton. He had put it to good use and soon found that the acquaintances and contacts he made by being a headmaster and a country gentleman were something he would find it difficult to relinquish.

Since his indiscretions though, she had kept him practically penniless but still deigned to give him complete freedom of the estates. He now had to run his social life on his headmaster's pay, whereas before he'd enjoyed the luxury of an additional, and virtually unlimited, expense account. She made him crawl to her to allow him to throw a house party. She denied him the use of her accounts with all their suppliers, and he had to justify every penny of his expenditure outside his own bank accounts. The estate staff were forbidden to sign for anything on his behalf, and she took a particular delight in hearing him request finance from her in front of other members of the family or even guests.

She was not going to let this snotty little social climber get away with taking her inheritance for granted. He would now have to grovel for it.

The reasonably invulnerable position he had held before he put the telephone down on the broker had been established by way of obtaining a substitute for the spending money hitherto denied him. He had done remarkably well out of dealing in the commodity market through this man and had even ceased having to demean himself for his pocket money. The markets had been kind to him and he had been able to produce a satisfactory supplement to his earned income.

He knew, however, that the visit from the commodity man would put an end to all that and even turn the situation dramatically against him.

Julian Hedley drove his Rolls-Royce with its personalised number plate right up to the front door of the Headmaster's house. Being well protected from the main school complex by a screen of oaks and beeches, it afforded sufficient privacy, but was indisputably the residence of the man in command of this spread of academic splendour.

If you were to take the short pathway from the side door and open the wrought-iron gate in the kitchen-garden wall, you would enter a small courtyard. Cross this and you would take three steps up into a small cloistered passage which in turn led through a low archway. Before you, lay the heart of this ages-old keeper of traditional middle-class ideals and principles called an English public school.

More cloisters bounded three sides of a patterned lawn. The fourth, and south–facing side, fell away in terraced grass banking to the main cricket ground, encircled by mature trees and bench seats, and thence to playing fields almost as far as the eye could see. Beyond the green-carpeted quadrangle your eye would be caught by more modern shapes of the science block, sports hall, music school and library, all creeping out and away from this centrepiece of educational inspiration, which was the mainspring of all that happened at Bradchester. Dominating the whole, and stepped along the whole length of the west cloisters, stood the magnificent chapel, its buttresses and stained-glass windows seeming to safeguard with spiritual reinforcement the moral and academic ideals strived for in this seat of learning.

You could, if so inclined, lose your soul to the temptation of the place and its mantle of protection from the dirt and squalor of the world outside its walls. You could easily be seduced by the peace and strength that enfolded you when crossing the threshold and entering to teach in the haven of the sanctuary within. You might find perfection here, some would say, in the most satisfying profession on this planet. You might find that elusive security so sought after and envied by those risking everything to have their sons educated by such as you.

High summer at Bradchester was, to some, a sultry, melodic sample of eternity, a brief glimpse of the life hereafter.

Julian Hedley didn't give a bugger about storing up treasures in heaven. He was behind with the payments on his Rolls and he hadn't been able to meet the horrendous fees needed to keep his son at school here. He needed the treasures in this life and he needed them now.

He rang the bell and Masterton himself answered the door.

It didn't take the two men long to come to verbal blows.

'You're a liar, Hedley,' said Masterton. 'You gave me your word that the deals would be sound and that there would be a two-month period within which to cover any shortfall.'

'Don't be so damn naive,' came the swift response. 'These operations take time. You can't sit here in your ivory tower and ignore the facts. The real world won't go away with cucumber sandwiches and a prayer at morning chapel.'

Hedley swigged at his whisky. He was the complete opposite to Robert Donaldson. He was overweight. He did have big lips and when he was in the City, he did wear blue, pinstriped suits. At the moment he was dressed in a light grey, single-breasted, summer-weight suit, cream-coloured shirt and tie, and grey leather deck shoes. He was also sweating profusely.

Masterton started his habitual room pacing. 'You can't just suddenly stroll in here and demand settlement. You know that's impossible. And you must face up to your responsibility for having misled us about the risks involved with those deals.'

'Now look, Masterton.' Hedley was starting to pinch his glossy lips together. It was a sign that he was expecting an unpleasant encounter. 'You people are always the same. When someone's investments don't turn out as they planned, particularly when they lose money, the first thing they do is look for a scapegoat. Somebody else to blame. It's never their fault. They were given the wrong advice, or they've conveniently forgotten they were warned of the risks involved. So don't start getting stroppy with me, because you knew full well what you were getting into. It was you who insisted I gave you the long lecture about the pitfalls before the account was opened.'

'Yes, but you were adamant that the risks were small and you even said that everyone in the City was onto this particular deal, and if we got in early enough, we would clean up.'

'Don't expect me to agree with you,' said Hedley. 'I'm used to people telling me what they wish I'd said to them, especially after a deal has gone sour. I've kept you in touch all the way along and I even encouraged you to get out of the operation not only when you were ahead, but also while your losses were relatively small. You've taken it upon yourself to stay in, completely against my advice. That's why I'm going to clear the cheque I'm holding from you, unless you can come up with the amount of your losses in cash from some other source. From what you've told me, I think that's most unlikely, so I'm giving you three days, and then that cheque gets presented. Do I make myself clear?'

Masterton had gone a sickly pale colour. He strode to the cabinet and poured half a tumbler of whisky, swallowing most of it in one.

'That cheque, as you well know,' he said, narrowing and

levelling his eyes at the broker, 'is drawn on the school's current account, and signed by me and the Bursar. Do you know what would happen if it were to clear through the bank account and the auditors were to ask for an explanation?'

'Frankly, I don't give a damn,' said Hedley. 'I've given you more than enough warnings, which you've chosen to ignore. You're the most intransigent bastard I've ever come across, Masterton, and I'll not put up with your arrogance any longer. I would remind you that none of us at the moment are in a position to allow clients to delay settlements, let alone rat on agreements, which is obviously what you're about to do. I would also remind you that, in order to accommodate you in this operation, I have undertaken the transactions in my own name. The deals are actually at my risk. You would have not easily found another commodity broker to take on deals on behalf of a school. Good God, man! It's obviously unethical. Schools aren't supposed to be in the risk business. I told you right at the start. What do you think your Board of Governors would say if they knew you were playing with the school's funds? They'd crucify you, and rightly so.'

Masterton drained his glass. He knew he was drinking more than he could adequately handle. He was also panicking. He was totally unused to being spoken to in this manner and it threatened his composure. He was accustomed to throwing his own weight about when dealing with subordinates. He could usually bluster his way out of a tight argument by pulling rank or using veiled threats, but when it came to an oral onslaught with a man obviously well used to squaring up to others under stressful circumstances, he felt very second-rate and extremely uncomfortable.

Hedley pushed home his advantage. 'You will now

understand,' he sneered, 'why I took the precaution of insisting that you deposit that cheque with me. It's when people like you snivel and whine that you make me sick. You want to play with the big boys but want someone else to take the rap when you get your fingers burnt.'

'All right! All right!' said Masterton. 'You've made your point. But don't forget that part of our agreement was that I persuade the board that you had a good case for a substantial reduction in boarding fees for your son for the rest of his time here. I suppose you've conveniently forgotten that.'

'No, I haven't,' said Hedley. 'On the basis of that arrangement, I agreed to undertake the deals. As I say, you would have been hard pushed to find another broker to do it for you. We both made concessions to accommodate each other. I'm not, however, going to be threatened as a consequence of you not taking my best advice to cut your losses and get out.'

Masterton tried to play what he thought was a trump card. 'So go ahead and present that cheque,' he said smugly. 'You'll find the bank won't accept it anyway.'

'I'm aware that that might be the case,' said Hedley. 'What do you take me for? It didn't take me more than five minutes to find out, even before I insisted on the cheque, that with an amount like this, the Chairman of Governors might have to be one signatory. Why do you think I got you and that fool Bursar of yours to sign? I've now got two of you in the hot seat. And incidentally, if the cheque doesn't clear, a copy of it will be in the Chairman's post within a week. You can bet on it. I'm sure he and the rest of the finance committee will be delighted to know how you are intending to risk school funds to cover your own speculative mismanagement.'

Hedley paused. This man was a complete walkover. He could see him crumbling before his eyes. The broker continued to enjoy the spectacle of Masterton adopting a 'cornered-animal' look. There was one chink in Hedley's armour, however, about which it would be better if the Headmaster remained ignorant. That was the fact that if it got about that Hedley had taken on a school as a client in commodity transactions, he could be in serious trouble in the City. The recent Financial Services Act had seen to it that the onus lay with the broker to fully inform every client through statutory procedures, and withdrawal notifications, of his rights and obligations concerning any transactions. This was to avoid clients, particularly private or uninformed ones, being enticed into just such a position as Masterton had. Hedley had certainly not abided by the new rules of the game, but instead had agreed to deal in his own name on Masterton's behalf, on condition that he was in possession of a school cheque, signed by both the Head and the Bursar, as his security against any 'mishap'.

Hedley had never intended that the deals should go disastrously wrong. It had been one of those occasions when the whole City had been swept along by the euphoria of a killing if you were on top of the situation. You had to be at your desk or dealing board virtually twenty-four hours a day. You had to be the first with the information that prices were moving and you had to act fast when things started to happen. It had happened in the currency market and the stock market many times. The commodity market was less affected, as here the movements in prices and the amounts of money involved tended to be less spectacular, and the press reporting less attentive.

What usually happened was that some international or political upheaval would put the main export or raw material of the particular country involved at risk. There would therefore be a mad panic to buy that commodity before it became unobtainable in the quantities required to service world demand, and before the price went through the roof.

You could buy low, if you were quick enough, and you really had to be a professional dealer to be that quick, and then sell almost immediately and take your profit. You could sell forward and also secure your profit, or you could do what a lot of people who came unstuck did, and hang on for a really big killing. The thing was in this case to know when the price had peaked. When it did and the word was out, the price could fall so fast that unless you were 'in the know', everybody was selling and there were no buyers. The price on these occasions often went back to a level below that at which it had started, and before the also-rans had managed to find a buyer.

That was exactly what had happened to Masterton's little joyride.

Hedley and he had been quite good friends at one time. His boy was doing really well at Bradchester and the Head had often invited Hedley and his wife to drinks or a dinner party at the school. Masterton knew what every parent's business was of course, as it was on the entry questionnaire for their child, and he was quick to cultivate friendships with those who might be of benefit, either financially or socially. Until quite recently Hedley had been doing very well for his clients and himself in commodities, but it had all started to go wrong when the recession really began to bite. The speculators had suddenly vanished. The credit bonanza had seized up. Rather than risk a flutter in the City, they were busy trying to sell their houses. The big investors were still there, but they had never dealt with the likes of Hedley. He had no pedigree. He was too flash. He had to rely on small portfolios, private clients. It was a shrinking market. He had also come unstuck on a couple of his own deals. More importantly, he wasn't the first person people rang with any hot financial news, and nobody was doing him any favours with prices either. He was not, therefore, the best person with whom to trust a lump sum with which to make a killing in a very competitive market.

Masterton had been captivated by the idea of a speculative gain in commodities. He could see himself at a cocktail party saying, 'Just taken advantage of a little variation in the price of aluminium.' Or, 'My people in the City, you know... saw a little opportunity in softs, and I gave them the nod.' Hedley had explained it all so clearly. He'd said the risks would be minimal, as he would personally be taking care of the deals. He wouldn't put him into anything he would not deal in himself.

Masterton had started small at Hedley's suggestion. The broker had dealt in his own name. 'Avoids the red tape,' he'd said.

He'd done quite well. Well enough to get hooked, but it was just about then that his wife had put the screws on his allowance. Masterton had become desperate. His position was being compromised. People were making polite enquiries as to his generosity. His life style seemed to have deteriorated. Was the school still in good shape?

He found it difficult to accept these sorts of comments in the same light as everyone else had to. 'The recession is still with us so we've got to tighten our belts,' they would say.

Masterton was damned if was going to tighten his belt. It wasn't the recession that had made him hard up. It was his wife, who had found out who he was fornicating with. If that hadn't happened, he would now have appeared to be flusher than most of his acquaintances. This he found irritating. He was therefore a sucker for the sort of quick killing Hedley said 'came along from time to time.'

There had been such an opportunity once before. Hedley had said the time was right but had insisted that Masterton give him a cheque, drawn on the school's account and signed by himself and the Bursar. Masterton hadn't wanted to go along with that, and so a golden opportunity had been missed. It had been a beauty too. There would have been a clear profit of sixty thousand pounds on an outlay of one hundred thousand. Hedley had shown him the figures. 'If only you'd gone along with it,' he'd scolded.

Masterton was livid. It'd taken him a little time to persuade Trent to sign the cheque on the second occasion, but he knew the Colonel was desperate and was on the point of having to move his wife to a mental hospital. He'd offered him a twenty per cent share of the profits, and shown him the figures for the deal they'd just missed. ' A similar deal was on the cards,' he'd said, according to the inside information he had from the City.

There was little risk. The hundred thousand was only to be used as collateral. It was not at risk. In any case, if there was a loss, the commodities would be sold very quickly, and the deal closed off. The hundred thousand would be intact, less that minute part of it that was the difference between the buying and selling prices. It was a tiny risk to take to share in an odds-on winner. The cheque would never be presented as the only one that would pass would be the one bearing their profit on it, and that would come from the broker to them personally. The school would never be involved, except to persuade the broker to do the deal for them in the first place.

Trent had finally been persuaded when Masterton had casually mentioned that there was a board meeting the next week and he was sure the Bursar wouldn't need reminding that the average age of the administration staff had been a subject discussed at the last one. The Colonel didn't need his memory jogged on that score. He was Clerk to the Governors himself and had produced the minutes to that meeting. He had also been requested to produce a list of such staff and their ages to present to the board for their perusal. He was the oldest on that list by far.

The cheque had been made out for one hundred thousand pounds, payable to Hedley, signed by Masterton and Trent, post-dated one month, and the cheque stub marked 'error – cheque destroyed'. Hedley had waited for the right opportunity which, as it happened, was not long in coming.

Press comment in London and New York had started a speculative rush in copper which, rumour had it, was something more than an overnight blip. Hedley had managed to buy in, not at the bottom, but near enough to satisfy him. His judgement appeared justified when the forward price also rose and continued to do so. He prepared to sell forward at a handsome turn, but was talked out of it by a very excited Masterton, who had phoned him at the office. The Headmaster had been chatting to some bankers and stockbrokers at a drinks party, and they had seemed convinced that if anyone had got in at or near the bottom of this copper business, they should stay for the ride. They had appeared quite envious of the price at which Masterton had apparently bought in.

Hedley had said it was risky, but Masterton had insisted he should let the investment run. Talked about stopping the cheque and cancelling Hedley's school fees reduction if he didn't. Said that everyone else was staying for the ride and so should they. Hedley had been tempted, as he had money of his own in this deal, and he really did need to land a big profit to recoup some of his recent heavy losses. He had checked around and it really did seem as though Masterton's contacts were right. The price was still rising. He decided to sell some of his own holding forward as a small hedge, but kept the majority of funds open-ended.

The price continued to rise the next day, and he sold another small amount of his own purchase. His instincts told him to get out now. He rang Masterton who said 'No! stay with it.' He was enjoying the ride and was counting the profits they were making by the hour. Hedley was adamant. The price was soaring, however, and they had cleared almost forty thousand pounds. Masterton wanted sixty thousand. He had heard about some of the really huge gains made in the past. People were talking about the historic, record-breaking price fluctuations that had made fortunes overnight. Masterton was convinced this was his chance and he was going to clean up.

Driving his company's Mercedes out of London on his way home having had another row with Masterton on the phone, Hedley was involved in an accident with a lorry and two other cars.

He'd been drinking for sure, but not to excess. The fact

that a blood test showed him to be under the legal alcohol limit was hardly the point however. The real problem for himself, Masterton and Trent, was that he was concussed and taken to hospital. Put under sedation while his other minor injuries were diagnosed and treated, he didn't come round until well into the afternoon the following day. By the time he'd realised that he had lost the best part of twenty-four hours, found a telephone and got through to his office, it was too late. The whole exercise was virtually over. The fortunes had been made, the price had fallen back, slowly at first while the early profit takers were coming out, and then, as always happens, the panic to sell off what was left was on. He couldn't even find a buyer. It wasn't until the price had fallen back way below what he had bought at that the market bottomed out, and a few buyers appeared.

Hedley was giving the nursing staff a hard time as he ranted and raved down the handset. Eventually a staff nurse pulled the socket out of the wall. Hedley lay back on the pillows exhausted. He hadn't sold any copper. Masterton's deal was still open-ended, and was showing a thirty thousand pound loss.

The broker was jolted out of his nightmare of a few days before to see Masterton sitting in a chair pouring himself another generous measure. He didn't offer Hedley one. 'I'd appreciate it if you were to leave now,' he said quietly. 'I've got some serious thinking to do.' His attitude had changed. He looked passive and dejected.

'You certainly have,' said Hedley. 'And you'd better be quick about it. Here are the up-to-date statements of transactions.' He thrust his hand inside his jacket and pulled out half a dozen sheets of paper which he threw onto the table. 'You'll see I've tried to recoup some of your losses by trading in other commodities, but I'm closing the copper deal tomorrow and giving you three days to come up with the difference. Otherwise your cheque goes to the bank and, if it doesn't clear, a copy goes to every governor on your board.'

Getting no reaction from Masterton whatsoever, he turned on his heel and strode from the room. As his Rolls left the driveway, he gave further vent to his feelings by letting the tyres spit gravel all over Masterton's front lawn. He didn't notice a scruffy looking individual sitting in an equally scruffy Y-registered Datsun, parked under a tree just outside the gates.

You had to give Masterton his due. He was a quick thinker when the going got rough, even if he did tend to dig himself an even deeper pit to fall into as a result of his impulsiveness. He certainly needed some rapid decisions now, as he believed Hedley when he'd said he had three days. There was no way he could come up with thirty thousand though. He would have to give Hedley a reason to delay presenting that cheque.

He could withdraw the considerable discount Hedley enjoyed against his son's school fees. That must surely be worth a lot to the broker at the moment, unless of course Hedley had covered his own dealing. Somehow he didn't think it would cut much ice. Hedley would no doubt consider Masterton's position as more precarious than his own, and he'd be right. No! It had to be something that would really shake up the man. Something to do with his son, on whom Masterton knew he doted. Drugs, maybe? No, too difficult to organise.

Although it was nearly midnight, Masterton picked up the phone and dialled Roger Hedley's Housemaster. I wonder if he's into little boys, he thought. It was not uncommon amongst boarders. Stick fifty or so young males together in a protected environment for two or three months at a time and it was inevitable. It was considered mostly harmless and little more than a prank at so young an age. It only became serious if senior boys or masters practised it, and such a problem was less common now than in the past, since all the recent publicity about sexual abuse and ChildLine and the Children's Act had brought it out into the open.

Masterton was well aware, however, that most parents thought their sons could never possibly be involved in anything like that. There was still an aura of Victorian disapproval and rejection of any reasoned understanding about the subject. Even the most harmless occurrence could be built up out of all proportion into something totally unacceptable – if the stakes were high enough, of course.

'That you, John?' said Masterton. 'Look, I'm sorry to bother you at this late hour, but I've been put in a bit of a spot.'

The Housemaster sounded sleepy but anxious to be of service. 'What can I do for you, Headmaster?'

'Well, look, it's a bit delicate, but I'll come straight to the point. I've just had a very distraught parent of one of your newer boys on the phone, saying that their lad has been the subject of homosexual advances by Roger Hedley, who is also in your house, I believe.'

'Yes, that's right, he is. Good God! I'll look into it. What's the name of the young boy?'

'Well, I'm afraid I can't divulge that at the moment as I've promised the parents I wouldn't tell you his name. Naturally though, they want it stopped, but in the most sensitive and diplomatic way. I'm sure you understand their reasons, John.'

'Yes, of course.'

'There's a good fellow. Just find out if Hedley has any relationship going on, however mild, and who with, and let me know, would you? You'll probably come up with the younger boy's name soon enough. There's probably nothing in it at all, but you know how parents can read all sorts of dramas into these things. Be discreet, mind, and get back to me tomorrow, would you? Best to put parents' minds at ease straight away, don't you agree?'

Masterton rang off, swallowed another large measure of whisky, and went to bed.

* * *

Try teaching a load of public school third formers history in the middle of June, when it's over eighty degrees in the shade. They don't want to know. They look as if they're concentrating, but that's an art they learnt and perfected in their 'formative' prep-school years. A scan across the classroom will show you quiet attention. Some will have their elbows on the desk and be taking notes. These will be the ones drawing sketches of Formula One cars or Round the World racing yachts. Others will be reading a prescribed passage and recording their comments in readiness for a form discussion to follow. These will be the ones doing newspaper competitions or filling in their pools coupon. The third group, always the same boys, will be those having a book propped up in front of them and appearing to be researching diligently. They will have a slightly vacant, studious look, and have a somewhat flushed expression brought about by attentive study. These will be the ones scrutinising thumbed and creased pornographic literature secreted behind their open text books.

All in all it's an impossible task, made the more difficult for me on account of the fact that I was meeting Maurice Tyler that night and having serious second thoughts about showing him the copied papers.

I had resolved to do it, however, and Richard and Christine couldn't offer any reasonable objection or alternative. I remained firmly dismissed and, as I had nothing further to lose, it seemed the only hope.

My mood alternated from desperation to anger, the latter being fuelled by Masterton bringing in an additional and much older staff member to 'assist' with the first eleven for the remainder of the term. This was actually unnecessary, apart from being imprudent, as it upset and confused the boys and was an embarrassment to both me and Brian Saunders, who openly admitted he disliked the idea. It was Masterton's way, however, of 'making a point'.

Walking across to the main school that evening after fielding practice, I took a slight detour and visited the chapel. The choir and members of Thaxbury Choral Society were rehearsing Parry's 'I was Glad', and I sat down in my usual pew and shut my eyes. It was hearing the emotive strains of that harmony and the hypnotic power of that majestic organ that made me decide to fight for the right to go on being able to sit in this seat. I'd always been told that if you wanted something badly enough, you had to be prepared to fight for it. I wanted this so badly that I could feel the tears starting to moisten my eyes as the organ seemed to reach a crescendo in sympathy with the strength of my feeling about this place.

I went out into the sunlight and walked away towards the benches round the cricket ground. The choir were beseeching me to 'Go into the House of the Lord'. The sound was stirring the trees surrounding the playing fields. It reverberated off the buildings and into my very soul, and I felt the immense authority of its domination over me. It made up my mind for me, and I was indeed 'glad' to surrender to its overture.

I drove over to Thaxbury in time to meet Maurice Tyler at nine o'clock. He was already there, in the hotel lounge bar, and jumped up with a welcoming smile when he saw me.

He thrust out a hand. 'Good to see you again, Alan. Drink?'

'No, thanks. Driving, you know. Can't take any risks these days.'

'Hmm. Know what you mean. You've got some additional information for me, you said.'

I handed him a set of copies. 'I don't know what you'll be able to make of those,' I said. 'I can tell you what I know about them as far as it goes, but whether they'll be of any use, I'm not sure.'

'What are they?' he said, leading me over to a table in the far corner of the room.

I told him everything that had happened since we'd last met, including how I'd been to see the Headmaster and pleaded with him to reinstate me. How I'd thought of challenging Masterton with these copies myself but had decided to ask the union's advice first.

Tyler listened attentively while perusing the figures. 'Very wise of you,' he said. 'You were right to show them to me.' His eyes shifted from me and back to the papers as he searched for some meaning in them. 'What do you think is incriminating about them?'

I told him what Robert Donaldson had said – that there was an open-ended deal which could be interpreted as a substantial loss if the deal had not subsequently been closed.

'What do you mean by substantial?' he asked. 'Are we talking about thousands, hundreds of thousands or what?'

'I think it was about thirty thousand,' I said.

Tyler put the papers down, took his glasses off and fixed me with an encouraging expression.

'Well, Alan,' he said. 'I may be able to help. But you'll have to let me have these.' He indicated the papers on the table. 'As things stand at present, I don't think, as I said to you earlier, you've got much of a case to make against your sacking, purely on the grounds of inexperience or even incompetence. We would have to challenge the statements of your Director of Studies and your Head of Department, and that would be asking too much. Apart from that, you could, I suppose be construed as still on probation as you are new there, aren't you? Even if your contract needs a full term's notice to be terminated by either side, which I believe is customary, the Head could have you out at the end of the autumn term, so you'd not gain much on that score. No, I don't think we could help you in that direction.'

He replaced his glasses, picked up the papers and started to look through them again. 'If, however, I could find something incriminating in these, then it would be a simple matter to write to your Head and state that the union, as your representative, was not satisfied with the reasons given for your dismissal, but considered that the underlying motive behind it was the inadvertent discovery by you of certain documents which the union would be submitting in full to a tribunal in order to support your case for reinstatement.'

Tyler smiled. 'We would then say "of course, this would be deemed unnecessary in the event of you being reinstated in full, with all your privileges and promotion prospects intact".' He looked at me for approval, and I immediately started to feel encouraged.

'I think I'll have that drink now,' I said. 'Get you one, can I?'

Tyler held up his hand. 'Just one thing,' he said. 'You must understand that all this depends entirely on me being able to prove conclusively that your Head has been a naughty boy. Don't forget, we're not in the business of bringing a case against him or anyone else for fraudulent misuse of school funds. That is not our intention. We would be merely providing evidence in order to persuade him to give you your job back. Nothing more. That has to be clearly understood by you. The union would be your representative in your problem only. It would not be judge and jury against the school or its headmaster.'

'Right. I understand that,' I said.

'Okay,' he grinned. 'You can get that drink now. I'll just have a half, thanks.'

As I returned with the glasses, I thought what a friendly chap he was. I'd heard that these full-time union blokes were really dour and morose characters with no sense of humour. Just facts and statutory procedures and 'democratic rights on behalf of the members' and all that stuff. I was rather warming to him.

Over his half of bitter he started to talk in general terms about the school and the Headmaster and what sort of fellow he was. Did he have a lot of influential friends? Did his staff respect him? Who was on the Board of Governors? What were the fees per term? Rather odd questions to a junior teacher, I thought, and indeed I didn't know the answer to any of them. He said he'd need a lot of background information if he was going to make a meaningful threat against somebody. But it didn't matter. He'd already taken the liberty of getting Norman Willett to send him a school prospectus that included most of that information.

He also wanted to know if I could tell him anything more about the Bursar. How did my friends, Richard and Christine, who he'd met last time, feel about the whole thing? Were they supportive of unions generally? Was Willett popular in the common room? How many staff at Bradchester were union members? Was the Headmaster's marriage a harmonious one? Had I heard any rumours about money difficulties?

I again expressed some surprise at his line of questioning, but was assured, most politely, that it was in my best interests to cooperate fully. 'The union needs your help if it is to help you,' he reminded me.

After another twenty minutes of going through exactly what I'd overheard when Masterton and the Bursar were having that first argument, he at last seemed satisfied and gathered up the papers.

'Don't forget, Alan. Anything, and I mean absolutely anything, you find out or remember, you must telephone me immediately. I have to consult to some extent with our legal people you understand, and they'll not be happy unless I can convince them that the evidence of foul play is watertight. Anything to do with Masterton or this Trent fellow or any names or suspicions that crop up along the way, you tell me.

Only with your help will the union be able to use its weight in your favour. I must, however, have a good deal more than I've got so far, okay?'

I nodded, and we parted on amicable terms although I felt slightly uneasy at his rather intimate line of questioning. I put it down to my being unused to dealing with someone whose business it was to deal with the more unseemly side of life on behalf of others. He was in a different league to me. His job was to protect his members from manipulation by those in positions of authority. I should be grateful to him for taking so much trouble to prepare a cast-iron case on my behalf.

* * *

As soon Maurice Tyler walked out of that hotel lounge, his smile and civil attitude left him. 'Damn and blast!' he thought. There was absolutely nothing to tie those papers up with Masterton. There was no name on them, no address, no broker's name or telephone number. This Headmaster was clever. No doubt so was the broker who'd made the transactions. No clue at all as to the identification of anyone involved. It would be a hell of a task to trace those deals to Masterton.

Chapter 6

It had been difficult for John Tanner to find out anything specific about homosexuality in his house without asking his house prefects and dormitory heads. They were the ones who knew everything that went on and from whom he had to try to ferret out any intimate pieces of information. He could do nothing during the day because they were all in school, as he was, so it was not until very late that he was able to ring the Headmaster and report his findings.

Masterton had insisted he come straight round and deliver the information in person.

The Housemaster was not to know it but he was to increase his stock with the Head that night by unwittingly giving him the information he had hoped to hear. Yes, the boy Hedley had been involved in general dormitory discussions about sexual fantasies. Masturbation and sexual intercourse were very common topics for analysis by boys of that age.

'Yes, yes! I know all that,' cut in Masterton. 'Are there any younger boys involved? I told you, I need to know.'

'It seems,' said Tanner, looking embarrassed, 'that the name of one particular younger boy has been mentioned by some, Hedley among them, as being rather attractive physically, purely as a joke I understand. There's no evidence, however, that it has gone any further than the walls of that dormitory.'

John Tanner waited. 'Do you wish me to divulge the name of the younger boy, Headmaster?' he said.

'What?' said Masterton, absent-mindedly.

'It may well be the same boy whose parents rang you yesterday.'

'Oh! Right, yes, of course.'

'Dawson,' said Tanner. 'Young Alex Dawson. New boy last September. Very nice parents. Father's in oil. BP, I think.'

'Yes, that's him,' lied Masterton. 'But you say there's nothing more to it than ribald dormitory banter?'

'As far as I can tell, no,'

'Well, perhaps you're wrong. Dawson would hardly be likely to tell his parents on the strength of that alone, would he? Anyway, keep your ear to the ground, will you, and be in touch if you come up with anything more.'

'Certainly, Headmaster,' said Tanner, and left.

Masterton felt he was due a bit of luck, and here it was. He would build this innocent little dormitory chat into a major sexual incident between young Hedley and the unwitting Dawson and use it to persuade the older boy's father not to do anything hasty with that cheque.

* * *

The morning after Maurice Tyler had seen Alan Carter, he answered a phone call from Ernest Diggens.

'It's time you paid me,' said the voice.

This was the code they had for when information was

available but it might be of such a nature that the recipient wouldn't want to hear it over the phone. He might have other people in the room or the line might be shared and picked up by someone else.

'How many hours have you done?'

This meant put it on tape and send it to my home address.

Next day a package arrived at Tyler's house and he played the tape before leaving for the Branch Office. Diggens always started his messages with a long moan about how boring the work was and an encoded request for payment, which he always considered well overdue.

He then went on to tell Tyler that having given him the information on Carter's flat, he had, as instructed, moved his location to one from which he could watch the comings and goings at the Headmaster's house. He had made notes of all the people who'd arrived at the front entrance either on foot or by car, but couldn't keep an eye on the back entrance at the same time. The notes would be available when Tyler wanted them, but there had been one incident indicating that a particular visitor had left the house on anything but amicable terms.

'A white Rolls-Royce, registration number JAH 100, had arrived at the house at six minutes past ten the previous evening, and a heavily built man of about fifty, dressed in a light-coloured suit, had entered the house. At three minutes past eleven he had come out in a state of agitation, run down the steps and slammed the door of the Rolls unnecessarily hard. He'd then left the premises, churning up the drive and narrowly avoiding colliding with the gates on the way out.'

Being thoroughly bored with sitting in his car for days and nights on end, the watcher had followed the Rolls. This had proved difficult as it was being driven in anger and it was all the follower could do to keep it in sight.

'Having travelled forty-eight miles in the direction of London, it turned east off the main road and, after three and a half miles of country lanes, drove into the forecourt of a large black-and-white timbered period house called Hanford Manor. The next morning, the same man, now wearing a blue pin-striped suit, drove the Rolls into London and, on reaching the City, turned into a private forecourt off Fenchurch Street. The car was parked in a bay bearing the notice "Reserved for Hedley and Co", and the driver proceeded through the back door of an office block. On an internal inspection of the building later, the watcher noted that on the fourth floor there were situated the offices of J. A. Hedley and Co, Commodity Brokers.'

Tyler's face broke into a calculating smile as he heard the rest of the tape out. There were details of the address, telephone number and also a description of the rather sumptuous premises from which Hedley ran his business. There was a final plea for payment of expenses for what Diggens considered services beyond the normal call of duty and, if the information led to anything positive, that Tyler would remember it when he paid him, which he hoped would be soon.

Things were looking up. Maurice Tyler now had the information that might enable him to connect the Headmaster of Bradchester to commodity dealing in the City. If this was as illicit as Carter seemed to be insinuating, then maybe the mere mention that Masterton's connection with Hedley was known would be enough to persuade him to reinstate the teacher. Tyler allowed himself another grin.

Getting Carter's job back, however, was not what he had in mind for the use of this information. Far from it.

During the past few days he'd not been idle where Bradchester School was concerned. From the prospectus that Norman Willett had obtained for him, he'd made a list of all the members of the Board of Governors and had then religiously checked each one out in Who's Who. There were some beautifully fat and juicy targets to be shot down from their eminent positions, if only he could prove that Masterton had been dealing in commodities and that such dealings had involved the misuse of school funds. If there had been a loss, that would be a bonus, and from Diggens' description of the commodity broker's acrimonious exit from the Headmaster's driveway there seemed to be at least a reasonable chance of that.

Tyler licked his lips as the list of the famous grew longer. One bishop, a High Court judge, two distinguished barristers, an Air Marshal, several prominent civil servants, a long list of very senior academics and educationalists and, what he had been hoping for all along, an Honourable Member of Parliament, holding a marginal seat for the Conservative Party.

He left for his office in a hurry. Not only had the playing of the tape delayed him, but he also had a great deal of plotting and planning to get through concerning this Bradchester thing, in addition to his normal heavy day of administering sound and helpful advice to the union's members. That would have to take a back seat for the moment, he decided. There were more important issues at stake.

Further investigation by his intrepid little band of helpers had uncovered yet more useful information. In Sir George

Beeson's constituency there was the customary dirty-tricks campaign going on amongst the opposition parties as they smelt the scent of victory at the approaching general election which was due at the latest in a year's time, next June, but might well be called in October – in only four months' time. Not only was the prospective Labour candidate under threat of being substituted in a takeover by the Left of the constituency party, but even the Liberal Democrats were embroiled in a none too tasteful purge amongst their local members in an attempt to select the candidate with the most chance of getting another seat at Westminster. There'd been rather a lot of dirty linen laundered in public just lately, most of it beneficial to Sir George, who had recovered some of his lost points in the local opinion polls as a result.

Maurice Tyler decided the time was right to offer his information for sale to the party or individual who would use it best to further their own political cause as well as his own, by selling it to the press, probably at a profit, and exposing Sir George as being involved with the fraudulent use of a charitable institution's funds by virtue of the fact that he was governor of a private school. If he couldn't find a buyer, he could always contact the press himself. It was better if another paid for the privilege though, as it would keep his name out of the matter and lessen the risk of the press bloodhounds uncovering his murky past.

He had already decided not to get involved with the Labour Party's official candidate. He had crossed swords with National Headquarters before and was well known to them as an activist having little concern for the party's political aims and ideals. He would be recognised as the Steven Winch who had sought to use the party as a platform for his own extreme anti-establishment views in the past. Such characters had been a massive liability to Labour's election prospects and, having taken virtually a decade to realise it, they were hardly likely to allow such individuals to put the clock back for them again. Maurice Tyler would, however, offer his information to the left of the constituency party, in addition to two or three other extreme candidates who had no hope of winning the seat but shared the same anti-establishment views as himself and would welcome the chance of some mud to sling in order to enhance their own meagre share of the forthcoming vote.

* * *

I left the hotel after my meeting with Tyler feeling relieved that at last I'd got it off my chest. There was no going back now. No agonising over whether to involve the union or to go it alone. Now the die was cast, and I would have to stick with it.

I told Christine and Richard all about the meeting, and Christine at least was pleased for me that I seemed more relaxed. I felt so myself, for I'd not been looking forward to 'spilling the beans' to someone so apparently adept at challenging such an imperious institution as a public school. Richard, however, had his doubts.

He wouldn't elaborate, but just put it down to a 'sixth sense' about Tyler.

'Come on,' I insisted. 'You must tell us why. We've agreed to back each other fully in this, and if you have any doubts, you owe it to us to express them.'

'That's absolutely right,' echoed Christine. 'It's because of your anti-union principles, isn't it?' She was about to launch into a tirade about Richard's privileged background again. I could see it coming.

'Hang on a minute, Christine,' I said. 'Let's not forget that without Richard's contacts, we would have no information or knowledge about those deals at all. We must pool all our resources, wherever we obtain them, and whatever our differing principles.'

'Hear, hear!' said Richard, grinning at Christine.

'So come on, Richard,' I said. 'Come clean as to why you have doubts.'

Richard wiped the grin off his face, and looked at me with a new-found respect.

'I really can't put my finger on it,' he said. 'It's honestly no more than a hunch. I just don't trust him, that's all. There's no proof, and even though I do have reservations about trade unions in general, so do many people. I just don't think you should be unaware of an uneasy feeling I have about him. What about all those questions he was asking you about the school and the governors and Masterton's marriage and all that? Seemed pretty irrelevant to me.'

'But he explained,' I said. 'He wanted a complete picture in order to prepare an accurate case if and when the time came.'

'Okay, okay', said Richard. 'I know that's what he said. I just don't happen to believe it, that's all.'

'Fair enough. Your doubts are noted,' said Christine with some impatience. 'So where do we go from here?'

'I think we've just got to wait for Tyler to decide when, or even if, he's going to challenge Masterton with the commodity deals,' I said. 'The trouble is that he won't until he's got cast-iron proof that there's been misuse of school funds, and he hasn't got that, and nor have we.'

'I just don't see any way at all we can get that,' said Richard. 'How the hell can we tap his or the Bursar's phone, or do a Watergate on Masterton's filing cabinet? We need the name of the broker who did the deals for him. Do we just go up and ask him for it?'

'God knows,' I said. We both looked at Christine for inspiration. There was none forthcoming.

There was a moody silence, eventually broken by Richard. 'I'm going to ring up Robert Donaldson again,' he pronounced with an attempt at enthusiasm. 'When we met him, I felt he was telling us only so much. He seemed to be hinting that there might be more he could do for us, but wanted us to go away and see how far we got with the information he'd given us. Didn't either of you feel that?'

'Well, he was certainly a little bit guarded, I agree,' said Christine. 'You may be right. I suppose there's no harm in having another talk with him.'

The summer term was slipping away fast. I could feel my chances of staying at Bradchester diminishing with every day that passed. I just knew that unless I could prove the dealings to be illicit, I was lost. My classroom was beginning to become a place of drudgery, and even the cricket had begun to pall. My mind was wandering and as time went by and nothing happened, I slowly grew into acceptance of the fact that I would have to go to Masterton again and accept my dismissal with good grace. I would then throw myself on his mercy and hope he would stick by his promise to help me obtain another post.

This idea was even starting to appeal to me as more attractive than battling away with a man who held all the cards and who would undoubtedly do me no favours were I to continue to threaten him.

Collins, the Captain of Cricket sought me out on the Friday morning to say that the first eleven were a couple short for Saturday's match against Harrow owing to illness. He wanted to know who I thought should be brought in to replace them. He felt that Peters from the second eleven was the only bowler who would fit the bill, and that Hedley, from the Colts, should be given the number four batting spot. Although only sixteen, Hedley had been getting a stack of runs lately, and as he would certainly make the first eleven next year, this would be a good opportunity to blood him. I agreed without much enthusiasm, and Collins went away to post the team on the notice board.

There was a certain amount of chaos next morning when Collins, in a state of great agitation, informed me that Hedley's bed had apparently not been slept in, and that he couldn't be found. The other members of his dormitory had reported that he'd been acting strangely after supper and, although being in the dormitory at lights out, had only been lying under the top blanket with all his clothes on. Two boys had said he'd left the room at about midnight and had apparently not returned. There was a bit of a panic on, and Hedley's Housemaster had been to see the Head during the morning, leaving his English class unsupervised for a whole period.

I didn't think much of the boy's chances of making the first eleven next year after this but couldn't really get too excited about it, as it would be somebody else's problem by then. Another boy was hastily selected and dragged out of class before the coach left for Harrow.

Hedley was back in the fold on Monday morning. He was delivered in time for chapel by his father. I noticed his arrival as my attention was drawn by a white Rolls-Royce pulling up in front of the cloisters. I saw John Tanner detach himself from a group of masters and hurry over to the car, out of which stepped Mr Hedley with his arm around the boy. Young Hedley looked dreadful. His eyes were red and swollen from continuous crying, and he was biting his lip hard as he struggled to control an obvious desire to flee as far away from his present predicament as possible.

Mr Hedley and John Tanner became involved in a heated exchange of views and, as I was the nearest, I offered to take charge of the boy. His father released him with 'He's to go straight into chapel' and continued his argument with the Housemaster. As the boy did not resist, I shepherded him, with the help of two of his classmates, into the cloisters where he was eventually persuaded to go into chapel. There were naturally many enquiring glances and secretive nudges as most of the rest of the school became aware that Hedley was in some sort of trouble, and one or two members of staff asked me what was wrong. I said I hadn't the faintest idea except that he'd missed the match on Saturday and apparently had been out of school all weekend.

I supposed I would get to hear the story sooner or later, but was surprised when the boy caught up with me at break time, still swollen eyed but now much more in control of himself, and asked if he could see me privately. Something made me agree to his request although if I'd not been present at his arrival back at school and hadn't seen the sort of state he'd been in, I would certainly have bawled him out for snubbing the chance to play for the first eleven and told him there was nothing more to be said. I'd become rather uncharitable since my own embarrassment, the news of which had permeated through the school, as no doubt young Hedley's would. I suggested he wait for me outside the common room in ten minutes' time.

He was there when I emerged holding a cup of coffee and it transpired that he wanted to apologise to me personally for missing the match against Harrow.

'Well, Hedley,' I said. 'I just can't think why a boy as keen on cricket as you would miss a golden opportunity like that. If you'd have got runs, you might have made the team for the rest of term. All I can think is that you must either have had an unbelievably good reason or that you're not at all interested in playing for the first eleven. In any event it would have been courteous to have informed somebody of your intention to be unavailable, instead of leaving it to the last moment.

He looked at me, the tears welling up in his eyes again. 'I really am sorry, sir,' he stammered. 'There was a good reason, but I just couldn't tell anyone.'

'Yes, I gather you left your house in the middle of the night. God knows how worried your Housemaster and his wife must have been. Where the hell did you go?'

The boy hesitated.

'Oh, never mind,' I said, rather losing interest. 'It's none of my business anyway. No doubt you're in enough trouble.' I turned to go back to the common room.

'Sir!' he said. 'Please.'

I hesitated. He was staring at me with pleading eyes. 'There's something else.'

A sixteen-year-old near to tears usually means that the

reason is rather more than trivial. The seriousness of this boy's plight was evident in his desire to communicate under difficult circumstances. I felt a twinge of compassion.

'What is it, Hedley?' I said.

'I've been told not to talk about the reason, sir,' he said, fighting to hold back the tears, 'but I'm so sorry to have caused you any trouble.' He pulled a grubby card out of his pocket and handed it to me. 'My father told me to ask you if you'd be kind enough to telephone him at his office as he insists on apologising to you on my behalf as well. That's his phone number. He realises you're in class all the time so he asked if you'd ring him when you're free.'

'Yes, all right, Hedley,' I said, turning away. 'I'll phone him when I've got time.'

I glanced down at the creased business card. It read: J. A. Hedley and Co., Commodity Brokers. There was a Fenchurch Street address in the City, and telephone and fax numbers. I strode off in the direction of the common room, putting the card in my jacket pocket.

Then I stopped dead in my tracks and my coffee cup went spinning to the ground. I wrenched the card out of my pocket again as I stooped to retrieve the broken pieces. No doubt about it. There it was: Commodity Broker. I stared after the boy as if to call him back. He'd disappeared.

I started to think. What of it? There must be loads of boys with fathers in the City, and some of them would be commodity brokers. It was just that I'd been clutching at straws, and here was one I needed to clutch at, even if it was a long shot.

I rang the number just before lunch and on stating my name was put through immediately.

'That you, Carter? Thanks for ringing. I was hoping for a word with you.'

'What can I do for you, Mr Hedley?' I said. 'Your son asked me to call you. He seems in an emotional state. I hope there's nothing seriously wrong.'

'Kind of you, Carter. I'd rather not talk about that but just wanted to apologise for his behaviour. Walking out on the team on Saturday like that. Unforgivable, I know, but believe me the boy did have a very good reason. Take it from me. Unfortunately, it seems best that it's not discussed at present, as another boy is involved. I've spoken to his Housemaster but not yet to the Head. There have been some allegations, of a nature I'd rather not mention, made against my son by the Headmaster, but I can assure you that they're completely unfounded and will be proved to be so. What I wanted to say to you, Carter, was that I hope this little incident will not jeopardize his chances of further selection for the first eleven. You see, him missing the match was not his fault, and I would consider it a favour if you were to ignore it. I'm sure he will repay you in the best possible way, by getting runs for you. After all, you had selected him, hadn't you?'

I didn't answer at first. I was amazed at the man's desire to get the boy into the first eleven before what should be his priority – to see him protected and supported during a very anxious time. I was so annoyed it jolted me into an aggressive form of questioning myself.

'Mr Hedley,' I said, summoning up all my courage. 'I will do all I can not to let this matter sway his further selection although I have to say that he was only selected because of the illness of another boy. If I'm to use my influence, however, you'll have to give me an honest answer to what you might consider a rather strange question.'

I'd decided to take the bull by the horns and go all the way. I would gamble on this man being insensitive enough to want his son in the team above all other considerations.

'If I can, of course,' he said. 'What is it you want to know?'

I swallowed hard. 'In your capacity as a commodity broker, have you ever had dealings, however minor, with the Headmaster here?' The question came out in a sort of intermittent croak.

'That is a strange one indeed,' he said, sounding surprised. 'I'm not at liberty to divulge things like that, I'm afraid. Why do you want to know?'

'To use your phrase about the allegations against your son, Mr Hedley,' I said, 'I'd rather not mention that.'

There was a considered pause down the other end of the line. 'Well, if you can do something to help my boy get over this problem, and putting him in the first eleven would certainly help, I don't mind saying that... yes... I've done a couple of very small personal deals on your Headmaster's behalf... just as a favour... very small amounts as I recall... a family matter, I think. I can't imagine why on earth you need to know but, as I've got my boy's best interests at heart, I don't mind telling you that. It must go no further, you understand, just as your influence on the team selection will remain my little secret.'

'Thank you, Mr Hedley,' I said, trying to keep a level tone to my voice. 'I'm sure we both have your son's well-being at heart.'

I put the phone down with a distinctly guilty feeling. God! Here was I, now getting into the business of using other people for my own ends. And how the hell I was going to force Hedley into the first team unless there were more absentees, I couldn't imagine. Oh well, maybe I wasn't. Maybe I should look after myself for a change, as everyone seemed to be advising me. At least I'd got the information I needed about those deals.

I thought about that for a bit. Hedley had said he'd only dealt with Masterton in a very small way. That wasn't quite the answer I was looking for. But he was hardly likely to tell me the real extent was he? That is, assuming that he had actually dealt much more heavily.

On the other hand, if he hadn't dealt in commodities with Masterton at all, he wouldn't then tell me he had. No, I reckoned this was as near as I would get, and I would now have to take the plunge.

Then I wondered what all this business was with the Headmaster making undisclosed allegations against the boy, and with another boy involved, Hedley's father had said. That usually meant one of two things in boys' boarding schools. Sex or drugs. I decided that as I was still actually in charge of the first eleven, albeit under notice, I would be quite justified in asking the boy's Housemaster what had caused his unexplained absence from the team and whether there was any likelihood of the reason affecting him during the rest of term in the event of him being selected again. I could not be expected to have a boy in the side who would be liable to 'do a runner' on another occasion.

John Tanner understood my point of view but seemed nervous and unwilling to go into the matter in detail. He said the Head had made the allegations, not him, so I had better go and see Masterton.

'But there'll be rumours flying about all over the place,' I said. 'Most of them will be products of fertile imaginations. You know what schools are like.'

'I'm probably more aware of what schools are like than you are, Alan,' he said testily.

'But surely you can give me some idea as to whether I should pick him.'

'No, I can't, and won't,' came the reply. 'All I can tell you is that Hedley is to be held under a sort of probation while the Headmaster decides what to do with him.'

'What about the other boy?' I asked.

'That's enough,' Tanner said. 'I've said too much already. Now please, don't press me further. As the Housemaster concerned, I've got enough problems without an interrogation by you.'

I didn't tell him I'd been speaking to the boy's father, but left it there. I'd noticed lately that the fact that I was leaving the school under a cloud, as far as the rest of the staff were concerned, didn't put me in a very strong position when asking favours of a slightly tricky nature. For all I knew, John Tanner might think I was involved with the two boys as well. Masterton's notice announcing that I was leaving for reasons of a 'personal nature' still adorned the common room board. He had not changed it to 'incompetence or inexperience'. Perhaps I should demand that he did so.

I didn't see Richard at all during the day, save for the usual fleeting glimpses, which were all you saw of a teacher during normal working hours. It was therefore not until quite late in the evening that we were able to pool our information. He was keen to tell me the result of the phone call he had made in break to Robert Donaldson.

'Well, I just asked him outright if he would be able give

us the names of any commodity brokers who, in his opinion, would be unscrupulous enough to deal in a speculative way on behalf of a school.'

'What did he say to that?'

'Pretty amazing answer,' said Richard almost laughing. 'He said he'd already written down the names of two brokers whom he felt, under certain circumstances, would do so.'

'Well, come on, who were they?'

'That's the amusing part. He wouldn't tell me.'

'I don't call that amusing,' I said. 'Not very helpful at all.'

'Well, I know,' said Richard. 'He was bloody well teasing me, you see. I'm certain he knows who it is, but he said it would be most unethical to disclose any names to us as we had absolutely no evidence to back up our suspicions. It's as if he's trying to encourage us. I really got that feeling. But I do see his point. He couldn't possibly go bandying about names of dodgy brokers just in case one of them might have done a slightly unethical deal.'

'No, I see that,' I said.

'What he did say, though, was that he'd written two names down on a piece of paper just after we'd visited his house. If we were able to find out anything our end in the way of a name, we were to let him know and if our name tallied with either one on his piece of paper, he would post us his names, with the wrong one Tippexed out. Rather odd, I thought, but I suppose it's his way of making sure he's not implicated himself.'

'Yes, I guess that's it,' I said.

'Bloody frustrating for us though. There he is, sitting on two names, one of whom I'll bet is the one we want, and we can't do a thing about it.'

'That's where you're wrong,' I said, in the most superior tone of voice I could muster. 'I've got it.'

'What are you talking about. Got what?'

'I know the name of the commodity broker who dealt with Masterton.'

Richard looked at me as if he was now convinced I had finally flipped. 'This is not the time for bloody silly jokes, Alan,' he said quite seriously. 'You're in no position to make stupid cracks. Don't be a fool.'

'No, honestly I have,' I said with a supercilious grin. I pulled out the card and showed it to him. 'Young Hedley gave me this earlier today.'

I proceeded to tell my bemused flatmate how the boy had asked that I ring his father and had given me his business card. I explained how even I had managed to put two and two together and had asked the man outright if he had dealt with the Headmaster. I explained that with a little persuasion he had admitted some small dealings, and that was going to be enough for me to act on.

'About time you had some luck,' he said, reaching for the whisky bottle. 'Well done. Let's celebrate. Does Christine know?'

'Not yet. I'm going to ring her now.'

It took me another ten minutes to convince Christine that this was indeed the first piece of luck that had come our way, and that it seemed a perfectly genuine missing piece of the puzzle. When she had finally accepted it as that, she told me that I had her full permission to get legless and, as it was too late to come over and celebrate with us, she would have a large Scotch herself.

As soon as I put the phone down, Richard grabbed it and

rang Robert Donaldson's number. Although it was late, he had not gone to bed, and I tried to listen down the receiver in my anxiety to catch bits of the conversation.

It was about the shortest phone call I'd been party to, however, and British Telecom wouldn't have got fat on us with that call.

I heard the ringing stop and a voice said 'Hello'.

Richard said 'Is that you, Mr Donaldson? It's Richard Pilcher speaking.'

'Yes,' said the voice, almost curtly.

Richard turned his head to me and winked. 'I have a name for you. We have good reason to believe this to be genuine.' He gave me another conspiratorial wink.

'Yes?'

'J. A. Hedley and Company. 143 Fenchurch Street.'

'Goodnight,' said the voice. The line went dead and that was it.

Two days later Richard got an envelope in the post containing nothing but a piece of paper having two things written on it. One was a date '7th June'. The other was the word 'Hedley'. Under this was a white smudge covering something else which looked about the length of one word but which was completely indecipherable. There was no signature, no address. Nothing. Only a postmark on the envelope, London SE, but the rest was too faint to read.

'There you are,' said Richard. 'Hedley's father. Would you believe it?'

'Seventh of June,' I said. 'That's the day after we went to see him. The crafty old so and so. He must have suspected all along.'

That morning I was late into my class after chapel on

account of my dashing back to the flat to phone Maurice Tyler with the good news. He had just arrived at the office, and I gabbled the details of Hedley's address and phone number, a short description of how I'd come by them, and why I was convinced this was the man who had sent Masterton the sheets listing the transactions. He didn't say much, but made affirmative grunting noises down the phone. When I'd finished, he was obviously pleased, so I pressed him to go right ahead and challenge the Headmaster in any way he felt was right in order to secure a reprieve for me and my immediate reinstatement. He was reluctant, however, to be rushed into anything and, to my disappointment, said that it would take some days to get his legal people to give the go-ahead, but he would be in touch as soon as he'd got their approval. I reminded him that time was running out for me, and even now my successor was probably in the first stages of being selected. Couldn't he see that time was not on my side?

He was very understanding and assured me that a few more days would not make any difference, especially as it would mean that the union, who really did know what they were doing, would then be in a strong position to settle the matter once and for all, quickly, quietly and professionally on my behalf. I should really not be in such a hurry to cast doubt on their ability to handle such matters, at which their track record of success was second to none.

I rang off feeling suitably chastised and had still not heard anything from him a week later.

There were a little over two weeks of term left when the three of us agreed that direct action was the only course left open to me. We'd had our discussions, our arguments, our excuses had been made and dismissed, and our doubts expressed. I'd rung Tyler three times, only to have a message relayed to me on the third call, that he was away on union business and the date of his return was uncertain. He had advised, however, that there was nothing to be lost by my submitting an ultimatum myself, as the union's legal department had given it the go-ahead, and the case was considered strong enough to succeed. If I wanted to proceed along those lines now, that was fine by him, and he would certainly back me at a later date if necessary.

It was decided that I should write to the Headmaster immediately, stating that I had been advised by my union representatives that the reasons given for my dismissal were considered unsatisfactory and, unless I was reinstated forthwith, the union would apply for an unfair dismissal case to be brought at a tribunal hearing. Evidence submitted at such a hearing would include copies of commodity transactions carried out by brokers J. A. Hedley and Co on the instructions of The Headmaster of Bradchester School. The inadvertent discovery of these lists of transactions, it would be alleged, were the real reason for my dismissal, and the above-mentioned commodity broker would be asked by the union to verify that such deals had taken place in the initial sum of one hundred thousand pounds sterling.

The case would be taken no further, however, in the event of my immediate reinstatement and a written confirmation on the school's headed notepaper, signed by the Headmaster to that effect, together with a notification to all teaching staff in the form of a signed notice on the common-room board explaining that the decision had been reversed.

When I'd written the letter and the three of us were pouring over it prior to it being dispatched, I gulped as I thought of the possible ramifications it might bring. 'Shut up!' I thought to myself. 'Just bloody well do it.'

So I did, and it was posted, first class the next morning.

There was, of course, a lot in it that we were taking for granted, but it was done and there was no going back. I was glad anyway. I'd had enough of reasoning everything out. The ball was now on Masterton's side of the net.

When the beanpole secretary ushered Richard and me into Masterton's study during the first period the day after I had posted the letter, she seemed almost to be acting in deference to us. To me in particular.

Richard had insisted in coming along because he had been reading up some of the bumf about dismissal and grievances, and it said you could have a colleague with you under such circumstances. I must say I felt a lot better now I was aware of some of my rights. We had decided that Richard would do most of the talking.

The Headmaster couldn't have been more charming. We had discussed this possibility and had decided that the more charming he was, the less charming we would be. Richard made a big thing about getting his notebook out. I had thought all along what a risk he was taking. After all, he'd only been reprimanded and, if this little ploy of ours didn't work, he would also be in danger of dismissal. I had nothing more to lose. I had the greatest respect for the strength of his friendship at this moment.

'Well, I can see you mean business,' Masterton opened when we were all three seated. He'd made a point of not sitting behind his desk, confronting us, but had brought another chair up so that we sat together, as if having a chat rather than an interview.

Richard was into the fray like a terrier down a foxhole. 'Mr Carter will be standing by the terms of his letter, Headmaster,' he said with an official edge to his voice.

'Am I to understand,' said the Head, 'that Carter cannot speak for himself?' He smiled benignly at the pair of us.

'I am entitled to have a representative to speak for me if I wish, Headmaster', I said. 'And until such time as I prefer otherwise, that is my wish.'

Masterton looked a little taken aback at our clinical approach, but nonetheless continued to be civil. 'Now steady on,' he said. 'I understand your desire to follow the correct procedures in this matter, but I have to say that you're wasting your time by threatening me and the school in the way you have.'

Richard remained silent.

'I must advise you that there is really nothing more to the matter than I have already explained in writing. I reiterate that I will of course do all I can to provide you with adequate references to enable you to obtain another post Carter, and, incidentally, you will find my influence not unbeneficial.'

He paused as if to test our reaction to his counselling and, when met with continued silence, appeared to take it as our agreement.

'As I said to you before, however, if you threaten... I mean... wish to proceed with your misinformed stand against Bradchester, and me in particular, then I have to tell you, most regrettably, I do assure you, that I will be unable to recommend you to any other headmaster or other kind of employer for that matter. Believe me, Carter, it will sadden me, but the choice is yours.'

He looked at me and then at Richard – nothing. I was

finding these deafening silences a great strain. It seemed so unnatural not to say anything. I had promised Richard though, so dumb we remained.

Masterton rose. We were getting to him.

'Gentlemen,' he said. This time with a touch more acidity than civility. 'I'm trying to accommodate you with as much patience as I can muster. If you are to remain silent, however, I must tell you that I am pressed for time, and there seems little point in this meeting continuing.'

Richard spoke. 'We are agreed on that, Headmaster,' he said crisply. 'The meeting was called by you, not by Mr Carter. We are attending it only to ascertain any likelihood of you, on behalf of Bradchester School, changing your position with regard to Mr Carter's dismissal. We have found nothing in what you've said so far likely to affect the position and therefore have to inform you that the proposals in Mr Carter's letter will be implemented with immediate effect.' He stood up and I followed suit. We'd agreed this move, almost rehearsed it. We made for the door without further comment.

'Oh shit! It's not going to work' was my immediate thought.

'Gentlemen. If you would consider one thing.'

We stuck to our prepared formula and ignored the request.

We were at the door when he said, 'Very well. You force me to say this.'

Richard turned. I stopped as well although we had agreed that once on the move under these circumstances, we would walk right out.

Richard had obviously decided that this might be worth hearing but he still said nothing himself.

'Please. Sit down again, if you would.'

This was better. I looked at Richard. I had obviously mirrored his thoughts.

'We will remain standing, thank you,' he said. God, the fellow was calm! I was practically wetting myself.

Masterton crossed the room to us with his forearms up and his palms outstretched, rather like the school chaplain about to administer the blessing at the end of a sermon. It was a sort of 'you give me no option' pose. Actually it turned out to be a last ditch attempt at placation.

'Look,' he said. 'This question of the papers that were removed. You seem to be placing great store by them. I must tell you that they really have no bearing on the case at all. Just a feasibility study. An exercise in investment possibilities. They're only examples. You'd be extremely embarrassed, I assure you, if you presented them as evidence. In any case' – his mouth showed the faintest hint of a smile – 'Mr Hedley, I think you will find, would certainly not be willing to do such an unethical thing as disclose the fact that he was asked to supply such examples in confidence, particularly as they have absolutely nothing to do with your dismissal. You would be a laughing stock.'

'Bloody hell,' I thought. 'I can't stand this bluff calling'.

Richard said, 'We'll be leaving now, Headmaster. We have classes to attend.'

'Wait!' It was an order delivered as a scream. 'Come here this instant, both of you.' The whole of the outer office heard it because the door was wide open and we had gone. We were half way across the quadrangle before either of us could find any words.

'Bullseye!' was Richard's offering.

'Don't ever do that to me again,' I menaced. We both succumbed to relieved and slightly tense laughter.

'What do you think?' I said.

'Well, we won't be sure until he makes the next move will we? But I reckon he's as rattled as hell.'

'I couldn't go through that again. Not even for my job back.'

'I rather enjoyed it,' he teased. 'Nice to see him wriggling like the worm he is. Rather fancied myself in the role of union negotiator... My God! What am I saying? Hope you noticed the skilful use of the buttoning of the lip. Works wonders saying absolutely nothing in a loud voice. Did you take note? Wish it worked in the classroom.'

He was really pleased with himself and the way things had gone. Me too, but I had been doubtful right up to the last minute when Masterton had screamed at us to come back. That's when I felt we had bowled him, middle stump.

It was Christine who put the dampers on my euphoria later that evening when she drove me over to the yacht club where she had to attend a committee meeting. I briefed her on the morning's events, and she did one of her finger to mouth, 'hold on a moment while I think' routines on me. Her silence was as effective as Richard's and mine had been with the Headmaster.

'What happens if you hear nothing from Masterton?' she said.

'We will, don't worry about that. You should have seen him.'

'Why should you necessarily? It's the union he'll listen to, and maybe he'll dance to their tune. But just you two? No, I don't think so Alan. You haven't got enough muscle.'

'But the letter clearly states the papers will be used as evidence, and he knows it.'

She nodded. 'Yes, yes. But the union didn't actually write the letter, did it? So Masterton only has your word for it that the union will act for you.'

It was my turn to be a little impatient. 'But there's an implicit threat that the papers will be used against him. That's the strength of our case. We know the union will back us because Tyler left a message saying so. We left Masterton in no doubt that the threat would be implemented.'

'Fine… Okay…' She looked at me with those big, compelling eyes. 'Hmm. I'd sooner it was coming from Tyler though. That's all. I just think you should get him to issue the demand. That way Masterton would have no doubt you mean business. Also, he may be right, and the broker, Hedley, may well decline to cooperate. You don't know that he will. He may be a buddy of Masterton anyway. But the union would have the know-how and legal backup to get the right evidence available at a tribunal I would assume, but we certainly wouldn't.'

'Yes. Well. You maybe right, but I honestly don't think so. You didn't see or hear Masterton's reaction.'

Chapter 7

I suppose a man who is appointed headmaster of a school on the threshold of the premier league of English public schools would possess many admirable qualities. Among them would be the ability to delegate.

It seemed that Masterton had this attribute in abundance, as he could apparently find the time to spend forty-eight hours out of school, albeit over a weekend, during the last fortnight of the summer term.

Immediately after a thrilling match on the Saturday against Tonbridge, which we'd won with two balls to spare, a hired car was waiting to take me a hundred and sixty miles to Hampshire, where I was to be the guest of the Headmaster and his wife, together with some friends, at their beautiful country home on the banks of the River Test.

Masterton had cornered me during the tea interval. He and his wife would be spending the weekend in the country and he would consider it a privilege to be able to give me some very good news concerning our little 'misunderstanding', if I would do them the honour of coming to dinner and staying overnight as their guest. A car would drive me there after the match and bring me back on Sunday evening. He must have taken an affirmative from me for granted as the car was ready for me at half past six, and Brian Dawkins had already been instructed to stay on and say our farewells to the Tonbridge team.

What really astonished me was that when I got into the chauffeur-driven BMW that was to take me from the pavilion back to my flat to grab some overnight things and then on to Hampshire, there on the rear seat was a dinner jacket and trousers, my size, together with a black tie, all neatly laid out in a shiny plastic bag. The chauffeur politely informed me that Mr Masterton had arranged the suit as dinner would be formal and he'd not been certain that I possessed one. He also enquired whether I would be good enough to collect a white shirt and black shoes.

'Am I going on my own?' I said. 'What about the Headmaster?'

'I believe he is travelling by air, sir. Helicopter most likely. He invariably uses that mode of transport.'

That shut me up completely, and I was also kept speechless by the speed at which we were propelled to my mystery dinner party. The man just sat the powerful car at ninety-five in the fast lane, with his main-beam lights permanently on although it was still bright and sunny. The eighty-plus brigade were 'tailgated' and overtaken on the inside if they didn't move over, the speedometer touching a hundred and twenty-five on more than one occasion. On enquiring what the hurry was, I was calmly informed that dinner was at nine fifteen.

I was sure we would be done for speeding, but amazingly we weren't. On three or four occasions the chauffeur slowed down to seventy for no obvious reason. Every time, there was a police car in a special lay-by, or lurking on a bridge, and once he even spotted a radar trap positioned on the opposite carriageway.

We turned into the long driveway at exactly ten minutes past nine and motored serenely up to the front entrance as if we had just come a couple of miles at thirty miles an hour. I had changed into the dinner jacket en route and was doing the final adjustments to the bow tie and retying my shoelaces, when the rear door was opened for me and I stepped out into the beautiful Hampshire countryside. I turned to survey the graceful sweep of the lawns down to the river but was gently ushered into the hallway, just managing to catch a glimpse of a yellow helicopter on the other side of the house, a dark blue Rolls-Royce and a couple of other cars in the drive that would have looked more at home at Le Mans.

Masterton detached himself from a sherry-drinking group and welcomed me like the prodigal son. It crossed my mind that I might be the calf, about to be fatted, but I was given no time to ponder that possibility. The Headmaster thrust a glass of sherry into my hand and steered me into an adjacent reception room.

'I'm so glad you could make it, Alan,' he said, shutting the door behind him so that we were alone. 'I want to tell you before we go into dinner that I'm extremely sorry for what has gone before, concerning our little disagreement. The fault is all mine. I have made a serious error of judgement about you and I wish to tell you here and now that it's my earnest hope that you will accept full reinstatement to the teaching staff and a written apology from me, together with an official notification of the reversal of my decision on the common-room noticeboard.'

In evening dress, and in some of the most beautiful

surroundings in England, 'gobsmacked' was probably not the most seemly adjective for the occasion. There was, however, no more accurate description for this slightly dishevelled, and astonished junior history and cricket master, slumped into a floral patterned armchair as if poleaxed.

I stared at him with mouth open and lower jaw inoperative. I felt as if I'd had three or four of those dentists' injections that make you dribble for an hour or so afterwards. Masterton helped me to my feet.

'I understand this might come as a bit of a surprise so soon after our recent meeting and your hard-hitting ultimatum, but I will explain everything to you after dinner. As it is, I want you to know straight away where you stand and that, if you accept my apology and your job back unconditionally, then I too may take it that the matter will rest there and that will be the end of a sorry affair for which I take the full blame.'

Well! What could I say but 'Of course, Headmaster, if that's the way you really feel about it'?

I knew I'd been softened up by the invitation, the drive down here, the helicopter, and the evening ahead with these elegant and important guests with the flashy cars. I knew it was all part of a game with him. He had to be softening me up for something. But I wasn't actually too worried, to be honest.

Richard, Christine and I had burnt so much midnight oil covering every possible angle of this affair and drunk so much whisky going over it time and again that I had a defence mechanism built in for practically every possible situation that could confront me.

I was therefore able to state firmly and without a trace of subordination, 'I would, as you say, Headmaster, have to have it formally, in writing and on school headed notepaper.'

'Anything you like, Alan. No problem.'

'And on Monday morning?' I ventured.

'Of course. I have already drafted a letter to you.'

'For the moment then, I am satisfied,' I said. 'This has all happened in a bit of a rush. You will forgive me if, for the present, I agree to do nothing more than accept your decision verbally and to discuss the details later. Formal acceptance can be made early next week.'

I was rather pleased with the way I had stood up to him. Maybe some of Richard's 'breeding' was beginning to rub off on me after all.

'Of course, Alan.'

I thought, 'All this 'Alan' stuff. Overdoing it a bit, aren't you?'

'Now come along, there's a good fellow. You must be ravenous after that journey. Hope Thompson didn't drive too fast. Get done for speeding he will, one day. And as for beating Tonbridge, well, that really is a feather in your cap.' He guided me into the dining room just as the other guests were taking their places.

'Here's the star of my school, ladies and gentlemen,' he announced. 'Alan Carter. At his feet lie the ashes of Tonbridge School cricket.'

Everyone turned to look at me so I smiled with my customary humility. It seemed to go down well.

'I give you a toast,' Masterton went on. 'To Alan Carter and Bradchester cricket.'

There was an enthusiastic 'hear, hear' and the remains of the sherry disappeared.

Fourteen of us were seated round the long, heavy

mahogany table down the middle of which was exhibited an amazing array of silver. A pair of rearing stallions, three enormous candelabra, two with seven branches and the centrepiece with eleven in two tiers. Right in front of me was a beautiful argent waterfall fully two feet in length with a magnificent pair of leaping salmon reaching to scale its solid silver cascade.

Carnations and lilies predominated in the floral decorations that interspaced the silver pieces and suspended some three feet above this glittering presentation was a blanket of natural vine leaves with trailing arms descending to the table at irregular intervals, from which bunches of black and white grapes had been cleverly suspended.

I looked at my five knives and four forks and wondered which knife I was supposed to use on its own. The three different shaped wine goblets I recognised, but what were the elegant little bowls half filled with what looked like water and having flower petals and pieces of lemon floating in them? Some sort of oriental gin and tonic, I speculated, making a mental note not to make a move before anyone else. I also had four different types of spoon, two of them apparently with precious stones embedded in the handle. Behind me, on one of three side tables stood silver platters with more glasses. Bulbous ones for brandy, yes, but what were the others? I remembered seeing a film once in which the port was passed round at the end of the meal and it was important to make sure it went the correct way. God!... clockwise, was it? I hoped they didn't start it at me, that was all. Richard would know. Why the hell wasn't he here?

I shut my eyes briefly and tried to receive a psychic message from him. Damn! The inconsiderate so-and-so wasn't tuned in. Well, it would have to be clockwise and to hell with it!

I was placed halfway down one side of the table with one of the sports car owners on my left and a very elegant lady of about thirty-five, who looked as if she'd just stepped off the front cover of Vogue, to my right. Across the table, just visible over the waterfall and through the rainforest of vine leaves was a distinguished-looking, white-haired man in his early seventies, who I thought I'd seen on the news recently. I discovered during the course of the evening the identities of some of these distinguished guests. The gentleman opposite me was flanked by Baroness Eleanor Stratford on one side. She owned the neighbouring estate and all the fishing rights on the opposite bank of the river. On his left sat Joanna Calverton, daughter of Sir Gerald and Lady Calverton, one of the brightest and most feared investigative financial journalists not only in the City of London, but also in New York, Hong Kong, and Tokyo. Somewhere up by the silver horses was Lawrence Hurd from Sotheby's, who'd travelled down from London with a Canadian stockbroker from Montreal and his wife. Two or three other guests whose names I never discovered made up the party, in which there was absolutely no mistake that I was the odd man out.

Nevertheless, I made a bold attempt at congenial conversation, encouraged by Masterton's heartening introduction and his limitless supply of alcohol. One of my wine goblets was filled with a chilled Chablis I think it was, and the chap on my left asked me what sort of car I drove.

'Ford Fiesta,' I said, which sounded pathetically menial compared with his ex-works racing Jaguar XKR 14, recently converted to road use by factory-trained mechanics.

Conversation between us ended there.

Masterton sat lording it at one end of the table, his wife at the other. I wondered how, if he'd just blown thirty thousand pounds of the school's money, this little gathering could be justified. Perhaps his wife had money, or perhaps he was fiddling his expenses as well. I'd heard that some public school headmasters were expected to entertain lavishly and were in receipt of very generous allowances for that purpose. I wondered how much of the school fees charged to parents was allocated to this kind of 'academic' event. Anyway, I couldn't help but be impressed and settled down to enjoy the occasion even though it would be as a 'poor relation' for me.

I didn't actually set the table alight with my sparkling wit or controversial points of view. The chap with the car on my left had already lost interest, and the elegant lady the other side of me seemed totally beguiled by the Canadian stockbroker. I managed to guess the correct spoon for the soup and noticed with satisfaction that the chap with the car didn't. A very appetising-looking piece of pinky-coloured fish came next and, having spotted the fish knife and fork, I reached for my glass of Chablis.

No luck. It was whisked away from under my clutching hand and a different white wine was poured into the next goblet. I asked the wine flunky what it was.

'A white Beaune, sir,' came the silky reply.

I had thought Beaunes were red, but apparently not all, and it was delicious anyway. I was correct in my assumption that the fish was one of the famous River Test brown trout and had actually been caught that afternoon by the distinguished-looking gentleman opposite. I was still trying to place him. A judge maybe, or a politician. Like most people, I could never remember names when introduced formally. I was always too worried about what to say or whether I was properly dressed to actually register them and was therefore useless when called upon to introduce them to someone else.

I was just in the process of deciding that I'd ask Christine to give me a book of etiquette for my birthday when the white head opposite poked itself through a sprig of vine leaves and asked me if I'd like to accompany it to the river tomorrow morning in the quest for another fish or two.

'I really would love to, sir,' I said. 'But I'm afraid to say I've never fished for trout.'

'Excellent,' came the camouflaged reply. 'Someone who won't criticise my casting. That'll make a change. I shall be your tutor and personal gillie then.' A hand and half an arm, clad in a white cuff and sporting gold links, appeared round a bunch of grapes. I shook it.

'Glad to make your acquaintance, young man, although I can't see much of you in this jungle. My name's Godfrey Baines-Fawcett. Just at present I suffer the appalling handicap of being one of Her Majesty's Lord Justices of Appeal, but I earnestly hope you won't hold it against me. I'd much rather go fishing.'

He insisted I call him Godfrey, and I spent the rest of the meal engaged in a most compelling conversation about the use of different types of flies for tempting the huge Test trout at different times of the season.

I'd done quite a bit of coarse fishing, mainly for roach and chub when I was a boy. The eminent man seemed genuinely interested in my experiences crawling through brambles and nettle beds to drop a maggot over a chub lying under the bank of the tiny millstream near my home.

'Ah! I can see you are a stalker of fish,' he said, beaming at me round a leaping silver salmon. 'We shall make admirable companions.'

From that moment, he made me feel completely at ease, as if I'd found a mentor in this frighteningly superior company, and the remainder of the dinner was a real pleasure for me.

Later on in the evening we partnered each other at snooker against Masterton and Lawrence Hurd and when I squeezed the black into the centre pocket to win, you would have thought I was his long-lost only son the way he slapped me on the back and signalled a hovering waiter to recharge my brandy glass.

Masterton was equally charming to me and took me aside into the study again just as the others were retiring for the night.

'I feel I owe you a further explanation about those papers,' he said, as we both wallowed in sumptuously deep armchairs with yet another glass of brandy.

'The reason I made an gross error of judgement about you, Alan, was one of being under stress you see, leading to a hasty decision, rather than anything else. The papers were indeed, as I said before, nothing more than examples, but taking away and copying them did rather upset the Bursar and me, purely from an ethical point of view, you understand. Just at that time, and with the pressures I was under from other, totally unconnected matters, which unfortunately are all part of my job... well, I overreacted, I'm afraid. Officially dismissing you for that offence would have been complicated, as people tend to read all sorts of things into absolutely nothing. I therefore decided to proceed with your removal the easier way for a school head, namely not being up to the job. This is less complicated and more easily substantiated.'

He paused and looked at me seriously. 'It was unforgivable. I'm very sorry. You shall, of course, have your conditions met, and I shall, I trust, have your word that the matter will be forgotten.'

I couldn't see anything wrong in agreeing to that. I knew I'd been softened up by the surroundings, the meal, the booze, even the Lord Justice may have had something to do with it. How was I to know? Masterton's timing was as sharp as ever, so he was now about to obtain my promise that the matter would rest there.

It was fair enough by me. I didn't want a post mortem, just my job back in writing and a few official assurances about my future. I was glad he had created an atmosphere outside the school environment and away from the rigid headmaster/teacher relationship of the campus. It had enabled me to see things from a distance and put them in perspective.

If I got my conditions from him, then there was absolutely nothing to be gained by pursuing the fact that I knew him to be lying about the deals. I couldn't really prove it anyway so why start a witch-hunt?

I felt on top of the situation so I told him that, subject to the conditions being fulfilled satisfactorily on Monday, I would be very happy to call off the union, and give him my word that the incident was closed.

'And any other copies of the commodity examples destroyed, or returned to me?' said Masterton intently. 'We wouldn't want anyone to misinterpret them out of mischief, would we?'

'Yes, Headmaster, I'll see to it,' I said, rather hoping I

could comply with such an assurance, bearing in mind that Maurice Tyler had become somewhat elusive of late.

'See you in the morning then,' he said as we hauled ourselves out of the chairs. 'Godfrey tells me you're fishing with him tomorrow. He's a good friend. You'll have a splendid time. You're welcome to borrow one of my rods – they're in the game room, across the hallway. I'll fix you up after breakfast.'

I didn't catch one of those elusive trout but I did get one to rise to a fly that, more by luck than judgement, I had dropped almost over it. For a brief second I had him on, but panic, excitement and a complete lack of experience made me drop the rod tip. The line went slack for a moment and he was gone. My distinguished companion seemed to be most impressed that I had even managed to rise a fish. He spent some time teaching me the art of casting, and I noticed that even though he considered himself no expert he could land a fly on the water like thistledown caressing some dewy lawn on a late summer morning.

During the lesson I learnt that Joanna Calverton was his daughter-in-law. This piece of information was delivered as no more than a passing pleasantry, but he seemed to want me to know it. 'Rather clever at exposing fraud and things like that in financial circles, you know, operates using her maiden name for professional reasons.'

His line snaked out in search of a long slim shape under the far bank. 'Want to keep well out of that sort of thing, a man in your profession. Other amateurs may play at it, but you stick to rugby and cricket, young man.' He retrieved some of his line with deft movements of his left hand and then his rod came up and back, and with one single movement the line was on its way again.

I looked at him quizzically. He smiled, never taking his eye off the end of his line. 'A little tip from Joanna. She knows everything that goes on in the City. Something about a commodity broker in trouble. Been seen with Masterton rather a lot lately. Know anything about it, do you?'

He drew the dry fly off the water and replaced it upstream of the dark shadow.

'Nothing at all.'

'Good lad, Alan,' he said. 'And that's the answer you should keep giving. Keep out of it, for your own sake. You never know what's lurking just under the surface.'

Thwack! His rod went back and then arched in a curve as it felt the fish. Where the line entered the water, it fizzed as it sliced across to our bank, paused for a moment and then returned to the other side under the pressure of the now horizontal rod. No thrashing around, no leaping out, just deep, powerful runs. The rod was up again in an instant, his left hand giving line through his right fingers clenched on the first section, just at the top of the butt.

'You take my meaning?' His smile confirmed the fortuitous timing of his remark. 'Now, get the net, would you? This'll take a bit of getting in.'

I landed the beautiful four-and-a-half pounder in the folding net twenty-five minutes later, and as it lay on the bank, he turned to me and put his hand on my shoulder.

'That's the end of the lesson for today, Alan.' His genial eyes searched mine. 'Do you think you've learned anything?'

'I most certainly have,' I said. 'If you hook something that might be too big for you, let someone else land it.'

'Right,' he beamed. 'You've got it.'

Chapter 8

Maurice Tyler wasn't too fond of the surroundings some of his clients chose for meeting places. This one was a converted toilet at the back of the 'Jack Rabbit' public house on the old wharf, just where the disused canal ran into the gravel pit.

The room had been recently decorated but still held an unpleasant odour from where the soakaway had opened up. It had been used as a betting office for the dog fights they used to run in the storehouse the other side of the yard. That'd been stopped three years ago when a reward was offered for information leading to the arrest of the organisers. The chap who claimed the reward had never got over his house burning down and his two children being killed in the fire.

If you ever wanted to describe a place as being 'the pits', this was it. A bit of wasteland on the outskirts of north-east London, it was more than a breeding ground for discontent. It was where the already discontented went to hatch their plots against the gratified and complacent. Fires could happen to the homes of 'squealers', so you kept your mouth shut if you had any sense. It was where Jack Simmonds said he would meet Tyler to hear what was so special about his information that it would swing a marginal seat at the general election.

'This will bring Sir George Beeson down at Stevensford on polling day,' said Tyler, 'and it's up to whoever gets the information to turn it to his best advantage. I don't really care who it is, as I'm not in that business any more. But as I think you'll pay my price for it and use it, I'm giving you first refusal in preference to those who can and will pay more.'

Jack Simmonds knew Tyler of old. He had been in one of the firebomb groups and remembered the night he lost the top of one of his fingers. Jack never thought bombing was a good idea, but he went along with it at first, just in case it did get results. He really preferred to stand up and air his social views, rather than plant a bomb and run away and hide so that you couldn't explain to people why you'd planted it. He'd suffered from the same problem as many like him in those days. Nobody would listen unless you did something violent. If you did, you were immediately a fugitive and couldn't air your views. Chicken and egg it was. There was only one way – to get yourself voted for, either onto the County Council or into Parliament, preferably the latter.

Now, seventeen years later, his ownership of a great many north London drinking, gambling and strip clubs, and his well-ordered protection rackets amongst those he didn't own, had made him a rich man. He was well groomed and self-assured and a small black moustache accentuated his pinched features. He was often called a 'spiv' and took pleasure in this description as it was usually used by someone he'd got the better of. He wore expensive but conventional clothes and shoes and no jewellery, which set him apart from his contemporaries. He felt no need to flash his success about.

He knew he was clever and wealthy but unlike most men felt no compulsion to advertise the fact.

It was somewhat inconsistent, therefore, with his apparently well-adjusted temperament that he harboured a fanatical hatred of members of the 'well-bred establishment' and would regularly show naive misjudgement in attempting to topple them. It was a sort of hobby of his which had its roots in earlier days. He wasn't very good at it and it was expensive, but he could well afford the price of his brushes with the libel courts.

The criminal law had never caught up with him. He was too well protected. His lieutenants were well trained, ruthless and loyal. Now the time had come to enjoy some of the fruits of other people's labours. He was as confident as hell and was going to run in Beeson's constituency. Despite his confidence, he was intelligent enough to realise he wouldn't get elected. But he would get noticed, and he would run a smear campaign against the class society, and the socialists for that matter. He knew Maurice Tyler's proposal wouldn't be anything trivial. The man didn't peddle schemes of no consequence.

Simmonds leant forward on the upright wooden chair and engaged his negotiating mode. There was mutual respect between the two of them. 'All right, Stephen,' he said with a wry smile. 'What have you got that I can't live without?'

'Listen! I'll allow you to call me 'Stephen' just the once and then the joke's over. 'Maurice Tyler' from now on and don't you forget it.'

Simmonds spread his hands in a conciliatory gesture. 'Okay, okay, Maurice. Don't get so worried. Never again, I promise.'

Tyler was businesslike. 'I'll give you the information verbally, then the price. If you agree, you'll have it in writing as soon as I'm in receipt of the sum in cash in used notes.' He looked up for approval.

Simmonds nodded. It was the customary way of doing business in his world, where the passing of information was involved. There was no way Tyler would abscond with the payment before handing over the evidence. Maybe he would in some circles, but not where a man like Simmonds was concerned.

'What I'm offering', said Tyler, 'is photographic evidence of some commodity deals transacted by a City of London broker on behalf of the Headmaster of Bradchester School.' He peered at his prospective client to check that he had his attention.

'For your information, that's one of the top public schools in the private education system, and a good example of the sort of institution that's responsible for the class society we have to endure today. It's also representative of the privileged few that keep the Conservative Party in funds.'

'Yes, yes, I know what Bradchester is,' said Simmonds with a sardonic grin. 'Couple of my mates send their boys there. Very good school, I'm told.' He saw the vicious look in Tyler's eyes. 'All right, so I'm a hypocritical bastard. That's my privilege. But this deal is all one way so far. Why should I pay you so you can have a place like Bradchester brought down when its existence doesn't bother me that much anyway?'

'Because the deals are on behalf of the Headmaster of this school, and he's using school funds to finance them.'

'So?'

'So, your beloved Sir George Beeson just happens to be a

governor of the school and therefore is implicated in the illicit transactions by virtue of the fact that he's one of the people who appointed the Head.'

'Expose the puppet and bring down the one who pulls the strings, you mean.' Simmonds was all ears now.

'You take the credit for uncovering a typical capitalist fraud in a top public school. You also bring down Beeson and establish yourself as the number-one hero of the working classes. You may not gain the seat but the party that does will certainly sit up and take notice of you. You can even sell the information to them if you like, or the appropriate anti-Conservative publication might offer you a handsome profit for proof of any allegations you might make. Providing you pay my price and keep my name out of it, I don't care what you do with it.'

The racketeer and intended Parliamentary candidate stroked his chin thoughtfully. 'The working classes aren't that naive these days, more's the pity,' he said. 'I'd need proof that all you say is genuine, that the deals are authentic, that school funds are being used, and that such use is illicit. Give me proof of all that and I'm still interested.'

'A teacher has been sacked because he found out about it,' said Tyler, 'and I was asked to bring the union in to represent him. It's on the unions records. I could get copies of those but I'd rather you took my word for it.' Tyler was bending the truth just a little, but he could see his client was tempted.

'Look,' he continued. 'I've got to protect my sources in this as well as my own position, which is useful to me. I'll let you have a look at some of the evidence right now, but the rest you'll have to rely on my word and my reputation for not dealing in trash.'

He took out the copies of the deals and went through them with his client.

'These are what the teacher found lying about, and they are the reason he will be unemployed at the end of August. He was dismissed because of what's in them, and the fact that he could hold the Headmaster to ransom with them.'

'Why don't you hold this Headmaster to ransom yourself then?' enquired Simmonds.

'Because they show a substantial loss, and if he's that short of money, he won't pay me anything. They'll just sack him as well and use him as a scapegoat to salvage what they can of the school's reputation. Besides, I'd like you to pay me, Jack, and then I'll know the information is in good hands.'

'How much of a loss?' enquired Simmonds.

'Thirty thousand pounds.'

'And the initial investment?'

'About a hundred thousand.'

'It's peanuts,' said Simmonds icily, eyeing Tyler with some contempt. 'What's your price?'

'Two hundred thousand, cash, used notes.'

'Who's the broker?'

'Not until we've agreed to deal, Jack. Then you'll have it; name, address, phone number and everything.'

'Asking a lot on trust, aren't you? I'm not so sure,' said Simmonds. 'From these figures there's no proof that school funds are being used, or that it's illicit if they are. And quite frankly, such a poxy amount of loss could easily be made up from another source I should think. Lend it myself.' Simmonds smirked, 'Cost a lot though.'

Tyler was ready for this dismissive attitude. 'Point taken, Jack,' he said. 'The amounts aren't important, but the principle of the thing is. Sacking someone who stumbles upon a fraud in an establishment organisation like that is dynamite if exposed. I know there are a couple of missing pieces, but I'm giving you first refusal as I know you'll make political use of it for yourself and help to bring down the school in the process, which would suit me very well.'

Simmonds thought that at two hundred thousand, Tyler was clever not to be greedy. 'Not for a miserable thirty thousand loss,' he smiled, 'one hundred thousand is what I'll pay.'

You know it's worth more, Jack. Certain publications would be interested.'

'Unless I have a chance of winning the seat, it's not. And not if there's no proof at this time that it's school funds being used. Too many loose ends, and with your background I don't think you'll be wanting to approach the press direct. One twenty-five. Twenty-five now and the rest when I've used the information to good effect'. The counter was accompanied by a knowing look.

Tyler was shaking his head but thought he would get a deal here. 'If you want to do it like that, seventy-five now, seventy-five on completion.'

'Done then.'

Chapter 9

I didn't get back to Bradchester until well after midnight and my mind was so reeling with the events of the last thirty-six hours that I decided not to ring Christine until morning. Richard had been away for the weekend, and in the absence of his thumping about in the bathroom, I overslept. The flat door banging finally woke me as my partner in crime rushed in, hurriedly grabbed a jacket and with 'come on if you're going to chapel,' rushed out again.

I made chapel, but was the last staff member in place before the Chaplain and Headmaster entered together, and the week's proceedings at Bradchester commenced.

I couldn't believe that the Head, in his lounge suit and gown, was the same man that had sat in a plush armchair in Hampshire in the early hours of yesterday morning, drinking brandy and apologising to me. I had to blink to confirm the reality of being here. Perhaps I'd dreamt it all. I'd been sacked and I was pretty certain that it was going to remain that way.

The Chaplain droned on. One of the school prefects read a lesson. A sparrow had got in and was battering itself to death against one of the clear bits of a stained glass window. We all trooped out in our allotted pecking order. Richard sidled up to me.

'Something's up,' he said. 'Come on, what's going on? Rumour has it that you were whisked away in the BMW after the match.'

'Well yes, I...'

John Tanner came up with his hand outstretched. 'Congratulations, Alan,' he interrupted. 'I felt sure you'd been misjudged. Glad to have you back in the fold officially.'

Richard and I stared blankly.

Richard said, 'What are you talking about?'

'Ah! I see you haven't been in the common room yet this morning then.'

'No. Why? What's in there?'

'The Head's noticeboard. You're reinstated. Wait, hang on a minute!'

We'd gone. I beat Richard by a couple of metres, and there it was – nine fifteen on Monday morning, in Masterton's handwriting, on school-headed notepaper.

'In the light of the presentation of improper assessment and misleading reports, culminating in the notification to staff that Mr Alan Carter would be leaving the school, I am most happy to announce that Mr Carter is forthwith reinstated to his position. Furthermore, he has accepted my fullest apology on behalf of the school for the unfortunate incident, the cause of which will be dealt with as an internal matter by myself. Mr Carter has behaved with the utmost discretion and sensitivity in the face of extreme injustice by others, and I know every member of staff will stand in admiration, as I do, of the manner in which he has conducted himself. I would therefore relay to you his personal wish that the matter now be considered closed.'

'Bloody hell! You incredibly brilliant, astute and talented

individual, Alan Carter. You will never cease to amaze me.' Richard flung his arms round me and gave me a totally uninhibited bear hug. Others were coming into the room and wanting to shake my hand. I was overwhelmed. It was seemingly a popular retraction by the Headmaster and I was, just at the moment, flavour of the month. I beamed at everyone who pumped my arm and slapped me on the back. Norman Willet was being slightly tiresome by trying to make capital out of the union's part in my reinstatement, which reminded me that Maurice Tyler had done precious little for me since I last saw him. But Edmonds and Dawkins seemed genuinely pleased for me, and I made a mental note to think through their part in the affair later. For the moment I was going to relish this acclaim.

I wanted no recriminations, no post mortems, no witch hunts, just to let it pass me by and get on with my career. The one person I really wanted with me right now was Christine. I wanted her to see this brief moment of adulation, which was as much the result of her shrewd and forthright thinking as mine and Richard's.

Richard had read my thoughts as ever and had got her on the common room phone. He beckoned me over, and as I shouldered my way through colleagues, I could hear him shouting to her, 'He's done it, it's official... On the notice board... Complete reinstatement...'

I grabbed the handset. 'Christine, you won't believe it. It's fantastic! Christine... what's the matter?'

She was crying. Sobbing like a baby. Unable to string two words together.

After a minute or two, she'd recovered enough to say there was no one who deserved a bit of good news more than I did, and that she loved me, and that the whole of her office were now surrounding her, wanting to know what was the matter. I could hear the hubbub in the background and could well imagine her embarrassment so I said I would come over this evening about eight thirty and tell her all about it.

There was only one week of term left, and that meant a very busy schedule. Speech Day, the start of Cricket Week, and I was miles behind with my reports. I'd received my letter from Masterton reinstating me and it was couched in much the same terms as we had discussed after dinner last Saturday. I noticed he'd gone on a bit about confirming that he'd notified the staff that my wishes for the episode to be forgotten should be honoured. Well, I suppose I did want the matter laid to rest, but I had the tiniest suspicion that the wish was more his than mine. Anyway, it didn't really matter. It was over, and in two or three months' time when everybody'd had a good holiday, I should most probably have come out of the affair with a few bonus points.

I made two more attempts to speak to Maurice Tyler at the union head office, to tell him to drop my case against Masterton, but without success. I was told he was unavailable on both occasions, so I finally wrote an official letter to the union in general with my instructions, and made sure Norman Willet got a copy.

Christine had welcomed me on the Monday evening like a lost lover returned from the battlefront. I'd secretly been hoping during that day that she might have something special in mind for the evening. I was not disappointed. She'd prepared a table for two in the middle of the sitting room. I didn't even get my finger on the bell when she had flung open the door and wrapped her long limbs all round me like so many randy snakes. I was told I was brilliant and that brilliant men deserved a special award ceremony. That was to come later in the form of a meal followed by what she described as 'personal service' here in the flat. I noticed she'd arranged about a dozen large cushions and bean bags on the floor by the table and that the curtains had already been drawn.

I looked at her and by her smile I knew our trains of thought were compatible.

'First of all,' she announced, 'I'm taking you to the Fisherman's Creel to soften you up.'

'Looking at this room,' I said with a lecherous grin, 'I think the opposite effect is more likely.'

She kissed me lightly on the lips. 'Hmm! I hope so,' she chuckled, wetting her lips with her tongue. 'Come on.'

We sat in the same alcove as before and I relayed the story of the Hampshire dinner party and Masterton's apology and his agreement to my conditions. I told her about my new-found fishing friend who just happened to be a Lord Justice of Appeal, and how he'd given me a disguised warning to have nothing to do with Masterton's City dealings.

'Bit late for that now, isn't it?' remarked Christine.

'Well, yes, but I think the advice would still be relevant. I certainly want nothing more to do with it.'

'That's right, Alan. You've had enough. We all have.'

'It's funny though,' I said. 'His daughter-in-law was there, at the dinner. She's a financial journalist and she knew there was something going on between Masterton and a broker in the City. She had told him about it.'

'Was he warning you in a threatening way then, or giving you a sound piece of friendly advice for your benefit only?'

'Good heavens! I'm sure he was genuine. I never thought

of that. No, I'm certain he was trying to be helpful. If you'd met him Christine, you'd know what I mean. He's a real gentleman.'

She seemed satisfied and started to ask me what she could do for me when we got back to her flat.

'Well,' I hesitated. 'A little wine perhaps to start with.'

'After that, you idiot. When we make love. Any special requests?'

'Your imagination is more fertile than mine,' I assured her.

'I'll be your slave girl if you like. Or how about a topless massage?'

'Only topless?'

'To start with, I think,' she teased.

'Here we go again,' I thought. 'We're going to be asked to leave if this develops much further.'

She directed my gaze to a couple who had sat down at the next table and whose thoughts were probably similar to ours. 'Do you think they give each other everything they want? I mean really everything?'

'I don't know. You'd better ask them,' I offered, choking into my beer.

'Oh, come on, Alan. Tell me what you really fancy. However outrageous or bizarre. Absolutely anything.'

I leant over and put my mouth close to her ear, whispering into it for about two minutes.

After thirty seconds she was nodding enthusiastically. After a minute she was starting to wriggle. At ninety seconds she was pretending to be shocked and had her mouth open in mock horror. During the last thirty seconds she was feigning protest and telling me my mind was warped and that I ought to be locked up. When I'd finished, she grabbed me and pulled me out of the pub and drove like a maniac back to her flat.

* * *

It took Jack Simmonds a week to be ready to let certain newspaper reporters know that in his next public speech to his "Independent Socialist for Anti-corruption" followers, he would be making a personal allegation against Sir George Beeson. The charge would be 'Bad Judgement', in being party to the appointment of the headmaster of one of the country's leading private schools. The headmaster concerned would be implicated in the illicit use of school funds, to finance personal gain from dealings in the City of London commodity markets.

Simmonds had been careful to ascertain from his lawyers that, couched in those terms, he couldn't be sued by Sir George for anything other than accusation of bad judgement. He could be sued by the headmaster concerned for the separate allegation, but he was satisfied that the risk he'd be taking on that score was minimal, as from Maurice Tyler's research and reputation the chances were that the allegation was sound.

Simmonds would release the little package of assistance to his cause in early July so that by the time the allegations had been refuted and the mud-slinging that Simmonds was determined should follow had died down, it should be just about late September. Everyone would be back from their summer holidays and the accusations would be starting to stick and capitalist heads starting to roll.

The Board of Governors or whoever was responsible for

these strongholds of class privilege would have to act at that time to either refute or verify the allegations. As they would have no alternative but to verify them, some heads would certainly have to be seen to roll. This Headmaster chappie Masterton's would be the first, and then Jack Simmonds would make it his business to see that Sir George Beeson's was close behind. The electorate in his constituency would be made well aware of just where the interests of their current Member of Parliament lay.

Jack Simmonds thought wistfully that if Labour got in at the next election, the private school system might well begin its descent into extinction anyway. Various socialist voices had been hinting at it for years, what with the injustice of it all and one law for the rich and one for everyone else and all that stuff. There was talk now of charging VAT on school fees and abolishing charitable status for fee-paying schools. The trouble was that last time Labour had got in they were so busy coping with 'Winters of Discontent' amongst the very classes they were supposed to be contenting, they had little time for legislation concerning the privileged few. Sticking up the top rates of income tax was as far as they got. But there still seemed to be plenty of money available to send the sons of gentlemen, whoever they were, to places like Bradchester.

* * *

At the beginning of July the weather turned from warm, with the odd westerly shower that had sent cricketers and spectators alike scuttling for cover, to simmering heat, at the mercy of a stationary high-pressure system over Scandinavia. Any breeze that did appear was no more than a brief interlude before more shimmering haze replaced it as if punishing us for the short respite.

Speech Day heralded the end of term, and the fields and walkways of Bradchester were filled with the sound of leather on willow and the chatter of fourteen-year-olds instructing their mothers in the art of leg break and yorker. Dark-suited and gowned schoolmasters wafted about as if trying to disturb the lifeless air into some primitive form of air conditioning. Sweating fathers showed some initial interest in classroom exhibits, in a vain attempt to uncover some justification for the enormous school fees they were asked to pay each term. Such little scenes were being enacted all over the school, interlaced with tea and cakes, tepid champagne and warm beer, all designed to refresh and relax the performers, but mostly giving them indigestion and a headache.

For me it was a pleasant experience, although tinged perhaps with a hint of superficiality. Parents strolling around a school with their sons would never really know what went on in the boys' minds. The younger ones would be on the threshold of adolescence and keen to establish their lack of dependence on anyone. It was the 'of course they don't tuck us up in bed at lights out, mother ' syndrome. The sixteen-year-olds were rebellious at even being seen with their parents at all, let alone if they actually took an interest in the school. 'Don't know... Not a lot...No idea'...was the most that could be extracted from them.

'How did your GCSE's go, son?'

'So-so.'

'How about a nice cup of tea, dear?'

'Please yourself.'

What they'd said about these sort of schools was right. They did seem incredibly durable places. They had a benign intransigence about them. Ninety-six per cent of the population hated them, but their representatives were invariably voted into power at a general election. They were class ridden and privileged by wealth. But those who had harboured such hatred but had suddenly acquired 'means' were often to be seen strolling beside you on Speech Day, happy in the knowledge that 'it wasn't right, of course, but my boy deserves the best, and this is where he'll get it.' These schools had always been one step ahead of the vagaries of human nature. To such foresight they owed their continued existence.

Handel's Hallelujah Chorus was thundering out across the cloisters from the Chapel as the school orchestra strove to outdo nearly two hundred visiting choristers. The sound and aura of the place was instinctive to a man who was weaned at such a school. To a newcomer to this way of life, however, it was inconceivably impressive.

It was Saturday afternoon and Christine had come over at teatime. Wives, girlfriends, husbands and lovers all descended on the school for the end of the official events. It signalled the end of the day from a professional point of view. Teaching staff were on stand-down. From this moment they were no longer expected to be available to comment on Johnny's poor grades in physics or his failure to be selected for the shooting team. With a spouse or a lover by one's side the pressure was off. We were free to laugh, joke, be trivial and to show any remaining clientèle still in the grounds that we were a good-humoured, well-balanced and mature team, dedicated to the educational well-being of their offspring.

Christine basked in my highly publicised resurrection. She clung to my arm and showed me off with a jealous pride. There were plenty of congratulations on offer. One or two parents had got to hear something of the matter and when enquiring further, she charmingly steered me away with 'internal misunderstanding' or 'case of mistaken identity'.

The highlight of the afternoon, and coming as a complete surprise, was the rather inadequate attempt of the Bursar to be civil to me. Christine spotted him lurking behind the Music School as we were walking across the quadrangle. He appeared, then disappeared, as if timing his moment to approach us.

'I think he wants to speak to you on your own,' said Christine.

We were up to the corner of the building, and he strode out as if surprised to catch us.

'Ah! There you are, Carter. I was hoping for a few words with you.' He stared at Christine, who remained unmovable.

'Ah! Yes, well... I just wanted to reiterate what I'm sure the rest of the staff here have said already, that I'm glad the little misunderstanding about the papers has turned out the way it has.' He glanced nervously at Christine, obviously wishing her somewhere else.

'It's quite all right, Colonel Trent,' she assured him. 'I know everything about it.'

'Hmm! Well, if you say so, young lady.' He turned to me again. 'I wouldn't like you to think I had anything to do with your dismissal. Far from it. Dead against it as a matter of fact. The Head was insistent you see. Thought it was a bit over the top myself, seeing as how the papers were totally innocuous. You are his employee, however. Little I could do.

Sorry I bawled you out and all that. Glad it's all over. No harm done, eh?'

'No harm done if you say so, Bursar,' I said. God! I really was beginning to feel sorry for this man now. It was pathetic.

'Glad to have you back then, Carter. See you next term. Have a good break.'

He turned on his heel and was obviously glad the embarrassing meeting was over. It was quite apparent that he'd been instructed by Masterton to make his peace with me. All right. As with the Headmaster, I was happy to bury the hatchet.

Christine looked as sorry for him as I did. 'I think he's actually harmless on his own, you know,' she remarked. 'When his kind get sucked into something they can't handle, they become just as much a liability as those who manipulate them.'

'You're right. You're always right. That's why I love you,' I said.

Chapter 10

Three national newspapers reported the allegations by Jack Simmonds against Sir George Beeson and Mr Duncan Masterton. It wasn't going to be headline news, not yet anyway, as the general election was months away. It did, however, make the front page of the Stevensford Chronicle and, since it was the report of a public statement, the local television people wanted comments from Sir George as he left the House of Commons.

'Can you tell us, Sir George,' asked one reporter, 'if there's any truth in the allegations of illicit financial practice by the Headmaster of Bradchester School, of which you are a Governor?'

'I've seen a copy of the report of Mr Simmonds' remarks,' said the politician, 'and you would not expect me to comment one way or the other until internal enquiries have been made. As Mr Simmonds has seen fit to name the Headmaster of Bradchester as being implicated, then I also trust he will see fit to defend his remarks in court when the time comes. Naturally Mr Masterton will be given the opportunity to dispel any such preposterous allegations, but as he is on holiday, you will have to wait until any such internal enquiries have been made.'

'And what is your reaction, Sir George, to Jack Simmonds' comments about your implication in the matter by virtue of the fact that you are one of the Headmaster's employers?'

Beeson had a statutory reply ready.

'Mr Simmonds represents a tiny minority viewpoint, little of which is shared by my constituents, and is intent on drawing attention to his political aims by the raising of false and libellous accusations. He is well known for his failure in the past to attract votes from an electorate that is far too intelligent to be hoodwinked by his underhand methods.'

The reporter was persistent.

'Mr Masterton and you will, I take it then, be making a complete denial of the accusations.'

Sir George drew himself up to his full six feet two inches as he produced his most patronising smile, specially reserved for tiresome reporters.

'You may take it the way you feel most comfortable,' he said. 'The fact remains that you would be insulting the serious voters if you think they will have nothing better to do than consider the irrelevant publicity seeking of the likes of Mr Simmonds. Now, if you'll excuse me.'

He brushed passed the small group of journalists, at the same time making a mental note to get in touch with Masterton as soon as possible. A direct allegation of this kind was not untypical of Jack Simmonds. He was as left wing as hell and had spent a lot of time and money settling similar unfounded accusations out of court. This, however, was a direct allegation against two named persons, the result of which, if it did not go his way, would be catastrophic financially. Much more so than any previous minor libel rap he'd faced. Sir George had an uneasy feeling that this time

Mr Simmonds was going for the 'big one', and it was just possible he might have done some serious homework.

He sat back in a taxi and considered the ramifications. There was no doubt it would be a pre-election stunt. Such ploys were in season. As Simmonds, along with the usual ragbag of deposit-losing irrelevants, had declared his intention to run against him, the reason behind it would be to embarrass him to the tune of a few thousand votes on polling day, regardless of where those votes might actually end up. The serious allegation, however, had been made directly against Duncan Masterton, not himself. It would be Bradchester's Headmaster who would be the focus of media attention when the time came. Still, he'd better have a word with Masterton, if for nothing else than to tell him to say nothing in public until a full and categoric denial was guaranteed.

I wonder if there's any truth in it, he mused. And if so, where the blazes would Simmonds have got his information from? Better ring Masterton tonight. He'd told the press he would be on holiday but although the school had broken up he might still on the premises.

Masterton was still at school but hadn't yet heard about the allegations. He was in his study in the main school building working through the new academic year's timetable with the Director of Studies when the call from Beeson came through.

'That you, Masterton? I've had to fend off some pretty awkward questions today. I suppose you've seen the news this evening.'

Masterton was immediately on his guard. 'No, Sir George, I haven't. What's the problem?'

'If you'd seen the news, you'd have watched me being interrogated on your behalf, and incidentally having to defend you against allegations made by one of my prospective election opponents concerning illicit dealings in the commodity market. Fortunately, I had been informed of the allegations minutes before the press and media attacked me with it. Now what's going on, Masterton? This could be very embarrassing for me, and the Government for that matter.'

'Good heavens!' Masterton had to stall to give himself time. He waved the Director of Studies out of the room. 'On the news tonight, you say. No, I didn't see it. What on earth did they say?'

The MP was impatient. 'I've just told you. Now look, I'm a very busy man. These allegations have been made quite obviously to embarrass me and in order to make political capital. The man who has made them is no fool, and I have to assume that he's done at least some homework before coming out with a libellous statement like this. I shall, of course, need your categorical denial eventually, and that in itself will have to be made public. For the moment you must say nothing to anyone. Is that quite clear?'

'Yes, of course, Sir George, but...'

'Well now, come on, man, what's it all about?'

Masterton was desperate. 'God Almighty!' he thought. 'If I deny everything, I'll look a fool if something is uncovered. But if I admit to anything at all, Beeson will bleed me dry for the rest of the details.'

'Where did this information come from?' he offered weakly. 'It must be trumped up surely.'

'Never mind where it came from. That's irrelevant at the moment.'

'I don't think I can really discuss this over the phone, Sir George. I'm sure you'll understand the reason for that. Better to talk it over face to face.'

'Don't play games with me, Masterton. I need answers now. If you don't give me a straight answer to a simple question, I shall personally have you crucified.' The politician sounded as if he meant it. 'And incidentally, if you can't make a public denial when the time comes, I shall be crucified alongside you.'

The Headmaster was shaking with indecision as well as fear. How the bloody hell had this got out?

'It's all a complete misunderstanding, Sir George,' he said, swallowing hard and trying to keep his voice smooth and his manner unruffled. 'I know what must have happened and there will be no problem explaining it away.'

'What d'you mean?' barked Beeson.

'There are no illicit dealings. Some examples of commodity transactions were accidentally removed from the office and wrongly construed by one of my staff as being authentic. They must have got into the wrong hands, I suppose. There's absolutely nothing in it though, I do assure you. They're just specimens. Somebody must have a grudge, I suppose. It's not uncommon you know, against headmasters. All part of the job, as they say.'

Masterton felt reasonably pleased with that. Not too bad under the circumstances.

'You're sure that's the case, are you? Absolutely sure, I mean. Enough for me to make a complete denial?'

'That's the only thing it could be,' said Masterton.

'Well, I'm going to sleep on it then,' said Sir George. 'And if you think any different in the morning, you let me know first thing. And remember, do not speak to anyone about this until you check with me. The press, television, they'll all be onto you shortly, but you must have absolutely no comment at all. Is that understood?'

'Don't worry, Sir George, you can trust me to do the right thing.'

The phone went dead. Masterton ran out of the main building and back to the house. Entering through the back door, he made straight for the drawing room and the drinks cabinet. His hands were shaking so much he knocked a glass over in his feverish attempt to calm himself with a huge whisky. He left the broken glass where it was, grabbed another, gulped down several measures of the burning spirit and slumped back into an armchair, spilling some of the liquid onto his jacket. He felt slightly faint, in a sort of mild shock, and his neck and shoulders had suddenly become rigid.

'It must be Carter,' he thought. 'There was no-one else who possessed the information. Pilcher? It could be him... or the Bursar. But he wouldn't want the information leaked for the same reasons as himself. He was implicated too. Pilcher. Yes, he was too clever by half. But he and Carter were friends. One wouldn't be likely to leak it without the other knowing. Carter would certainly be party to it, probably along with that girlfriend of his. But why? Why on earth should they? Carter had got his job back. What would they gain by dragging it all out into the open?'

Masterton's eyes narrowed as the drink started to fire his anger. 'Yes, it would be that vindictive little swine Carter. Grammar-school type. Knew I shouldn't have taken him on. Blast! After all my consideration to him. Meeting influential friends, having him to dinner. Taking him into my confidence.' He poured himself another large measure and started to pace the room. It was bloody frustrating. 'You give someone a chance in life, a good position, good prospects. All right, there's a misunderstanding, so you apologise profusely, entertain the person lavishly, and they stab you in the back anyway.'

He hurled the second glass into the grate, and stood there clenching and unclenching his hands. He knew full well that the headmaster's statutory method of getting rid of difficult staff by maintaining incompetence, was no longer available to him. He had, as they say, 'blown it' in that direction where Carter was concerned.

'And who the devil was this character who was threatening Sir George's career? Some political opponent, no doubt with a massive chip on his shoulder, who was private-education bashing. Why would Carter want to furnish such a person with ammunition for their cause? Carter's future lay with such a system. It would surely be in his best interests to protect it. The same would apply to Pilcher.'

He would have to get hold of Carter anyway now and confront him with going back on their agreement, despite Sir George's warning not to speak to anyone about it. He couldn't have a junior teacher holding him to ransom indefinitely.

Masterton was furious at himself for having let the situation get this far. If only he hadn't been quite so hasty in sacking Carter in the first place. Well, what was he to do? Run the risk of those blasted papers falling into the wrong hands? The problem was how to wriggle out of it. No, he'd done the right thing by telling Sir George that the commodity papers were only specimens. That was definitely his best line of defence. If he stuck to that story and told that idiot Trent to do the same, then the real truth need never come out. The allegations could be denied, and there was no way they could be proved, unless of course Hedley substantiated the deals publicly. But then he had him over a barrel by threatening to expose his son as a homosexual should the need arise. Yes, that had indeed been a clever move.

It then came to him that he would now have to face interrogations by other governors, some parents, maybe even the media. Damn! He would welcome such publicity under normal circumstances, but this was impossible. He went to the cabinet, got another glass and downed a treble. On his way back to his study in the main building, he vented his fury on every single door he passed through, by slamming it shut behind him with every ounce of force he could muster.

The wires were buzzing between the governors of Bradchester that night. The Chairman, Sir Harvey Wainwright MBE MA, was in constant demand at his ex-directory number, fending off polite but anxious enquiries, not only from the rest of his board, but also from close personal friends. Some of these queries came in the form of consolation, some as advice as to what action to take. Almost all were tinged with apprehension as to whether the enquirer's head was likely to be among those seen to be rolling if and when the time came.

Colonel Trent also lost control of a glass that evening. It had been full of neat gin, and he didn't actually knock it over. He dropped it, while watching the local television news, which included a report of Jack Simmonds' speech.

Attempting to retrieve the empty glass, he staggered into the coffee table, bringing it down with him. The doctor had warned him about his heart and his drinking, but he had this feeling that because he was an ex-Army man he would be able to cope better than other men in his predicament. Sick wife, not really up to his job, totally dominated by the man he had to work with... money troubles.

As he started to get up, he felt the tightness in his chest and waited for the pins and needles feeling in his arm. It didn't come. He remained sitting on the floor, the gin soaking through his sock and into his shoe. He adjusted his position ever so slowly, and sat propped up against the sofa, loosening his tie. He thought about taking his shoes off, but it was effort enough under normal circumstances. Managing to remove his jacket, he felt for his pulse at the left wrist. It seemed to be fine, but every now and then he lost it.

Indigestion, he kidded himself. Another gin will calm it all down again.

He remained where he was for another ten minutes before rolling over into an 'all-fours' position and pulling himself onto the sofa and up.

Ah yes! He was fine now. Then he started to think about what he'd seen on the news, and the tightness came back again. Having removed his tie completely, he refilled his glass and gingerly sat down.

Chapter 11

Christine had decided that I needed a complete break from Bradchester after the end of term and her therapy was very appealing. She'd taken a week off to look after me, and we would sleep, eat, drink, sail, make love and sleep again, until the world started to appear less complicated.

It had been a beautiful week so far. The sun shone from dawn to dusk, and the wind had got up enough to provide some exhilarating sailing. There was a big Wayfarer meeting at the yacht club in ten days' time and as Christine, in her capacity as Sailing Secretary, had plenty of administrative jobs to keep her busy, we were spending every day over there. There was plenty of time for sailing, however, and she made sure that it formed a major part of my 'therapy'.

She was a very capable helmswoman in her own right and was currently lying second in the club's 470 class. I'd crewed for her in quite a few races, mainly handicap events, on Sundays earlier in the year, but very often we'd just gone sailing together. I was pretty inexperienced and consequently not good enough to partner her in the 470 fleet races. She had a chap called David Harmer as her regular crew. 470s were no toy sailing dinghies. They were powerful racing machines with a big enough sail area to require the use of a trapeze to obtain the ultimate performance. I had been absolutely spellbound, not to mention scared out of my wits, when foolishly, before the season started, I'd asked her to show me what the boat could really do.

It was blowing about force three. 'Probably gusting four', she'd said.

'It'll shake you up a bit, Alan. Are you sure?'

'Oh, come on. I can take it if you can,' I said. 'I'm not a geriatric yet.'

She smiled and said. 'Right oh, then. Don't say I didn't warn you. Out on the trapeze you go.'

'Aye, aye skipper,' I teased, and then wished I hadn't,

She balanced the finely tuned machine on a beam reach on the starboard tack by spilling a bit of wind out of the sails until I'd got myself organised.

'All right, Alan?' she shouted as we began to pick up speed.

'No problem,' I yelled back. I was finding it easier than I'd expected. I could balance myself out on the wire with my feet on the gunnel and felt quite confident. 'It's a doddle,' I smirked.

'Good,' she shouted. 'Hold tight then. Here we go. Let's have that jib sheet in.'

I thought we were already going damn fast and wondered what she meant. I obeyed and immediately found out.

The power of the boat was amazing and I was totally overawed at being strung out over the whistling ocean. Occasionally my backside caught the water with a wrenching thump when I was too slow in spotting a change of heel angle. Christine just laughed when this happened and I marvelled at her casual manner.

'Try a tack now?' she enquired.

I bit my lip in acknowledgement.

'Stand by then, tacking, three, two, one, come in now.'

I was already in, and she shifted her position slightly in adjustment.

The tiller went behind her back, the boom came over and I sat out on the gunnel as I fumbled to hook on the port wire. We were already shooting away on the new tack and heeling severely. Christine hung right out of the boat.

'Need you out here, Alan'

At last I got hooked on and climbed out. The boat seemed to be waiting for me, straining at the leash to be levelled out and be off. I threw my weight on the wire and the 470 leapt away again.

'Well done,' shouted Christine. 'Not too bad at all.'

Somehow I didn't think David Harmer would have been impressed. My fear was subsiding just a little, when she said, 'Right, let's really go for it then.' My heart sank. 'Beam reach, and we'll get her up on the plane.'

'Are you sure?' I protested.

'You're doing brilliantly, Alan, and you asked me what the boat could do. I did warn you! You're lucky it's not windy today.'

'Bitch!' I yelled, as she bore away laughing and easing the main.

I grimaced. The motion of the boat was steadier now but we were going twice as fast. I hung on, trying to concentrate on balancing the speeding craft as the spray stung my face and eyes. It was an unbelievable sensation. Christine was spilling no wind now and as I looked over my right shoulder, she smiled broadly.

Suddenly I was higher above the water and travelling

faster still. The motion of the hull seemed to have gone light, and as I glanced down I could see the reason – the front half of the boat was not in the water at all. We were planing on the aft section and now I was really scared. Surely a slip of a girl couldn't hold this arrow-like projectile in this unstable attitude for long. There seemed to be nothing in the water to steer the boat with, and here was I, completely at her mercy, not even in the boat, but hung out on a thin wire about to die.

She had it totally under control and was laughing at me as she made very deft movements on the helm. 'How d'you feel?' she teased. I mouthed an obscenity.

I didn't really have time to think about it in depth, but I do remember having the utmost confidence in her skill from then on. I never felt I was going for a swim, as she handled the flying craft with a featherlike touch. I had the greatest admiration for her as she leant right out with the end of the tiller extension held between her fingers like a violin bow, switching her gaze from sails to water ahead and back again. She appeared to be enjoying it as we rode the uneasy motion of the crests with apparent abandon, slewing about like a skidding car. Her black hair flew back from her shining face as the spray whipped into it, and I felt a touch of envy for David Harmer.

Then the wind freshened briefly to force four, and Christine got every ounce of performance out of the 470 that was available. It was certainly a 'brown trouser' moment for me, and my expression of sheer terror must have caught her eye, for she bore away into a run and told me to come into the boat. I needed no second invitation and crouched there very quietly. She nursed me back to good humour, and sailed the boat herself until I had recovered enough to be of use again. I'd had enough of the trapeze for one day.

'Bloody hell, Christine,' I stammered. 'It's terrifying. I'm absolutely shattered.'

'You did really well, Alan,' she smiled. 'I remember my first plane in a force four. It's a hair-raising experience.' She nudged me with her elbow. 'Fun though, isn't it?'

'I could use a double brandy,' I said.

'Right you are,' she grinned. 'Stand by to gybe then.'

She turned the boat downwind and I lowered my head as the boom whipped over. Easing both sheets again, we ran back towards the clubhouse.

As I sipped my double brandy in the bar afterwards on that day back in March, I'd made a vow never to ask anyone again to show me what a high-powered racing dinghy could do.

As it turned out, I'd been so exhilarated by the experience that when I'd recovered and thought about it, I decided that I'd like to get used to it, especially if it meant sharing Christine's love of sailing with her.

I'd progressed quite well and, when time had permitted during the summer term, had spent many a Sunday at the yacht club, either being taught how to crew by her or later on sometimes doing a handicap race with her. On one occasion, when I'd had a little experience, one of the 470 class helms was short of his regular crew for a club championship race and pleaded with me to help him out. He needed points to hold his place in the table and was very persuasive. I wasn't keen as I had no wish to let him down but, after many promises of free pints of bitter and guarantees not to get angry with me, I consulted Christine. She said it would be okay, so I agreed.

I wouldn't have missed the start of that race for anything.

In the handicap races, Christine had always taken it easy with me, but now I was to be in the same race as her, I was interested to see how good she really was.

She had a reputation for not being afraid to 'mix it', and as the five-minute gun went, the heat was really on. My skipper, a chap called Pete Matlock, was a pretty accomplished helm and was anxious to be well up at the start. He manoeuvred skilfully and several times we passed close by Christine. There was not a flicker of recognition from her though as she fought for position at the line. With one minute to go, tempers started to fray and the shouting started.

Christine was right in the middle of it. I was too busy handling our own boat to watch her but I could hear her all right.

She was screaming 'starboard' as I caught a glimpse of a white hull going about and missing her by inches. The white hull was much too late reacting and another boat caught it at the stern, shearing off the rudder pintles and causing it to capsize. 'Ten seconds,' I called out to Pete, who'd already started his run. He'd done well and as the gun went there were five of us up there including Christine. We left the debris behind and went off on the starboard tack and very quickly went about onto port. She was the other end of the line and held her course on starboard. We were on a converging course but Pete had got us slightly ahead.

'Going to be a close one this,' he yelled. 'Keep her as flat as you can and we'll make it.'

If I'd done what he'd asked, we would have crossed in front of Christine. As it was, I suppose I just wasn't good enough. David Harmer was out on his wire and steady as a rock. I was nervous and kept trying to see where she was. We rolled a little. Then again. It slowed us enough to make a collision just possible. Pete stuck to his course. But so did Christine. We were just ahead and could probably have held our line to pass in front. Christine anticipated a slight gust and produced just enough extra speed to instil the tiniest bit of doubt in Pete's mind. Maybe we couldn't make it.

'Starboard!' Christine sensed our doubt and kept on coming. Pete held his line and obviously thought he had enough water to get across without forcing her to alter course to pass behind us. He knew she would raise a protest if that happened. The two boats were screaming towards each other. It was decision time. I glanced anxiously at Pete. His jaw was set in a rigid display of determination not to give way. We were going to hit her. It was too late now.

'Christ Almighty!' I yelled at Pete.

It was Christine's right of way but it was too late to tack.

'Starboard! Pete Matlock.' Her voice had a clinical edge to it.

'Shit!' he mouthed and slammed the boat round. I was slewed into the gunnel with a bang as we lurched about and clambered inboard as best I could before unhooking and clawing myself over to the starboard side.

Christine sliced her boat past not four feet away. 'Watch their boom Alan,' Pete Matlock yelled at me as the aluminium spar missed my head by inches as she swept by. The wake from her 470 hissed arrogantly as she deviated not an inch from her course, finally showing us a clean pair of heels as we gathered ourselves together some ten or fifteen metres behind.

'Bloody women drivers,' shouted Pete after her, drawing a

two-fingered response without even a backward glance.

I looked at Pete. He was smiling and shaking his head ruefully. We'd lost four places in that little encounter.

'I suppose she was right?' I offered tentatively.

'Yes, she had starboard. I had to give way. Beats me though where she got that bit extra to make me go about. I was sure I had enough water to go across her. She's a brilliant helm, Alan. Make no mistake. Hard as hell with it too. Miles better than I'll ever be.'

'Bit over the top though, wasn't it? Cutting us up like that.'

'Not at all. She really knows what she's doing. Actually, Alan, I take it as a compliment that she held her line at me. I think if she hadn't known me, and that I'd go about in time, she'd have gone behind me and protested. Would have made her mad though. As it is, I don't mind at all being cut up by someone as good as her. I'll probably just throw my beer over her afterwards and give her a kiss. Mind you, some of the visiting opposition don't take kindly to receiving that sort of treatment from a woman. Seem to think it's a man's prerogative to dish it out. Come on, let's get racing again. I've got some places to make up.'

'Right!' I agreed, rubbing my bruised leg. I was as proud as hell of her. 'Let's get after the bitch.'

Christine had won that race and had kept her wet suit on in the bar, fully expecting Pete to throw his beer over her, which he did. She didn't expect any special treatment from the male members of the club, nor did she receive any. The banter was good, and it was obvious they were very proud of her. Three of them had told me I was a lucky bastard, with which sentiment I heartily agreed.

And so it was in that kind of atmosphere during mid-July that she and I sailed and drank some beer, and ate and slept and made love, and chatted with friends and relaxed. It was just what we both needed, and looking back, I think it was probably the happiest week of my life.

That is until one of the members casually asked me if I knew that the Headmaster and one of the governors of the school I taught at were hot news for fiddling the books, or something of the sort.

Christine and I were sitting in the corner of the bar and what he was saying didn't really register at first. I smiled at him over my beer and said something to the effect that I wasn't surprised, and the remark seemed to be forgotten. It was when he threw a copy of the local paper under my nose that the back of my neck suddenly started to go hot. I felt Christine's hand take hold of mine under the table as I read the bold newsprint alongside the pictures of Masterton and Sir George Beeson.

Member of Parliament and Headmaster implicated in illicit financial dealings.

It leapt off the page at me like a punch between the eyes, and the happiest week of my life was over.

Chapter 12

An Extraordinary General Meeting of the Governors of Bradchester School had been called as soon as the news of the allegations against Sir George and Masterton had broken. There were seventeen members of the board, of which five were women. The Chairman, Sir Harvey Wainwright JP, MA, FREng, had been keen to get things settled as soon as possible and, in order to do so, had had to get his own secretary to make the arrangements. Normally he would have relied on Colonel Trent, as Clerk to the Governors, to organise things, but his poor health meant he had to be disregarded.

The school secretaries had been asked to work in shifts to deal with the deluge of enquiries that swamped the switchboard. Ex-governors, parents, old boys, even some senior current pupils all wanted to know what was going on. The answer was of a stalling nature. 'In order that internal enquiries can be made, a statement will be issued to the press at the appropriate time.'

This did not satisfy everyone by any means and some outraged callers were offering a certain amount of abusive comment. Several prominent and distinguished former pupils insisted on attending the meeting, even if only in an advisory or consultative capacity, so serious did they consider the situation. Sir Harvey made more enemies in two days refusing to let them attend than he had in a lifetime.

Governors' meetings were usually held at the school, but on this occasion, to avoid the reporters and television cameras that had been hanging around the Headmaster's house for some days, an obscure residence near Wimbledon, home of the sister of the least prominent member of the board, had been chosen as the venue.

It was a morose gathering, called under somewhat bizarre circumstances on a Friday evening. Sir Harvey had instructed the Headmaster to attend but to wait in an adjoining room until called. He'd also told him that there would be a short discussion by the board to start with, at which he would not be present. If at any time the board wished to put questions to him, he would be sent for and whatever was discussed could be minuted. Sir Harvey then asked his Headmaster, 'strictly off the record at this time, you understand,' whether there was any truth in the allegations made by Jack Simmonds.

Masterton had decided he could bluff it out, principally because his secret would be safe with Julian Hedley.

'Absolutely none, Sir Harvey,' he said with great innocence and sincerity. 'As I said, it's a complete misinterpretation of the contents of the copied papers. They are examples only. Specimens printed to advertise the services that are available from a broker in that field.'

'And the broker concerned would testify to that fact if called upon?'

'He could do nothing else, and I'm sure would be glad to. He's a personal friend of mine and his son is at the school. A fine boy who will be a credit to Bradchester.'

'Very well, Masterton,' said Sir Harvey. 'But remember, if the rest of the board are not satisfied with what you've told me, you will have to convince them yourself. Do you understand?'

'Perfectly,' said Masterton. 'But you have my word. A full denial can be made with complete confidence.'

'I hope for your sake you are right. Don't forget, there are two most able and distinguished barristers on the board.'

The door closed quietly and Masterton was left on his own.

The Chairman whistled through the requisite formalities for such a meeting, and then said, 'There's only one item on the agenda and you've all been notified of it – namely to discuss the allegations against Sir George and the Headmaster made by Mr Jack Simmonds and reported in certain national and local newspapers, and subsequent comments made by the media relating thereto.'

He'd decided to get through this unpleasant business as quickly as possible and hopefully before some of the more ponderous board members could prolong the proceedings unnecessarily. This needed fast, decisive action from the most professional of his colleagues.

'I think it best to ask Sir George to speak first to the item,' he opened, 'giving us the facts as they presented themselves to him and then to give us his opinion as to why the allegations have been made in the first place. I'm sure you all know why, but we should hear it from Sir George, who is no stranger to the mysteries of political skulduggery, in a purely passive sense, I'm sure.'

He surveyed his audience and adopted a more serious tone. 'I will then put a point to all of you, to which I wish you to give very serious consideration before those who would like to speak on the matter do so.'

He turned to the politician on his left. 'George! If you'd be so kind.'

The big man rose. Sir George recounted clearly and precisely the media interviews he'd had outside the House of Commons and the reasons for his evasive replies to reporters' questions. There was nodded agreement all round the table. He conveyed his regret to the board that the incident had occurred at all but confirmed he was in no position himself to comment at present on the undertakings of those who were directly responsible for the financial running of the school. This meeting would, he felt sure, get to the bottom of the matter without delay. He mentioned that he'd felt it necessary to speak to the Headmaster briefly on the telephone after the news had broken and had received an emphatic denial of any untoward behaviour. The whole thing was an easily explained misinterpretation apparently.

He finished his brief explanation by confirming what he was certain they all knew – that the whole thing was a clumsy attempt by a political opponent to discredit him and all he stood for, by involving his support for the private education system. The attempt he felt sure would fail, and the school authorities would be absolved from any involvement in such allegations.

Several governors started to speak at once.

Sir Harvey interjected. 'If members would kindly address the chair,' he rebuked. 'Before discussing this very serious matter, I'm going to ask you all to consider this. I have spoken to Duncan Masterton and asked him outright to what specifically the accusations refer. He has told me that the dealings concerned are not what Mr Simmonds claims them to be, but merely copies of examples circulated by a commodity broker. Such practice is, I believe, quite common these days in the search for new clients and investors in the very competitive financial services markets.'

He broke off and turned his gaze to each governor in turn. It was his customary method of preparing to influence individuals to agree with him.

'I do not wish this meeting to become a court martial of the Headmaster, nor do I think it necessary to subject him to an interrogation to ascertain the facts. We are here merely to decide the best course of action in the light of present circumstances, in our capacity as governors of the school. Sir George, I know, will be the first to admit that our primary duty lies with the protection of the reputation of Bradchester. His personal political position will be best served as a natural follow-up to our success in that duty.'

Sir George was nodding.

'Furthermore,' continued Sir Harvey, 'I would remind you that both Sir George and I have received categorical denials from the Headmaster of anything amiss at the school with regard to this matter. Whilst not wishing to influence you in any way, I would ask you to bear that in mind in your deliberations.'

He sat down. There was an uneasy silence. The Chairman had insinuated that discussion should not seek clarification of the Headmaster's statement of denial. The remark might well be aimed at any type of cross-examination of Masterton, particularly by the barristers amongst them. Both remained silent. It was Lady Ellen Bourneford JP, MA who spoke.

'Chairman,' she began. 'It's quite clear that this board must be absolutely confident that a statement can be put out, making a complete rejection of the allegations. Only in that way can the seeds of any doubt that have been purposefully sown for political ends be dispelled and any consequential slur on the school's reputation immediately repaired. In order to have that confidence, we must not allow the Headmaster to shoulder the whole burden of responsibility for the denial of any untoward financial practice in the school. We must remember that we are not asking him to be a financial expert but a Headmaster first and foremost, and in my opinion he is one of the finest in the country.'

There were a few 'hear, hears'.

She went on. 'There are those among us who have expert knowledge of the financial services market, and they should have the opportunity of satisfying themselves, on the board's behalf, that these commodity dealings, are what the Headmaster says they are – namely an irrelevance, and can be proved to be so in public.'

Air Vice-Marshal Sir Peter Smithson KCB DFC RAF (Retired) intervened.

'Mr Chairman!' He looked cross. 'You'll forgive me, I'm sure, but because I agree with the last speaker's sentiments about the quality of the Headmaster, I feel it uncharitable to cast doubt on his ability to decide whether there is anything underhand going on in his school. In my opinion, if he tells us there is no truth in the allegations, we should do him the courtesy of taking his word for it.'

Sir Harvey looked at Lady Bourneford for some response. She was poker-faced. She considered the Air Vice-Marshal to have some useful contacts, but otherwise to be comprehensively naive. He was on the board for the former reason, not for his powers of logical reasoning.

'Furthermore,' blustered Sir Peter, 'we should sue for libel at the earliest opportunity. That will put the matter to rest.' He sat back in his chair and threw his pen onto the table in a gesture of disgust at the whole affair.

Muttered agreement was again evident.

Sir Henry Melling MBE MA DL, Chairman of the Melling Group of Companies, offered his raised arm.

'Yes, Henry,' said Sir Harvey.

The Melling group had worldwide interests in banking, insurance and financial services generally, including the ownership of foreign exchange and commodity broking concerns in London, New York and the Far East.

'These alleged illicit deals, copies of which this Jack Simmonds says he possesses. If we could be allowed a sight of the originals, it should be reasonably easy to ascertain whether they are specimens only, or authentic, as Mr Simmonds suggests. My company would be able to apply to have them authenticated as genuine if there are dates and reference numbers. If they are not, it would seem reasonable to assume a full denial of the allegations could be made with complete confidence. And, as the Headmaster has told you no such deals ever took place, perhaps he would be good enough to show us the offending papers in order that his opinion can be substantiated.'

The Air Vice-Marshal made huffing noises as a sign of his disapproval.

'That seems a most logical suggestion,' said Sir Harvey. 'I should like the agreement of the board to the Headmaster being asked to produce those papers for us to look at.'

Sir Peter was the only dissenter.

Sir Harvey turned to his secretary, who was taking the

minutes of the meeting. 'I wonder if you'd be good enough to ask him to make them available to the board, preferably right now if he has them with him, and at the earliest opportunity if he hasn't.'

She left the room and returned within two minutes to explain that the Headmaster apologised, but owing to the seriousness of the allegations, and in the light of Sir George Beeson's request for absolute silence and discretion, he had perhaps overreacted in destroying all papers having any bearing on the matter. He realised that it was a foolish and hasty thing to do, but in the heat of the moment, that had been the first action he had taken.

There was silence round the table, punctuated only by the tapping of several ballpoint pens.

'How convenient for Mr Simmonds.' The remark, by Sir Thomas Whittle QC was calculated to make a few hackles rise.

'What are you insinuating?' enquired Lady Bourneford with an aggressive edge to her voice.

'There is no insinuation,' said the barrister, sitting well back in his chair with his arms folded in a slightly disinterested attitude. 'I merely make the observation that the loss of physical evidence is to the benefit of the originator of the allegations, and detrimental to us, engaged as we are in the quest for a means of denial.'

'It certainly is a pity,' said Sir Harvey. 'But we shall have to take Masterton's word for it that the papers are not incriminating. I for one would be happy to accept his explanation and make a public denial. I trust that the rest of the board will support me. After all, we have appointed an honest and trustworthy man to maintain the reputation of our fine school on our behalf, and we should stand firmly behind him. I have no doubt at all that the matter will end there, and personally I would discourage any feelings of vindication in the form of a libel action against Mr Simmonds. That sort of thing brings unwanted publicity, and in my experience, even if one is in the right, any publicity of that sort would be detrimental.'

'With respect, Chairman,' it was Sir Thomas again, 'your wish to exonerate the school from involvement is understandable, but overhasty.'

It was too much for the Air Vice-Marshal. He was on his feet. 'You go too far, sir. Explain yourself, if you please.'

'Gentlemen, gentlemen,' interrupted Sir Harvey. He turned to Sir Thomas. 'I'm sure we would all like to hear any constructive criticism you may have,' he said icily. He was aware that the eminent barrister had not been in agreement with the appointment of Duncan Masterton as headmaster.

Sir Thomas continued. 'Jack Simmonds is a man whom the police would dearly love to bring to book, and the board would be well advised to know the sort of person they are up against. This character has been held on suspicion of pimping and extortion, but released when prosecution witnesses notified their refusal to testify. That was over twenty years ago. Since then he has kept a clean sheet, but is known to be involved in extortion rackets amongst certain communities in North London. He is well protected by silence and, as Sir George will tell you, he latterly has aspirations that are not so much political but more as a nuisance value against those who are politicians. He has very substantial sums of cash at his disposal, and in the recent past has obtained a reputation for imprudence where libel cases have been involved. However, one thing he is not is a fool. To have kept one step ahead of the law for twenty years shows two important characteristics; loyalty among his closest followers verging on the fanatical, and a highly complex and efficient information network. Believe me, no successful criminal can exist without either, and our Mr Simmonds has both in abundance.'

There was a sort of stunned silence round the table induced by the sudden transportation from the relatively virtuous environment of an English public school to the sleazy depravity of prostitution and racketeering north of the Thames.

Sir Thomas clarified his point to an utterly captive audience. 'We would therefore be wise to assume in the first place that Mr Simmonds has the contacts to have been able to get hold of these papers, and secondly that he will have learnt enough from his previous flirtations with the libel courts to have checked his facts before inviting another such action against himself. With these two assumptions very much in mind, I would strongly advise the board to make absolutely sure those papers are what the Headmaster says they are.'

'How are we to do that if they've been destroyed?' said Lady Bourneford.

'Possibly by contacting the broker who circulated them to Masterton,' came the ready reply. 'I suppose that would be possible wouldn't it, Henry?' He looked at Sir Henry Melling for confirmation.

'It should be, yes.'

'Then perhaps,' said Sir Harvey, ' you would be good enough to get the information from Masterton and establish from the broker concerned that the papers were just specimens.'

Sir Thomas spoke again. 'Mr Chairman,' he said wearily. 'Why don't you ask Mr Masterton to come in and sit down with us, so that he can help to clear this thing up here and now? We'll be here all night if we have to keep running to and fro asking him for bits of information.'

'Because I know of your dislike for him, Sir Thomas, and that you will take unfair advantage by confusing him.' Sir Harvey couldn't conceal his own doubts about the barrister's motives and felt sure he would behave like a prosecuting counsel if the Headmaster were present.

'Nonsense,' snapped Sir Thomas. 'In any event I'm well outnumbered by those who would automatically leap to his defence, while ignoring any conflicting evidence I may turn up. Believe me, the facts must be crystal clear. If you make a mistake, Mr Simmonds will crucify you.'

The Bishop of Peterborough looked uncomfortable and cleared his throat.

'Begging your pardon, Bishop,' said Sir Thomas. 'My apologies.'

'I don't think the board take kindly to your insinuation that some of their number are prone to blind acceptance of the Headmaster's word,' said Sir Harvey. 'Perhaps you would like to rephrase.'

'No, I would not,' insisted Sir Thomas. 'And furthermore, I would like it minuted that I strongly disagree with the board not being given the opportunity to question the Headmaster. I don't think you quite realise, Mr Chairman, what the press will do to this school if he is mistaken. There will be no second chances, you may be sure about that.'

Three or four governors rose to protest, but the Bishop

was too quick for them. He had already risen and, in his most commanding pulpit voice with arms outstretched, urged them to consider the importance of a conciliatory attitude at this time. He asserted sufficient authority amongst them to persuade those standing to be seated, whereupon he asked for The Good Lord's guidance upon the meeting. Most of the governors said 'Amen', and he sat down again.

Sir Harvey was at a loss as to how to follow that.

Sir John Glazebrook helped him out. He had remained silent so far but now seized the opportunity to get some decisions made.

'Possibly the Chair would call for a proposer and a seconder to Sir Thomas's suggestion that the Head be asked to attend. Assuming that to be what Sir Thomas had in mind.'

Sir Harvey was furious at having been outmanoeuvred but admitted that would be in order.

Sir Thomas then made the proposal and was surprised to hear it seconded by Sir John himself.

This had the effect of changing quite a few minds round the table, particularly those belonging to governors who had sworn blind allegiance to Sir Harvey and had combined to put him in the chair some six years ago. Sir John also had the respect of the majority of the board, but in this particular case, a fine line was to be drawn between implicit loyalty to the Chairman and the need to side with the likely survivors if heads began to roll.

As the doubters would have nothing much to lose at this stage anyway by voting for the motion, they decided to keep a foot in both camps and supported Sir Thomas and Sir John.

The proposal was therefore carried by a slender majority, but watered down somewhat by Sir Harvey insisting that all questions to the Headmaster were to be put through the Chair, and not direct. When making this condition, he was staring threateningly at Sir Thomas.

'Before calling the Headmaster in, Mr Chairman,' said Sir John, 'I wonder if I might enquire whether the Bursar should not be able to throw some light on the matter. After all, he is responsible to the board for the financial running of the school, and as such should be aware, should he not, of the existence of these so called 'incriminating papers'?

'I'm afraid he's not at all well,' replied Sir Harvey. 'It seems he's had a minor stroke. Nothing he won't get over, I'm informed, but he will be out of action for some time.'

'Perhaps he would be well enough to answer a few simple questions,' pressed Sir John. 'Maybe he also knows what the papers contain and could therefore corroborate the Head's explanation. I could drop by his home, if he's well enough, and have a few words with him.'

'Yes, an excellent idea, Sir John, thank you. You'd better check on his state of health first though. His wife, I understand, is none too well herself.'

Masterton entered the room showing the outward signs of confidence that he felt would be expected of him. Beneath his assured exterior, however, he harboured some trepidation of the next half hour or so. When confronted with the circle of stern and forbidding expressions, he inwardly groaned at the realisation that by insisting that the papers were irrelevant, he'd blatantly lied to the whole lot of them. Too late to back out now. He'd have to stick with his story. Part of it was true at least. He had destroyed the papers, both the originals that Carter had returned to him and the copies that the Bursar had found in the flat. The fact that he'd only done that last night was neither here nor there. His real worry was if the copies that Carter had obviously leaked to this Simmonds character came to light or were shown to the press. There was a good chance that wouldn't happen, however, and anyway he'd virtually guaranteed that Hedley wouldn't verify them as genuine. No – it was better to stick with his story.

There was a formal note in Sir Harvey's voice.

'Come in, Headmaster.' He motioned Masterton to a chair beside him.

'The board would like clarification of a few points before deciding the action to be taken in this matter concerning the allegations made against you and Sir George. It goes without saying of course that we expect you to make a complete denial, but in order for us to be able to give you our full backing, it's important that we are clear in our minds about certain finer points that some of us might be invited to explain.'

'Of course, Sir Harvey. I understand.'

'I will therefore invite members to address their questions to the Chair and would ask you to wait until I have clarified them for all of us before answering. Is that clear?'

Masterton nodded. 'He's protecting me,' he thought. 'That's good of him, but he must be expecting a rough ride if he considers it necessary. Damn!'

Sir Thomas was speaking. 'Chairman,' he said pointedly and with a touch of sarcasm. 'We are informed that the foundation on which these damaging allegations are based are some copies of commodity deals which the Headmaster claims are nothing but examples sent to him by a broker for marketing purposes. We assume that Mr Simmonds, who is supposedly in possession of these papers, considers them to be proof of illicit dealings by the school, and in particular by the Headmaster. Mr Simmonds, by his very action in making the allegations public, will have put himself at risk of a very substantial libel case. I wish to know why, if the Headmaster is so confident that Mr Simmonds is mistaken, he would seemingly place himself in such a vulnerable position so willingly?'

Masterton glanced at the Chairman who nodded his agreement to answer.

'I can only think, Sir Thomas, that a man like Mr Simmonds is so driven by his fanatical desire to attack the democratic and capitalist system he's powerless to change that he would be prone to extravagant mistakes of this kind in his desperate bid to seek publicity.'

Masterton felt very pleased with that. There were several heads nodding in agreement, including the Air Vice-Marshal's. A point scored against the eminent barrister was a good start indeed.

'Where did Mr Simmonds get his information?' The question came from Lady Bourneford.

Again the nod from Sir Harvey.

'It seems that one of my junior teachers inadvertently stumbled upon the papers in the office. The originals were recovered, but not before he'd made some copies. I can only assume he harboured a grudge of some sort and thought to use the copies to make trouble. When the copies were recovered, I'm afraid I destroyed them with the originals.' Masterton was sweating a bit now. He hadn't wanted to go this far, as it was possible the governors might wish to know who the teacher was.

'Who is this teacher?' enquired Sir John Glazebrook.

'Just one moment,' interrupted Sir Harvey. 'I don't think

it's terribly relevant at this stage.'

'I assume the teacher has been dismissed,' said Sir Peter.

There was a pause while the governors waited on Sir Harvey's next comment.

He looked at Masterton. 'Well, has he been dismissed?'

Masterton was in trouble. 'No, Mr Chairman, he hasn't.'

'Good heavens, man,' said the Air Vice-Marshal. 'Why ever not? Is he a lefty or something? He obviously has no business being employed at Bradchester. Get rid of him. That's my advice.'

'Now just a minute, ladies and gentlemen,' said Sir Harvey, with a hint of impatience. 'We really must stick to the subject. Hiring and firing is the Headmaster's job, and we have employed him to do it. Now is not the time to question his judgement on such matters. He will no doubt have his reasons, but they are not for scrutiny at this time.'

Sir Thomas had been sitting back with his arms folded and his eyes shut. He opened them briefly to catch a glimpse of his fellow barrister on the board eyeing him in similar fashion. No word passed. No other expression was necessary. The message was clear between them. There was food for thought here indeed. Both men appeared to go back to sleep.

Masterton certainly had a stalwart defender in Sir Harvey. Some of the board were beginning to wonder why.

'I think, Mr Chairman,' said Sir John Glazebrook, 'that we should be told his name, if only to be aware of his possible involvement with Mr Simmonds, and in case it comes to light from any other source. We can then be on our guard. I for one am quite in agreement that the decision to dismiss or not is the Headmaster's and have no wish to interfere with that process. I also think we should know the name of the commodity broker concerned in order that any checking of the figures may be carried out without delay.'

There was general agreement.

'Very well,' said Sir Harvey, turning to Masterton.

'The broker is Julian Hedley, who has his offices in Fenchurch Street in the City. As for the teacher, he's a relatively new young man in the History Department by the name of Carter. Joined last September. Takes a bit of sport as well. Not one of my better appointees, I admit, but we were in a hole at the time. I really don't think he's any threat to the school. Pretty harmless really, but of course I'm watching him carefully. I think he'll move on soon anyway. Not the right type for Bradchester.'

Sir John raised his eyebrows and made a brief note.

'Yes, all right, thank you, Headmaster,' said Sir Harvey. 'I'm sure you know your business best.' He turned back to the table. 'Any other questions?'

Sir Thomas had opened his eyes again. 'Yes, Mr Chairman.' Sir Harvey sighed audibly. 'May I ask the Headmaster whether the Bursar has any knowledge of these papers?'

Masterton was willing Sir Harvey to divert the question. He was out of luck.

'I'm pretty sure he doesn't,' said Masterton. 'They were addressed to me personally as I'd requested them myself. I have made a point of trying to keep up with the various forms of investment available for school funds in order that the very best returns on our liquidity may be made. This was one of very many examples of opportunities that come through the post. Of course, it goes without saying that there's no question of the school entering into such speculative forms of investment. Quite the reverse. We do, however, strive to be aware of what's going on in the financial markets, but of course are well served by those members of the board who are professionals in that field.'

He glanced at the banking representatives round the table.

'Unfortunately,' he continued, 'it does not prevent us receiving much unsuitable advisory material through the post. I'm almost certain, though, that Colonel Trent would not have seen these particular examples.'

'All right, Headmaster, thank you,' said Sir Harvey. 'I think, ladies and gentlemen, that if there are no more questions, we will ask the Headmaster if he will be good enough to leave us again.'

Masterton made as if to continue speaking but was cut short.

'If you wouldn't mind just waiting in the other room for a moment,' said Sir Harvey firmly. 'We'll call you when necessary.'

The Headmaster left the room biting his lip.

The Chairman turned to face the meeting. 'The position seems to be as follows. 'We have to make a very strong rejection of the allegations, that is quite clear. There is too much undercurrent of doubt and uncertainty flowing about this matter already. The school switchboard has been jammed with calls, not all of them civil and there is obviously doubt amongst some of you as to the authenticity of these papers that have been destroyed. The Headmaster assures us they are irrelevant. Some of you would like proof of that.'

He again fixed the doubters with a meaningful glare.

'As we cannot have the proof, then we must consider this. We either take the Headmaster at his word and deliver a full denial, or we say nothing and hope the situation will eventually slide into obscurity. Either way, we must expect Mr Simmonds to continue to press his allegations, at least for the time being.'

Sir George interrupted. 'I will have the media hounding me from first thing tomorrow morning,' he declared. 'If I don't make a statement soon, people will come to their own conclusions.'

'If I might suggest, Mr Chairman.' It was Sir John Glazebrook again. 'I think we must continue to hide behind the statement that we are making internal enquiries, for a little longer. I would recommend that I and one or two others, if they are willing and could make the time, do just that and make further enquiries. I am willing to visit the Bursar, and I would also like to speak to the teacher, Mr Carter. I've made his acquaintance on several occasions at the school and should like to hear his side of the story. It may conflict with the Headmaster's of course, but the stakes are too high now to leave any stone unturned. In any case, he is one of the people who have seen the contents of the papers.'

Sir Thomas raised his hand to the Chair. 'I'd be happy to assist in these further enquiries,' he said. 'My time is limited, but I'd like to speak to the broker who furnished the Headmaster with these documents. Perhaps he will have copies of them.'

'Thank you,' said Sir Harvey grudgingly. 'The board I'm sure would be grateful, and the Headmaster will no doubt give you the address. I think it best though that any enquiries be carried out with my full knowledge. So, in order that I can keep the rest of the governors fully updated with the situation, you should phone me every evening.' He looked at the whole table. 'And I think that should apply to anyone of you who turns up information which has a bearing on the matter. Time is not on our side.' He consulted his diary. 'Today is Friday. I would like any enquiries you are pursuing to be completed if possible by next Tuesday evening.'

There were muffled protests.

'I know that's not long, but I must have some idea as to whether or not you are likely to come up with anything that will confirm the Headmaster's assurances.'

He called for any more relevant questions, dismissed a few that weren't, and closed the meeting.

Masterton was nervous when Sir Harvey took him aside briefly afterwards. 'What's going on?' he said. 'Am I on trial here?'

'We're all on trial for the moment, Masterton. But if what you've told us is true, then there's nothing to worry about, is there? Some of the other governors feel that your assurances should be substantiated, that's all. It's a natural reaction.'

'Surely they can take my word for it, Sir Harvey. Are they insinuating I'm lying to them?'

'No, they are not,' said the Chairman. 'But you must understand that in the final analysis, responsibility lies with the board, not you. As your employers, we have not only to protect you, but also we must make sure that no mistakes are made. This matter goes much deeper than you think. There are political motives to be considered, and you are fortunate in having governors with such a wide range of experience in all walks of life outside the school to assist you. Believe me, Masterton, you can't handle this on your own, and the board are quite entitled to insist on further enquiries'.

He put a hand on Masterton's shoulder. 'Apart from

which,' he confided, 'if it weren't for the fact that I believe you to be right, I would have found it difficult to dissuade Sir Thomas Whittle from cross-examining you in front of everyone. That would have been most uncomfortable for you, right or wrong.'

The Chairman and his Headmaster were the last to leave the house and so were unaware that Sir John Glazebrook had followed Sir Thomas Whittle home, the two of them fully intent on further discussing the matter well into the night.

Masterton had made up his mind that despite what Sir George Beeson had said to him about being discreet and saying nothing to anyone, he was going to find Carter and have it out with him. He would also visit the Bursar at his home on the pretext of wishing him a speedy recovery and make damn sure he kept his mouth shut. Sir Thomas it was who'd asked whether Trent would have known anything about the papers. He'd lied pretty convincingly he thought, but Sir Thomas might have it followed up. He must be first to Carter and the Bursar.

But where the hell was Carter? He wasn't at his flat, and neither was Pilcher so he couldn't ask him either. And incidentally, he thought, Pilcher was another one who might know something about the leak. They were close friends those two. He looked up Carter's home telephone number in the file but there was no reply from there either. He was certain he'd be at his girlfriend's place but didn't know her surname or address. It would have to be the Bursar first.

Sir John Glazebrook was also looking for Carter, and the following morning had phoned Masterton from Sir Thomas's home to ascertain his whereabouts. The Headmaster had said he couldn't be traced at present but had almost certainly gone off on holiday with his girlfriend, but had no idea where that would be. Sir John had a feeling that Masterton was quite anxious to catch up with Carter himself and was perhaps not being as helpful as he might. He therefore decided to take a trip to Bradchester and make his own enquiries.

He and Sir Thomas both had their own ideas as to what enquiries to make and from whom. Sir John had always held the theory that if you want to know something about someone, enquiries to the people who do the everyday mundane jobs for them were very often productive. People like cleaners or postmen often seemed to be a mine of information about a person's habits or interests. He therefore set out just after lunch for Bradchester. Two hours later he parked in the staff car park and took an easy stroll in the direction of the common room.

As luck would have it most of the buildings were still open, as the cleaning staff were working overtime and weekends to prepare for an influx of foreign students who would take over the school for educational courses during the holidays. Wandering into the common room, he spied a buxom lady on her knees, trying to get coffee stains out of the carpet.

'Excuse me,' he said. 'I wonder if I might have a word?'

'Be with you in a moment, dear,' she replied, continuing to scrub. 'How these teachers get this place in such a mess is beyond me. Suppose it's because they don't have to clear it up themselves. Wouldn't let my home get into this state, I can tell you.'

'Perfect,' thought Sir John. 'Just the right type. She probably knows more about what goes on in this school than the teaching staff.' He wandered over to the noticeboards until the good lady was ready to talk to him.

He was aimlessly reading a few of last term's notices when he caught sight of the Headmaster's announcement that Mr Carter had been reinstated after dismissal. It went on to praise his conduct during some unfortunate misunderstanding, and an apology on behalf of the school was also expressed. The Headmaster, it mentioned, would be dealing with the cause of the misunderstanding himself.

Sir John was making a few notes when there was a tap on his shoulder.

'Funny business that was I can tell you, dear,' said the smiling cleaning lady.

'What do you mean?' said Sir John, slightly taken aback.

'Well, dear, of course, we're not supposed to read the notices really, but you can't help it, can you, what with cleaning and dusting all round them?'

'No, I suppose not.'

'Caused quite stir that did and no mistake. Poor lad. Such a nice boy. I clean the flat for him and his friend that lives with him. Upset something terrible he was, till they gave him back his job.'

'Why did he lose it in the first place?' said Sir John, anxious not to abuse this lady's trust.

'There was another notice earlier, just where that one is now. Funny it was, something about it being private or confidential or something. Anyway, whatever it was he was supposed to have done, they decided he didn't in the end. We was so glad. Such a gent he is, doesn't look down on us cleaners like some of them do.'

She suddenly put her hand to her mouth. 'Oh, I say. You're not one of them inspectors are you, dear? Talk myself into trouble I will and no mistake.'

'No. It's all right,' Sir John assured her. 'I was actually looking for Mr Carter. I don't suppose you'd know where I could find him?'

'Course, dear. He'll be with that lovely girl of his over at Thaxbury. Said he wouldn't be using the flat this week as they'll be sailing at the club most days. Lovely couple they make. So upsetting for them that business was.'

On his way over to the car, he spied the head groundsman working on the cricket square and went over to him. Bill Timms recognised the distinguished figure approaching over the outfield. Sir John had often complimented him on the standard of the wickets he produced and was quite knowledgeable himself about pitch preparation.

'Afternoon, Sir John.'

'Afternoon, Bill.'

After a short discussion about the square and the weather, the groundsman gave Sir John directions to the yacht club and watched him walk back across the outfield to the car park. 'Takes a real interest does that one,' he thought. 'Even remembers my name.'

'Well, well!' thought Sir John as he climbed into his car. 'So Carter was dismissed and then reinstated. Now that is most unusual and would lead one to believe that the dismissal was made in haste. Masterton had certainly not mentioned that at the board meeting. An error of judgement perhaps that, after consideration and in the cold light of day, was better reversed. The cleaning lady had said there was a previous notice to the one he had seen. Something about dismissal for confidential reasons.' He consulted the notes he'd made.

Sir John felt it would be very embarrassing for the Headmaster that there had been one notice of dismissal, and then another of reinstatement. The staff would be suspicious and making their own minds up as to what was really going on. There would be numerous theories flying about. It might be interesting to hear some of those theories in private if he could. The trouble was, time was so short and everyone was away on their holidays. But maybe some of the staff would have been engaged for the holiday courses. It was quite common for staff to offer their services after term had ended. It provided a useful addition to their income. Yes, maybe if he came over next week he might glean some interesting information.

It was now five thirty on Saturday, and he fumbled with the car's phone until he eventually got the yacht club number from directory enquiries. He was told that Alan Carter was out sailing but would most likely be in the clubhouse in about an hour. Sir John explained who he was and asked that Mr Carter be told that he would very much appreciate it if they could have a talk. He would be at the club at seven o'clock in the hope of seeing him then. He replaced the handset knowing that the teacher might indeed be disinclined to see him and would prefer to put the whole unfortunate episode behind him. Well, he'd have to cross that bridge when he got there.

Collecting some rather unpalatable-looking packaged sandwiches from a corner shop, he followed the directions the groundsman Timms had given him and after three quarters of an hour saw the dinghy masts strung out one side of the clubhouse, along the sea wall. He stopped the car on a track overlooking the water and well away from the building.

Taking out his sandwiches, he settled down to wait. There were many craft weaving their diagonal patterns to and fro across the estuary, which was over half a mile wide at this point. Some were racing, some just sailing. From the balcony of the clubhouse an assortment of square and cone-shaped flags stood out below the crosstrees of a white flagpole. Occasionally a hooter sounded, to be greeted by a wave from a finishing dinghy. Sir John took his binoculars from the glove compartment and started scanning the milling craft, but found it impossible to follow one crew for long as it was soon lost behind two or three others. He waited contentedly for ten minutes until there were a number of boats on the slipway and then picked up the glasses again in an attempt to recognise Alan Carter. He thought he spotted what might be him, with a dark-haired girl who'd been helming, but there were so many young men with dark-haired girls, he could easily have been mistaken. He did, however, want to make sure that his message would have been well and truly delivered, rather than embarrassing the teacher by presenting himself unannounced.

Chapter 13

When the boats had been put in the dinghy park and covered up, Sir John gave it another half an hour and at seven fifteen drove along the track to the car park. Enquiring of the barman where he could find Mr Carter, Sir John was directed to a corner table where a couple were engaged in what looked like an intense conversation. It was Carter all right and they'd seen him. The girl rose and came over.

'Are you Sir John Glazebrook?' she enquired. There was a defensive note to her voice.

'That's right,' he said.

'I'm Christine Walkham, Alan Carter's girlfriend, and one of the club secretaries. I'm afraid I'm going to have to ask you what it is you wish to see Alan about as, if it's what I think it is, he is now on a well-earned holiday trying to forget all about it. You'll have to have a very good reason to raise the matter again, Sir John.' She looked at him earnestly and stood firmly in his path.

Sir John immediately had the greatest respect for her. 'I understand perfectly what you are saying, Miss Walkham,' he said, 'and I realise it's a great intrusion on his and your privacy.' He paused as a tall, very well-built young man placed himself at the girl's side.

'Everything all right, Chris?' It was a mild threat to Sir John.

'It's quite all right, David, but thank you,' she said, waving him away.

'This young lady is highly thought of,' mused the School Governor. 'I shall have to watch my step.'

'I think I will be able to persuade you that it is important for me to speak to Mr Carter,' he continued, 'and I would consider it a privilege if you would be party to any conversation you allow me to have with him.'

'Very well,' she said. 'We'll go into the committee room.'

'May I buy you a drink?' he enquired.

'No, thank you. But if you'd like something, I'll have to sign you into the visitors' book. Perhaps we should see what this is all about first.'

Sir John knew he was on probation under the careful scrutiny of this rational and very attractive club official. She and Carter must have suffered considerably to cause this sort of wariness.

She steered him past the visitors' book and shutting the door of the committee room behind them, motioned him to a chair.

'I'll come straight to the point,' he began. 'I expect you'll have heard that there have been serious allegations made against the Headmaster of Mr Carter's school, and also a statement implicating one of the governors.'

Christine nodded but said nothing.

'There's been a meeting of the Board of Governors,' he went on, 'and naturally they wish to issue a formal denial of the allegations. Having done that, the matter will rest there unless the originator of the allegations, a left-wing politician called Jack Simmonds, can and does produce evidence to support them. If he does, then it will cause great embarrassment to the board and the effect on Bradchester and its reputation will be catastrophic. The board wish to be able to substantiate that any such evidence, particularly in the form of copies of some commodity figures issued by a London broker, in no way constitute proof of unlawful financial dealings by the school, and the Headmaster in particular.'

'How could Alan help you do that?' said Christine. 'Surely the Headmaster is the person to ask.'

Sir John cleared his throat with a certain amount of embarrassment. He would have to give out some information if he was going to get anything back from this young lady. 'I have to say, Miss Walkham, that the board feel the need to substantiate the Headmaster's assurances before making a confident denial.'

'You mean you think he's lying.' It was a statement not an enquiry.

'He may have found himself in a position of not being aware of the implication of the papers.'

'Then if he wasn't aware of it, there's absolutely no way Alan Carter would be. You'll have to take your Headmaster's word for it.'

Sir John decided he would have to put his cards on the table.

'I should say that I'm one of the board members who feel that Mr Masterton is not divulging all he knows to us and as a consequence may be putting the school's reputation at risk in an attempt to cover up something he may be involved in. Now obviously I couldn't say that to you in front of witnesses and, believe me, I would not say it to you at all if I didn't feel really concerned for the good name of the school. The issue as I see it is this. If Masterton has done something unlawful, then he must be the one to pay for it. The school will suffer – of course it will – but not as much as if the Board of Governors issues a full denial on behalf of the Headmaster, only to find it proven that he was engaged in something underhand after all.'

He expected some comment from the girl but there was nothing.

'What I need to ask Mr Carter is whether he knows anything at all that would help in establishing that there was nothing in those papers that would prove unlawful dealing by the Headmaster. If he can establish that to the satisfaction of the board, then a formal denial can be made with complete confidence. Conversely, if he can show us that there is substance to the allegations, then the board will take the necessary course of action.'

'I don't understand the need for your question,' said Christine. 'The Headmaster will have the originals and as he's obviously told you about the copies, otherwise you wouldn't be here, you will know that he has those as well. Alan handed him back the originals. His flat was searched in his absence apparently on the Head's instructions and the copies taken.'

'Unfortunately the Headmaster has told us that he saw fit to destroy all the papers "in a moment of extreme anxiety",' said Sir John weakly.

'To save his own neck more like.' Christine couldn't keep a patronising tone out of her next comment. 'I'm sure you'll forgive me for saying so, Sir John, but you should be concentrating on keeping your own house in order and not coming around upsetting people by asking them to do it for you.'

Sir John felt suitably chastised and said as much. 'I would still like to ask Mr Carter if he could help the school,' he added, 'or perhaps you yourself if you've a mind to.'

He decided he would have to push a little harder.

'I suppose you will have realised that Mr Carter is the obvious candidate to have been responsible for the leak of the contents of the documents to this Mr Simmonds.'

Christine had trouble keeping her composure. 'How dare you say that?' She managed to remain in her seat, despite a violent urge to call some of the members and have him thrown out.

Sir John held up his hand. 'I'm sorry,' he said. 'I desperately don't want to believe it, but you must understand that it is the way most people would interpret the facts. I would like Mr Carter to prove them wrong and give us the real truth of what was in those papers.'

'I know what was in those papers,' said Christine, 'and I can tell you there was certainly enough for the Headmaster to have panicked for fear that the contents might be leaked. But Alan was not responsible for the leak and neither was I. I'm not going to let you speak to him, as your precious school has done enough to him already. You'll have to take my word for it or your Headmaster's. The choice is yours. Alan Carter is a fine man with nothing to hide and he's a credit to himself and your school. Now if you don't mind, Sir John, you must go and look elsewhere for a place to wash your dirty linen.'

Her voice was raised in a burst of emotion as she opened the door to see him out. Sir John knew he'd gone too far and as he passed through the door he could see that the girl was crying. Four club members immediately surrounded him.

'What the devil d'you think you're doing?' said one. 'What's he been saying to you, Chris?'

'Damn you,' said another. 'You're going to answer for this.'

Sir John was jostled and seized by the jacket.

'Stop it,' shouted Christine. 'It's all right.'

'No, it bloody well isn't. It's that bloke who wanted to see Alan. Chris has stood in for him and look what he's done to her. Come on, lads, let's see how well he swims.'

'Oh, please stop it!', she pleaded, almost screaming. 'Stop it, stop it, stop it!'

* * *

I couldn't take any more of this, so I rushed over to the door shouting 'Pack it in all of you,' and pulling them off. I'd wanted to see him thrown in the estuary as much as anyone, but the sight of Christine in tears, pleading with them to stop made me act.

'You will please leave these premises immediately, Sir John. That is, after you've apologised to Miss Walkham for whatever it is you've said to upset her.' I signalled the others to leave us alone and waited while he brushed himself down.

He didn't turn on his heel and stride out of the clubhouse as I'd expected. He sat down again looking rather shaken and pale and asked if he could have a glass of water. I thought perhaps the lads had gone a bit too far although he'd certainly asked for it. Christine went for some water and he drank it slowly as we watched him closely, half expecting him to be ill. He was by no means a young man.

Putting the empty glass down he looked up at us. 'I owe you both an apology,' he said, 'for coming here in the first place and presuming you would see me, and to you Miss Walkham for making the remark I did which upset you so. I really am sincerely sorry.'

'What did he say to you?' I said, addressing Christine.

She looked a little forlorn and her eyes still held some tears. 'Only what we both know and had been discussing the very second he walked through the door. That you will be accused of passing on the contents of those papers to this Jack Simmonds character.'

Some of the other members were hovering near the bar and looking anxiously in our direction. I quickly went over and reassured them all was now well.

Turning back to Sir John, I lowered my voice. 'Miss Walkham here was trying to tell you, no doubt, that I'm not to be pestered by anyone concerning this wretched business. She has the right to do that, and I am certainly under no obligation to answer any questions about it, even from an envoy of the governors which is obviously what you are.'

'Alan, careful. Are you sure you should...?'

'It's all right, Christine,' I said. 'There's just one thing I will tell Sir John, as I believe him to be a man of honour, providing of course he realises I will not repeat it in public.'

I turned to face him. 'I was sacked by the Head because he thought I knew the implication of what was in those papers. In fact, I didn't and still don't for sure. The official reason given to me in writing, however, was that I was not a competent-enough teacher.'

Sir John listened without comment.

'So, after consulting my union, I wrote to the Head stating

that unless I was reinstated immediately, the union would take my case to an unfair dismissal tribunal at which evidence of illicit commodity dealings would be presented as part of my case.'

Sir John had raised his eyebrows at me.

I went on. 'The next day I was officially reinstated.'

I leant closer to him. 'You can make of that what you will, Sir John. But I can tell you that I've had it up to here,' I indicated a point in the middle of my forehead, 'with the treatment I've received from your Headmaster. I want to hear no more about it. I don't know anything about this Jack Simmonds or how he got his information and I don't want to know. I wish to be left alone and I'll be back at the start of next term ready to do the job for which I'm paid.'

Sir John rose rather unsteadily to his feet. He was unaccustomed to being manhandled but felt it was a small price to pay for obtaining confirmation of his own view that Masterton had been lying. The unpleasant truth he had divulged to Miss Walkham about Carter being considered the source of the leak to Simmonds had brought him into the conversation. That had led to a brief but nonetheless telling insight into the teacher's side of the story, which he believed.

'I don't suppose,' he said as I steadied him, 'that you would by any chance still have copies of the papers in question? And that if you did, you would allow me to show them to the board in order to prove Masterton's liability?'

I was dumbfounded and speechless with indecision. It was Christine who spoke.

'No, Sir John. That's not fair,' she said, raising her voice sufficiently to attract more inquisitive looks from the 'minders' among the club members. 'Even if we did, the matter is over as far as we're concerned. You must solve your own problems and leave Alan alone, otherwise you could be accused of harassment.'

Sir John raised his hands in acknowledgement of defeat. 'I apologise again,' he said. 'Just a forlorn hope that would make our job easier. I respect your comments, however, and will leave now. I've already upset your holiday and I hope one day to find the opportunity of making it up to you. I'd like to thank you for the way in which you've shown so much patience with me in the face of extreme provocation. Believe me, it has not been at all pleasant for me to see you both so distressed.'

He turned as he reached the door. 'And incidentally, you and your friends would have been quite justified in chucking me in the drink.' His face showed the signs of a boyish sense of humour. 'I think I'll make a strategic withdrawal now, before you change your mind.'

With that he was gone, leaving Christine and me staring after him in complete silence and in a state of mental confusion.

'Well! What did you make of that?' I said when we'd sat down again and I'd had a pint shoved into my hand.

'What I make of it,' she said, tidying up her face and downing some lager, 'is that you have a friend and supporter in that man. In my opinion he placed himself in a hostile environment solely to try to get to the bottom of Masterton's devious goings-on. It can't have been easy for him to accept some of our comments, let alone the roughing up by some of our enthusiastic chums.'

I felt relaxed now he'd gone, but somehow wished I could have been more help to him. 'He's always been very supportive,' I said. 'Encouraged me no end with the cricket and rugby. Seems to take a real interest in everything. Comes to nearly all the matches.'

'He's a nice man,' said Christine, 'and no fool. I'd love to have been a fly on the wall at that board meeting. What a situation they've got on their hands, some of them believing the Headmaster, others taking him for a liar, and Sir John hopefully trying to establish some evidence that will salvage the school's reputation. I think he knows that there isn't any, and that you were his last hope. I wonder what they will do now.'

'Don't know,' I said. 'But I can't help feeling we should give him a copy of the papers. After all, it should really settle the thing once and for all. The governors will then have to swallow the fact that they've appointed a devious man, he's been found out, and they'll have to get rid of him.'

'I don't think it'll come to that,' said Christine. 'And in any case, I'm not having you thinking any more about it. It's their problem, of their making, and they can sort it out. Now come on, we're on holiday, drink your pint and forget it.'

'Right!' I nodded but was left with a niggling feeling that it wasn't going to go away.

Chapter 14

Sir John had telephoned Sir Thomas Whittle when he'd got home on Saturday night to find that the barrister had also not been idle that day.

Men who reach eminent positions in public life become party to a network of information and influence at the highest level. It enables them to reach out and touch almost anybody, from the lowest history teacher to the corridors of power in the Civil Service, the City, the Law, Government, even the Cabinet itself.

In this case, Sir Thomas had simply picked up the phone, dialled the ex-directory number of the Chairman of one of the clearing banks, who was a close personal friend and to whose eldest daughter he was godfather. The banker knew all about the trouble at Bradchester and had been expecting a call of this nature late at night during the weekend. Sir Thomas had to waste no time explaining the seriousness of his reason for calling, and it was barely fifteen minutes later, but well after midnight, that he received the information he wanted.

His friend had rung back and informed him, 'strictly unofficially, of course', that he'd just come off the phone from the Chairman of the Securities and Futures Association, another close friend as it happened, and a member of the same golf club. He had confirmed Sir Thomas's worst fears, that the Association had been suspicious about Julian Hedley's activities for some time. There'd been doubts about his adherence to the standard of ethics required by its members, particularly in the light of the strict guidelines laid down in the Financial Services Act. The Association were very close to making an inspection of his trading methods and would be glad of the opportunity to have him removed from their membership. This had been difficult, hitherto, without proof of malpractice, but if Sir Thomas were to 'slide a little evidence their way', Hedley's licence might be suspended without the word Bradchester ever being mentioned. The Association would then be rid of one member who had been a possible liability to the 'good name' of the City for too long.

Sir John Glazebrook listened to this account of Sir Thomas's investigations with increasing concern and then recounted his own discouraging tale of the day's events.

His main concern, he told Sir Thomas, was that copies of the commodity transactions would almost certainly not be forthcoming. The Board of Governors would not therefore know for sure whether Masterton had actually transacted the deals or not. They would no doubt be able to get hold of copies eventually, as Sir Henry Melling had suggested at the board meeting, via the City's investigative channels, but that would take some time and time was something they didn't possess either. In any case, as Sir Thomas pointed out, this fellow Hedley might have dealt in his own name for the school and be relying on Masterton to come up with the cash. In that case, until the Headmaster actually put the school's money at risk, the board would have no proof that the allegations had foundation. That was unless Mr Jack Simmonds let them have a look at his copies, and that would be most unlikely, as no doubt the press would have first call on those, at a price.

Both men agreed that to offer to buy any copies from Alan Carter would be extremely counterproductive, again assuming there were any more copies in existence. If approached in that way, Carter would be quite justified in telling the media as much, and that would as good as prove the school's guilt.

'I'll put some pressure on this chap Hedley on Monday,' said Sir Thomas. 'Not personally, but through some people I know. There'll be no comeback. I've as good as arranged it already. He may produce some names if he knows he's going to lose his trading licence. Bring somebody down with him – you know what I mean.'

Sir John nodded gravely to himself. 'It seems that we're going to have to face the fact that Masterton and the school and therefore Beeson and all of us are likely to be implicated after all.'

'Frankly, John, I had no doubt of it when Masterton said he'd destroyed the papers. No, we've got big trouble here, and the sooner we wake up to the fact the better. The problem will be how to get out of it with the least amount of damage. I can tell you, we'll have enough on our hands persuading some of the board there's a problem at all.'

Sir John was shaking his head at the handset. 'I don't think it'll come to that. Somehow I feel things are ready to break very soon, and time is so short we'll have to be talking to Harvey direct anyway. I'm going to try and see Trent if I can. He should be able to throw some light on it, if he's well enough to see me, that is.'

Sir Thomas sounded sceptical. 'And if Masterton hasn't got there before you.'

Sir John sighed in agreement as he put the receiver down. He knew exactly what Queen's Counsel meant.

At eleven o'clock on Sunday morning, Sir Thomas's words gained even more pertinence as Sir John pulled his car up outside the Bursar's front gate. There was a police car and the doctor's car already there, together with an ambulance. Masterton's BMW was parked a little way up the lane.

* * *

At about one o'clock Christine had driven me from the yacht club to my flat to pick up some more clothes. I hadn't been there for over a week and when I opened the front door, I found a small pile of mail on the carpet. Richard was also away, so I separated his and mine and noticed a white envelope marked 'Alan Carter – Urgent'. I took it and the other letters into the front room while Christine headed for the kitchen to make some coffee. We hadn't much time, as our handicap race started at three fifteen, and I didn't want to come back here again until I needed to. The white envelope contained a note from John Tanner, asking if I would go and talk to him urgently concerning young Hedley.

We were finishing our coffee when there was an exaggerated knocking on the door. I opened it and Masterton forced his way past me and strode into the sitting room.

'Come here, Carter, I want a word with you,' he insisted. Then he saw Christine. 'Oh, it's you, is it? I want to speak to Carter in private, if you don't mind.'

Christine stood her ground.

'If you wish to speak to me, Headmaster,' I said, 'you'll have to do it in front of Miss Walkham. She stays. And you've no right to come barging in here in this manner.'

He was fuming. 'You've broken your word to me, Carter. You agreed that the matter between us was closed and that there were no more copies of the papers in existence. Now I find you've deliberately leaked the contents to the press. I've got accusations and allegations coming at me from all directions. I suppose you watch the news in the holidays? You'll have seen then that the contents of those documents have been misinterpreted as we agreed they might. I hold you responsible, Carter. You deliberately gave them to this Simmonds character, one of your scheming left-wing cronies no doubt.'

He was breathing heavily and opening and shutting his hands. Christine had risen from her chair and was making to speak. I motioned her to be silent. I was taking a leaf out of Richard's book and saying absolutely nothing. She sat down again.

Masterton's fist smashed down on the table. He turned and placed his face six inches from mine. I could hear his teeth grinding in the effort to control himself.

'I can't help you now, Carter. Do you understand? The Board of Governors is involved and I can't protect you any more. They will instruct me to dismiss you, and there'll be no reprieve this time. You're finished, do you hear? And there'll not be one member of staff sorry to see you go.'

With that he marched out of the room and slammed the front door behind him with such force that a picture in the passageway fell to the floor, smashing the frame and glass.

I sat down in a state of shock and put my head in my hands. For all my assertive silence, I was shaking. I couldn't handle such a verbal onslaught from a man who spoke with such venom, but who held such a position of authority over me, even though I knew him to be totally in the wrong. That's what made it so hard to take. And I felt so sorry for Christine. I could see she was in tears. All her efforts to drag both of us away from all this, to protect me from any further stress had been all going so well, we'd been so happy for the past week, and now it was all in ruins again.

I went over to her. She rose from the chair and I took her in my arms. She clung to me and cried loud and long and unashamedly, her mouth buried into my shoulder in an attitude of bewildered despair.

The tears welled up in my eyes also. This girl had fought like a tiger for my peace of mind. She'd taken all the flack for me, argued my case, been insulted on my behalf, and been treated with contempt in my place. I held her very tightly until her sobbing had subsided. Lifting her tear-stained face away a little, she looked at me and put her finger up to my eyes to gently wipe away a tear. She placed her wet cheek on mine and we stayed like that for a long time.

After a while, she wanted to talk, mainly to persuade me to continue to stay away from school, this flat, the whole wretched affair. But, as I'd suspected at the yacht club when Sir John had left, the business was obviously unfinished as far as Masterton and the school were concerned. It seemed I couldn't escape, and wherever I went, someone or something would find me and rake the whole wretched affair to life again.

I told her I would probably have a good ally in John

Tanner for, although we'd had words when we last spoke, I knew him to be an honest and reliable man at heart. Eventually she agreed so we went straight round to his house.

He was surprised to see Christine with me and was at first hesitant. 'It's rather a private matter, Alan,' he said, looking doubtfully at her.

'Well,' I said, I'm not leaving her on her own. We've just had an unpleasant encounter with the Head, so we're sticking together. Also, we haven't much time, so if you could let me know what it is you want to see me about.'

He looked startled at my slightly terse manner. 'I'll tell you both then, as I know how close you are. But I'd ask you not to repeat what I say.' He paused for confirmation. We both nodded.

'It's about young Hedley, the boy who was away from the house one night last term and who missed a first team match. I wanted to ask you if you think I should keep silent about what I feel is an attempt by the Headmaster to set him up as guilty of something he didn't do.'

Christine got up and moved towards the door. 'I think I'll go and have a chat with your wife,' she said. 'I know what you're going to talk about, and you'll be inhibited if I'm in the room. Better that you talk openly to Alan if he is to help you. This is not the time for holding anything back.'

The Housemaster looked embarrassed so I assured him she was right and he should speak freely.

He waited until Christine had closed the door behind her. 'I can't stand idly by and see that boy suffer for something I know he didn't do.'

'What is he supposed to have done?' I asked, knowing full well.

'Well, it was my wife who got it out of him in actual fact. After he came back that Monday morning with his father, he didn't say a word for a week. Refused to go into the dormitory and insisted that he sleep in a room on his own. Eventually we put him in the sick room by himself. I'd been warned by the Head that there'd been some complaint by another boy's parents about him and their son, but I made some enquiries and there was just no foundation to it at all. He blurted it all out to my wife one evening, that the Head had accused him point-blank of homosexual activities with a younger boy in the house and that he was going to make a public exhibition of him. That was what made him run away that night before the match.'

He paused and searched my face as if trying to establish that I was taking in what he was telling me.

He went on. 'I know there's no evidence, but the Headmaster has insisted on making something out of nothing. The boy could have committed suicide that week, he was in such a state. If it hadn't been for my wife, I honestly think he would have attempted it he was so low. And then, when this news about Sir George Beeson and the Head and some dealings in the City came out, I started to put two and two together. I know the boy's father is a commodity broker and the allegations being made could be so serious for the school, I wondered if the boy was being used by Masterton to protect himself. God knows how, or what it's all about, but you've been the victim of some damned odd goings-on here lately, and I can't think they're unconnected. That's why I'm asking you what I should do. Should I keep quiet and let the boy suffer, or should I tell someone the truth, and if so, who?'

The fact that someone else had been going through the same sort of anguish as me made me feel that perhaps not all the world was against me and me alone. I felt sympathetic towards John Tanner. He and his wife must have had a terrible time with the boy in that condition, not knowing what he might do next. I decided that if I were to help him, I might be able to share some of my problems with him, thus taking some of the pressure off myself and Christine. I didn't really want to have anyone else involved, but in the absence of Richard on holiday, I felt he might be an able substitute. It would mean he would tell his wife, of course, and that would be yet another person who perhaps knew too much. But maybe it was no bad thing to have another woman in the picture.

'I think you should do nothing for the moment,' I advised. 'I've had a visit from one of the governors, Sir John Glazebrook, and I can tell you without saying anything you won't have guessed already that there's doubt amongst some of the board about Masterton's honesty. They wanted me to produce evidence that would prove him either guilty or innocent. Well, as it happens, I can't, although a lot of people probably won't believe that. Nor would I if I could. It's not my problem, it's theirs, and they'll have to sort it out.'

The Housemaster looked doubtful. 'Putting two and two together, Alan, it does rather seem that you must have had something to do with this left-wing character getting the ammunition for his allegations against the school. All that business between you and the Head last term, and now this. Too much of a coincidence most people would say. Personally, I tend to think you've got caught up in it by accident, knowing you as I do, and that's why I'm asking for your advice. If I thought you were mixed up in it for vindictive reasons, I wouldn't be talking to you now.'

'That's good of you to say so,' I said, 'and I can assure you that is exactly what has happened. I stumbled into it quite by accident and was sacked for that reason. Masterton has something to hide and it's something to do with young Hedley's father. Hence the commodity dealing connection. Some of the governors are on to the Head, and it's my guess that he's using the boy to buy his father's silence. If Hedley Senior ever divulged the fact that Masterton had been dealing in commodities and putting the school's money at risk in the process, Masterton would be finished and he must know it. That's why he must have a hold over the man, and what better way to do that than by threatening to expose his son as a raving homosexual?'

John Tanner was shaking his head. 'This is too fantastic,' he said. 'I can't believe it can be happening, although what you say all seems to make sense. My wife and I have been sitting here for the last few nights since the news broke, going over and over it, trying to prove to ourselves that there's no connection between Hedley and Masterton, and now you come along and neatly confirm it.'

'Well, there's still a lot you don't know,' I said, 'but I don't want to get pulled back into this business again, so I won't say any more at this stage. But I'm very concerned for young Hedley and would like to help if I can. From what I know, it is imperative from the Headmaster's point of view that Hedley Senior does not spill the beans about the commodity deals, so we have to assume that they are dynamite to Masterton. I've been told, by another senior City broker, that Mr Hedley is at risk of losing his dealing licence if it were to come out that he'd been dealing with Masterton under questionable circumstances. It seems likely now that Hedley will be exposed and therefore will have to close down, in which case he would have nothing to lose by confirming having dealt with Masterton – except for the fact that his son's reputation is being held to ransom.'

I leaned closer to John Tanner. 'If you were to remove that threat by telling Hedley that you would testify if necessary that his son was totally innocent, then Hedley might let us all know the truth. That truth would almost certainly be that Masterton was in it up to his neck. Events would then have to take their course.'

Tanner's face took on a worried expression. 'I don't want to be responsible for getting the Head sacked,' he said. 'I only want to do the right thing by young Hedley.'

'Well, you'll have to let your conscience decide,' I said. 'It'll be either the Head or the boy who'll suffer. The decision will have to be yours. But to tell you the truth, when this is all over, I'd sooner have the Board of Governors on my side than Masterton. But it's up to you.'

He looked at me as if he wished he'd never asked for my advice in the first place. 'I'll talk it over with my wife,' he said. 'Thanks anyway for giving me the facts.'

I turned to leave.

'Just one thing, Alan,' he said. 'And I'm sure you won't answer this if you don't want to. How did the information get to this Simmonds fellow? Norman Willett was rabbiting on before the end of term about how he'd been instrumental in getting you reinstated. Could it have had anything to do with the union?'

'I've really no idea,' I said and left the room. 'Damnation!'

I thought. 'Here we go – this is where all the rumours and suppositions are going to start. That bloody man Tyler. Should have realised he was only using me. Now I'll get all the flack for him giving Simmonds the information.'

* * *

Masterton was not a happy man. Things were definitely not going his way. Some of the governors were going to look under a few stones. That was quite obvious from the Chairman's comments to him after the board meeting at which he'd felt he was in the dock. The Chairman of the Headmasters' Conference had telephoned him to imply that whatever the outcome of 'this sordid little matter', he was sure that Masterton could be relied upon to consider the good name and reputation of the public school system and act accordingly.

What the hell was that supposed to mean?

He was going to get no change out of Carter and that girlfriend of his. Carter probably still had some copies of the papers and would no doubt use them if threatened again, so he'd better be left alone.

And now this Trent business. Masterton had only gone to see him to remind him of the delicacy of their position and to give him the helpful advice to say nothing to anybody about the commodity deals. The Bursar, however, had seemed determined to panic and was beside himself with worry. He'd been drinking heavily as usual and was not thinking rationally. He'd intimated to Masterton that he felt he should make a clean breast of the whole thing to the governors, and that Sir John Glazebrook was indeed due to arrive in two hours to see him about something. It was bound to be about the Simmonds allegations, and he didn't feel he would be able to hide anything.

Masterton had felt the Bursar needed to be brought to his senses and had remonstrated with him, even physically shaken him, to force home the fact that if he let the cat out of the bag to the governors he was finished.

Ten minutes later the Colonel was dead, having suffered a massive heart attack which Masterton had struggled to treat there and then by massage and violent blows to the chest in a panic-stricken attempt at revival.

By the time he'd thought to ring for an ambulance, there was no hope at all of saving the Bursar. The crew had found Masterton with one dead body and had alerted the police. When Sir John arrived, he found that, in Sir Thomas Whittle's words, Masterton had beaten him to it.

As Masterton was the last person to see Colonel Trent alive and had indeed been present at the time of death, he was reminded by the police that he would be required for further investigations concerning the cause of death in the near future. When he was finally permitted to go home, he had really only one last card to play. That was to make sure that Julian Hedley would not divulge to any investigation, be it by the police, the media or by the City authorities, details of his transactions with the deceased Bursar and himself. He was not totally confident of the broker's silence and so would telephone him on Monday to remind the man of the vulnerability of his son's position.

Julian Hedley was another one on whom the gods were not disposed to look kindly. Things had gone from bad to worse since Bradchester School had got itself mixed up in the 'dirty tricks' campaign that always preceded a general election.

He'd started to receive discreet suggestions from those few friends he still had in the City that his days were numbered. The powers that be were on the warpath against any hint of contravention of the Financial Services Act that could give ammunition to opponents of the City's supporters. Sir George Beeson himself had been on the phone demanding a complete denial of anything untoward involving the school. He'd been quite unpleasant, suggesting that his office would be closed down if full cooperation was not forthcoming to save Bradchester's reputation and his own political neck.

Hedley was aware that he'd be investigated anyway, and it was odds on that his licence to trade would be suspended at the very least, so he told the politician to get lost.

He had two further phone calls which gave notice that his days as a commodity broker were numbered. The first, on the Sunday night from his son's Housemaster, was not at all acrimonious. The second, from Masterton, was.

As a result of the first call, Hedley was in a strange way quite looking forward to the second, when and if it ever came, and he was in his City office when it was put through on the Monday morning.

'I'll come straight to the point, Hedley,' said the voice with a crisp edge to it.

'I wish you would, Masterton.'

The Head didn't like being called 'Masterton' by people he considered to be his inferiors. It riled him. Hedley was used to it. As a broker he was the man in the middle, and as such, accustomed to put-downs and points scoring by clients on both sides of a deal.

'You'll probably know by now,' said Masterton, 'that the

school and I are under a lot of pressure as a result of these allegations.'

There was no comment from the other end of the telephone.

'I just thought it prudent to remind you that I am totally denying the charges of tinkering with the school's funds and am depending on you to do the same.'

Still no comment. Masterton didn't like silence as a form of argument. He felt more comfortable in a violent verbal confrontation.

'All right then, Hedley, if you're determined to remain silent, I'm sure I don't have to tell you that the only way the allegations can be substantiated is if you let them. And I'm sure neither of us would like to see that happen, bearing in mind how well your boy could continue to do at Bradchester with the even larger discount on his fees I propose, and the fact that his unfortunate homosexual habits could easily remain a secret with me and need never be made public.'

Masterton was pleased with the way that little piece of oratory had rolled off the tongue. He was smiling with satisfaction to himself. This common City wheeler-dealer who'd been so bloody rude to him the other day would be cringing at the other end of the line.

Hedley would, under normal circumstances, actually have been smirking with satisfaction, knowing what he'd been told the previous night by John Tanner. His enjoyment was tempered, however, by the fact that he was in deep trouble himself and the only satisfaction he could get out of it was bringing down Masterton with him.

He decided to enter the conversation. 'Bugger off, Masterton,' was his contribution.

Masterton's smile widened behind the receiver. 'A comment

befitting the father of a boy to whom such a physical undertaking is no doubt commonplace,' he sniggered.

'Such a threat against my son, if carried out,' said Hedley, 'would have that cheque down at the bank within twenty-four hours, and copies of it to every governor on your board.'

'I think not, Hedley. I have the support of my board,' bluffed Masterton. 'Any such action would finish you and your boy. Now we don't want that, do we?'

'What's that Bursar fellow got to say about all this? He's implicated as much as you are.'

Masterton put on his most sympathetic and grief-stricken voice. 'I'm afraid he's recently deceased. Yesterday lunchtime. Most lamentable.'

'What! Dead, you mean?'

'A sad loss.'

'How the hell did that happen?'

Masterton had made his point and was not anxious to continue the confrontation further. 'Stroke or heart attack, I believe, but it's irrelevant how the poor man passed away. It's his wife we should feel sorry for. Awful for her, don't you think?'

'If you're thinking of pitying anyone, Masterton', said the broker, 'you should reserve some for yourself, because I doubt if anyone else will have any for you when I confirm your involvement in those dealings.'

'Well, we both know that you won't, don't we?' smirked Masterton confidently. 'Good morning to you, Hedley, and, as they say, have a nice day.'

He replaced the receiver gently and felt a lot better.

Julian Hedley pulled himself out of his huge executive chair with the resigned air of a man whose only recompense now was to make sure that when he fell, others fell with him. He'd already had notice earlier that morning from the Securities and Futures Authority of the impending inspection of his trading records, accelerated, unbeknown to him, with Sir Thomas Whittle's assistance. That would lead to suspension for sure.

Any investigating team would eventually uncover the fact that he was vastly overexposed and they would also be certain to want verification of the alleged deals to which Jack Simmonds was referring. Even though these were in his own name, it would come out sooner or later that he'd breached the Financial Services Act rules, not only with Masterton but also in many other unconnected transactions. An acknowledgement of his guilt and a plea for clemency might lead to a temporary suspension, rather than a complete denial, which would mean a lifetime ban.

He opened his office safe and took out the Bradchester School cheque, signed by Masterton and the late Colonel Trent in the sum of one hundred thousand pounds. He then went into the outer office and instructed his secretary to address envelopes to every governor of Bradchester School and handed her a current copy of the Boys Independent Schools Yearbook, which contained their names. Their addresses she would have to ferret around for, and those that were unobtainable by research could have their copy of the cheque sent care of the Chairman, whose home address he was in possession of.

He then made twenty-five copies of the cheque, and later that afternoon posted, first class, as many as his secretary had obtained addresses for. Having presented the original cheque for payment at his bank's branch in Fenchurch Street and obtained a receipt, he left the City in his Rolls, and drove for an hour and a half to Sir Harvey's home and deposited all the others in separate envelopes, care of the Chairman of Governors, Bradchester School, through the letterbox.

Twenty-four hours before his deadline of Tuesday evening therefore, a much harassed Sir Harvey was in possession of more than enough evidence to make some decisions, approval of which would necessitate another Extraordinary General Meeting. He had also taken a call that day from the Secretary of State for Education that had left him in no doubt just how important the Conservative Party hierarchy regarded such decisions.

Such calls were usually of extremely short duration and this one was no exception as Sir Harvey and Bradchester were not ranked very highly in the private-education pecking order. As the outcome of such a potentially damaging allegation could have serious repercussions for a marginal seat, however, a call from the top was considered to be merited.

It had been all over in less than two minutes.

'Sir Harvey Wainwright?'

'Speaking.'

'Would you hold a moment, please, I have the Secretary of State for you.'

There was a slight pause. 'Listen, Wainwright. I've been on to the Chairman of the Headmasters' Conference but I wanted a word with you personally. The Prime Minister wants this Simmonds business out of the way. It's an embarrassment to him and the party, especially at this time.'

'I understand, Minister,' said Sir Harvey.

'You'll be so good as to deny any truth in the allegations

- if you are able to, that is – or, if not, openly admit the error of the school's ways, and be seen to remove the people responsible without delay. Do I make my position and that of the Prime Minister quite clear?'

'That is quite clear, Minister,' choked the Chairman. 'But if I may say so...'

'Just do it'. The line went dead.

On the strength of that call and his receipt of the copies of the cheque from Hedley, Sir Harvey had already set in motion another governors' meeting, at which he would have no option but to propose the acceptance of the Headmaster's resignation in addition to his own.

His final call that Monday night was to tell Masterton that he wanted his letter of resignation in his hands by the following evening, in order that it could be accepted by the Board of Governors on Wednesday.

As there was nothing but silence from the other end of the line, he advised his ill-fated employee that he would not be expected to attend the funeral of Colonel Trent as the school would be represented by himself, one of the last duties he would perform as Chairman of Governors. When Sir Harvey rang off, he knew, by virtue of Masterton's complete absence of comment, that he had heard every word that had been said to him.

Chapter 15

Christine should have been back at work on the Monday but had pleaded with her boss to be allowed an extra two days, principally to make sure I had plenty to occupy me during the remaining weeks of the holiday. She insisted that I should not remain within range of the school during the week, when I would be on my own, but nonetheless should place myself under her protective custody at weekends – at the yacht club during the day and in her flat at night. She made me promise that wherever I went between Monday and Friday, I should telephone her at least every other night and be back in time to pick her up at the office on Fridays at five o'clock without fail.

It relaxed me to feel that during the week she wouldn't have time to worry about me for a change, but could concentrate on her job by day at least. I took the opportunity to head for the Cotswolds. It was a part of England I'd never seen, but from what some of my friends, and Richard in particular, had said about it, might well suit my need for tranquillity. Richard's parents had a house near a place called Stow-on-the-Wold, a name that conjured up the atmosphere and flavour of rustic old England with visions of sleepy stone houses, thatched roofs and clear-running, gravel-bedded streams holding wily trout.

Richard had told me he would be spending some of the holiday with his parents in the Cotswolds and this was where I was to contact him with any messages. He was there when I did phone and I was immediately invited to stay indefinitely. He was desperate to hear my news and was anticipating that blood might be about to flow at Bradchester.

I threw some things into the back of my car and headed west across England.

To have Richard Pilcher for a friend was my good fortune. He belonged to one of those families that was full of individual characters, everybody being an expert at something in their own right. They all seemed to have the greatest respect for each other most of the time, and when they didn't, their agreement to differ was a mark of their maturity as a family. I was welcomed with open arms by Richard's father and mother and given a room at the far end of the landing, which looked out over one of those streams I'd envisaged. Richard's elder sister and her husband were also staying for an indefinite period. Nobody had any particular plans and yet everyone seemed incredibly busy. Meal times were varied and do-it-yourself, and I was told I was to sleep all day if I wanted to but if I went fishing, I was to please keep a note of what I caught for stocking purposes. They would love me to have dinner with them on Thursday, and would I not remove the wire mesh from my bedroom window, as a tame barn owl would come in, usually with a dead mouse.

I relaxed so much in this sort of atmosphere that I barely made it to Christine's office by five o'clock on the Friday.

And so it was in this way that I was rehabilitated by the people who cared for me in a beautiful environment of countryside and congenial company during the week, and salt spray, sailing and the woman I loved at weekends. I made a few runs for one of the local village teams during their Cricket Week and put to good use my recent fly-casting lesson by landing five beautiful brown trout from the stream at the bottom of the garden. Richard plied me with pints at The Unicorn down the road, while I pieced together for him the missing components of the Bradchester puzzle. Friday nights, Christine and I demonstrated how much we had missed each other during the week, and we spent Saturday and Sunday sailing and recovering from Friday night.

By halfway through the third week of this idyllic existence Richard and I had discussed every possible outcome of the Bradchester affair and had kept our eyes glued to the newspapers for further developments. Our opinions as to the likely conclusions to be drawn and acted upon by the governors changed as additional snippets of information were picked up and reported on by the media.

* * *

There were three extremely eventful days at the beginning of August in which most of the serious repercussions of the whole affair took place.

August being the month when most of the working population of the country, with the exception of those in the leisure industry, are on holiday, it was in the Conservative Party's interest to remove the embarrassing wart called Bradchester from the political scene at this time. As the school could now be seen to have been caught red-handed with its fingers in the till, it was also in the interests of many of the governors, particularly those with City connections, to abide by the Education Secretary's advice to acknowledge what had happened, with as much grace as could be mustered, and sack those responsible and most closely involved with the minimum of publicity. Mr Simmonds' party, which hoped to reap some reward from his revelations, would have their thunder largely stolen by virtue of the fact that nobody could really give a toss about political points scoring when they were on holiday. The left-wing candidate's timing was bad in that all the events that might sway any floating voters were going to take place when nobody would notice.

The most important scoop for the press was the low-key announcement that Sir George Beeson would not be defending his seat. As most MPs were away, including Sir George himself, the Constituency Party Headquarters was able to put out the statutory announcement without having to explain itself to any great extent. 'A new and energetic candidate would be selected in due course' seemed to satisfy most people, and the relief felt by senior party members, not to mention by the Prime Minister himself, was strikingly evident.

Less evident, but in its own way causing a great deal more anger and scorn, was the minor announcement in no more than half a dozen lines on an inside page of the resignation of the Headmaster of Bradchester School, together with that of the Chairman and eight members of the governing body.

Jack Simmonds had immediately staged another public meeting which was so poorly attended that the television people went home early, and only the press were left to pick up the barely newsworthy crumbs. He made an 'I told you so, and aren't I a clever fellow?' speech, which was reported in detail in left-wing papers, but made no more than a few lines elsewhere. Damage to the Conservatives was light, but enough for Central Office to see to it that the word went out to snuff out any further liability from Bradchester's direction. It would be made an example of and isolated from the traditional image of leading public schools. The party wanted its private-education house put in order and, so that it could be seen to be taking a tough line with defaulters from the highest standards of morality, it would sacrifice this relatively insignificant member to the irritating victimisations of the left.

Sir Harvey Wainwright himself could see no alternative but to try to salvage whatever he could from the wreckage by coming clean concerning Simmonds' allegations and instigating the head-rolling procedure, starting with his own.

The next Extraordinary Meeting was therefore preceded by a great deal of lobbying amongst the present governors, in order to establish which of them should become past ones. Sir Thomas had already made it clear to Sir Harvey that he would be supporting Sir John Glazebrook as the new Chairman and had suggested, most politely, that several of the existing board should consider resigning. This came as no surprise to Sir Harvey as there would have to be a clean sweep if Bradchester was to have any chance of survival.

There had already been a ten per cent cancellation of registered future pupils, as well as a substantial number of withdrawals of boys currently at the school, and it was still only the beginning of August. Sir John again found himself in the unenviable position of having to clarify which governors he felt unable to work with if he were elected by a majority. It was apparent that, subject to the sanction of the Charity Commissioners, he was certain to be voted into the chair, so to save further embarrassment those unwelcome few, numbering eight in all, were persuaded to withdraw.

The more intelligent among them had seen it coming and realised that they had 'backed the wrong horse'. They would have to wear the mantle of 'scapegoat' for having wholeheartedly gone along with the appointment of Masterton as Headmaster in the first place and having buried their heads in the sand during the last few weeks in the second.

Sir John and Sir Thomas knew exactly what was required to satisfy the general call for Bradchester to be punished, in the shortest possible time and with the minimum amount of bloodletting. Their appointee had been caught with his fingers in the school's till and nothing less than the removal of his supporters would do. The Education Minister and the Department of Education and Science had been instructed by the Prime Minister himself to vet and approve the proposed new Chairman and every governor before the Charity Commissioner would be given the nod to rubber stamp the newly constituted board. The Commissioner's office was also detailed to make a toothcomb check of Bradchester's bank mandates and to draw up very stringent financial directives to avoid any recurrence of such a misdemeanour.

These new regulations were to go right down the line to every registered charitable private school, which meant virtually every independent educational establishment in the land. It was nicknamed the Bradchester Directive, a term instigated and encouraged by the Secretary of State himself. It meant that the blame for all the extra scrutiny of schools' accounting practices in future, and the inconvenience and extra work it entailed, could be laid firmly at Bradchester's door. The school therefore was understandably no longer flavour of the month.

When the new board had been approved, one of its

first tasks was to admit liability for the cheque that had been presented to the bank for clearance by Julian Hedley. The bank was instructed, however, not to honour it as it didn't have the requisite signatures for so large an amount. Nonetheless, Sir John felt that the school should be seen to be willing to confirm its guilt in every way possible, and a good starting point would be to honour the amount owed on Masterton's hapless commodity dealings. The cheque for one hundred thousand was therefore returned and destroyed, but the outstanding loss, to the tune of approximately thirty thousand pounds was made good by the board, thus purging the school's debt once and for all.

A frank statement was prepared for media consumption which held nothing back. The facts were presented to the public in a way that could leave little room for further witch-hunting, and the blame laid squarely at the feet of the Headmaster and those whose job it should have been to supervise him. Their resignations were confirmed and notification given that their replacements, where relevant, were under consideration. For the time being, the current Deputy Head would take over the day-to-day running of the school. A Board of Governors, reduced in number, but approved by the Charity Commissioners would administer the Trust, and the school would be open for business as usual at the beginning of September. This was the bravest face that could be put upon the situation, the consequences of which would make their mark on the school for many years to come.

The appointment of a new Bursar to replace the recently deceased Colonel Bradley William Trent was not publicly announced as Trent's involvement in the affair was considered ineffectual. He was, however, given a diplomatically 'quiet' burial in deference to his sick wife's feelings, she herself being accommodated in a suitable residential home, paid for out of the Colonel's meagre estate, with a 'top up' from school funds.

* * *

The usual pre-term staff meeting took place amid an atmosphere buzzing with excitement and apprehension. Senior colleagues had been called back early, and a great deal of departmental reorganisation and administrative reshuffling had taken place in the days before the rest of us arrived.

Sir John was to address the assembled and extremely curious company and, as he rose to speak, Richard gave me a nudge and said 'This should be interesting.' I lowered myself further into my chair in the expectation of some enquiring glances as the story unfolded and people began to read between the lines. Some teachers were still unaware that there was anything amiss, and I heard more than one enquire where Masterton was.

'Ladies and gentlemen,' began Sir John, 'Those of you who've been able to follow the very unfortunate events that have taken place during the last few weeks will be well aware of the drastic changes that have been forced upon the school. There may be some of you who are as yet unaware of the facts, and it is those primarily that I wish to put in the picture.'

There was an ominous silence in the hall as the realisation sank in that it was unprecedented for one of the governors to make the opening address at this meeting. Sir John's first words had concentrated the minds of his audience and they were now 'all ears'.

He continued. 'I wish to scotch any rumours or speculation by telling you the position as it has been, and as it stands at present, in order that there may be no doubt in your minds as to what has happened to your school. There has been comment in the media, some of it accurate, some less so. The facts, however, are as follows.'

He paused to take a drink of water.

'The Board of Governors of the school has been reconstituted, and I have been elected its new Chairman. There have been nine resignations including that of the previous Chairman. A complete list of the changes will be given to you on your way out of this meeting, together with a simplified account of what I'm going to say to you. The Headmaster Mr Duncan Masterton has resigned his post, and his successor is being sought. In the meantime Mr Alistair Norton, the current Deputy Head, will take over the Head's duties until the appointment is made. I feel sure you will give him your full support during this time.'

There was a murmuring in the hall and heads were turning and nodding. Richard and I kept ours still and lowered.

'Media reporting,' went on Sir John, 'of the reason behind these resignations has been varied. The true facts are that there have been certain financial irregularities carried out by those in a position of trust, which leaves no alternative but for them to be replaced. Those governors who felt they failed in their responsibility in overseeing that part of the administration of the school have seen it their duty also to resign their positions.'

Again an outbreak of animated discussion and general hubbub.

Sir John raised his voice. 'Ladies and gentlemen, please.

If you will permit me.' He waited until order had been more or less restored.

'I know you will be speculating on exactly what I mean by financial irregularities. It would be unnatural if you did not. I know full well that the common room will be rife with rumour and counter-rumour the moment this meeting is over. I would ask you to consider, however, that if the school is to continue to function properly, and we are to survive during what will be a most difficult period, it is you as the teaching staff and the flag bearers of the school at the sharp end of its operations that will have to show the most resolve in putting the events of the past weeks behind us. You are being asked to pick up the pieces from events which are not of your making, and I would naturally expect to have to justify my request for you to do that.

'I will try to do so by being as frank as the situation permits and confirm that the reports of irregular commodity dealings are quite correct, and as far as it is in my power to do so, I have overseen the resignation of those responsible. The school, which I hope will have the benefit of your continued support, is now in a position to shake off a sad episode in its history, and engage in its proper function – namely the education of the pupils whose parents will continue to place their trust in us. Registrations have already taken a knock and will most likely continue to do so for a while. Some current pupils have been withdrawn for the new term. The standing and prestige of Bradchester will undoubtedly suffer as the system will not easily forgive us. But we have a fine school and our numbers are such that at the moment we can operate. I feel that the best way to keep the student population up to an economic level is to admit our mistakes openly, be seen to have purged ourselves of the reasons for them, and get our heads down in a professional manner and offer a first-class service as before.'

He paused to wipe his brow with a handkerchief. 'That is why, ladies and gentlemen, I have produced a written explanation of what has happened, so that you can quote it if questioned, as some of you most surely will be. The true facts are all there and I would ask you not to deviate from them. The sad fact is that, as a member of the previous Board of Governors, I feel an immense sense of responsibility for having been unable to prevent the occurrences. That I'm standing up here addressing you as the new Chairman means that those who have felt it their duty to resign and particularly those who, in my view, rightly remain feel that I am the person best able to preside over Bradchester's recovery. I hope I will prove them right and will be taking particular care to pick individuals who have the right qualities to make up a well-balanced and vigorous board for the future. In selecting them and a new Headmaster for Bradchester, highest of all on my list of those priorities will be the quality of honesty, and I would ask you most humbly to support me and each other during the next few, most difficult months.'

He sat down and I was reminded of the occasion when he had been manhandled at the yacht club. He looked similarly drained as he again reached for a glass of water. There was silence in the hall. Nobody wanted to clap, or shout 'hear, hear' as the situation did not warrant it, but I could sense that he'd done enough to win many of us over. It was an amazing effort under the most formidable pressure, and the way he'd insisted on 'coming clean' proved to me, not for the first time, that he was himself a man possessed of many fine qualities – honesty being numbered highly among them.

Alistair Norton then rose and outlined his feelings about the matter, namely that he agreed with the new Chairman's views about the future and that he was accepting a difficult challenge as being the best way of maintaining some continuity in the school's programme. Sir John left the hall to allow him to try to inject some normality into the proceedings by reminding us that we had a school to run, and this meeting should now get on with the customary pre-term business of administering that process.

It was a tricky task for the Acting Head, as most of those present were more interested in trading rumour for counter-rumour as Sir John had suggested.

I was tapped on the shoulder. 'You know what's going on, Alan, don't you?' said a voice.

'Is it about that trouble you were in last term?' said another.

'I knew Masterton was up to something. Never trusted him,' said a third.

When the meeting finally broke up, the questioning continued into the common room and even out into the car park. It seemed that I'd not only been the catalyst for the whole sordid business but was also the fountain of all knowledge about it. The problem was that it was true, but I found being in that position most distasteful. Richard defended me with honour, however, and when we eventually reached the sanctuary of our flat, we slumped into armchairs, feeling quite drained from the inquisition.

Gradually, over a period of a few weeks, I began to feel more and more isolated from the good relations I'd enjoyed with some of my colleagues. It was nothing I could put my finger on. Nobody accused me of anything, but I could sense apprehension in the way some staff members approached me for an opinion about something, and in their lack of trust in my judgement about quite minor matters. It was as if some of them considered me a 'mole' in their midst, and I found it distressing.

I discussed it with Richard. 'It's mainly the older ones,' I told him. 'It's as if I'm a spy in the camp. I know we've got some pretty intransigent people on the staff, and I've never gone down a bundle with them. Now it's happening with some of those I thought I got on well with. If I ask their advice about something, I get the minimum answer and "must dash, Alan, catch you later," or something like that. I'm being avoided, Richard and I'm getting depressed about it. What's going on?'

'I've got to be honest with you, Alan,' he said... 'There is a bit of a problem.'

'Well, come on then, out with it.'

'It's the union business and Norman Willett. He's been going around telling everyone how it was him who got you your job back, and if it hadn't been for the union you wouldn't be here now and Masterton wouldn't have been exposed. Naturally he's using the whole thing as a sales exercise to enrol more of us as members. How brilliant the union is and how none of us can afford to stay out, all that sort of stuff.'

'Well, surely they can see through that,' I said. 'And in any case, they surely can't take it out on me if Masterton's got his due reward for looting school funds.'

'Not quite as simple as that, I'm afraid,' said Richard.

'You see, despite the fact that most people think Masterton got what he deserved, human nature, being what it is, will make people want to look after number one at the end of the day. It's their own comfort they're most interested in. They couldn't actually give a damn what's happened to Masterton. That's all history now, as far as they're concerned. There is a general worry, however, that the union has apparently had enough clout to remove the Headmaster and nine governors from a school as prestigious as Bradchester... well, as Bradchester used to be, shall we say. That makes people nervous. And I'm afraid that as you're considered to be the member of staff who gave the union the information to act on... that makes them nervous of you.'

'But that's so unfair,' I said, 'I never gave the union permission to leak the contents of those papers, only to use them at a tribunal if necessary.'

'You know that and I know that,' he said. 'But you're being naive if you think anybody else here gives a damn what you meant to do. The fact is that you're a member of the union, everyone knows that, as Norman has made it his business to make sure they do, and they're just putting two and two together in assuming you are linked with the leak. Norman is encouraging their suppositions for his own interests and there you are – you are the "mole". Unless you want to stand up in front of everybody and explain the whole thing to them, including how I copied the papers for you and how you gave them to the union, you're lumbered with a certain amount of suspicion. You're considered to be a powerful person, Alan. After what's happened to Masterton and the Board of Governors, nobody will be keen to get too close to you.'

'But I can't go on working here under those circumstances,' I said. 'It'll be impossible. And I'll never be able to apply for a post at another school. Who would take me on knowing I'd exposed and got rid of a Headmaster and half the governors of my previous school at one fell swoop and all in the space of ten weeks?'

'No, it is rather a singular achievement!' He grinned and then said, 'I'm sorry, Alan,' as he saw the look of dejection on my face. 'You asked me what was wrong and I've told you. I really do understand how difficult it's going to be for you and, believe me, I sympathise. I also feel guilty about having got you into this mess in the first place by copying the papers. We do have the option of putting out a statement or even telling everybody individually what happened, but I have to say I think it won't make any difference now. It will only stir it all up again and we'll be in trouble for that for sure. You'll have to try and struggle on. Things will improve, I'm sure. It's only the older staff who are nervous of you. I've spoken to a lot of the others and they're not that bothered, believe me. It'll take a bit of time, but things will settle down.'

I looked at him in a disbelieving manner and shrugged my shoulders. 'Well, I can tell you it's getting to me, Richard. I don't know how long I can stand it.'

Richard's explanation of my position had depressed me because of the injustice of it all, but it had at least made me aware of the reason behind people's thinking. I was angry at the situation, which was partly of my own making, with a little help from Richard, but at least I was able to understand why I was getting the cold shoulder from some quarters. When I analysed a list I drew up of the members of staff whose attitude had changed markedly towards me, Richard was in fact correct in saying it was mainly the older teachers who featured. There were some exceptions, but in the main I could identify about the same number of friends as before. I had perhaps lost a few and gained a few. My main concern was that the ones I'd lost were those who were able to have some influence on my position on the promotion ladder. My relationship with Alistair Norton, never an entirely smooth running one, was a case in point. I was definitely now not one of the favoured ones, and it seemed as though some of the established staff to whom I had not really appealed before the Masterton affair were encouraged to be even less communicative towards me than before.

Anyway, I had no option but to buckle down to it and give of my best. I was still assisting with the Rugby 1st XV, although our fixture list was noticeable by the number of top school fixtures that had been cancelled. Radley, Harrow and Haileybury were gone, but we still had Tonbridge and Rugby. Many of the blanks had 'to be arranged' written alongside, so it was obviously going to be a difficult convalescence.

I was an object of curiosity in the classroom, particularly at the start of term when some of my questioners were embarrassingly blunt and to the point.

'Did you get the Headmaster sacked, sir?'

'No, I didn't. Get on with your test, Johnson.'

'My dad says you're a communist hangover, sir. Are you a lefty?'

'Do you think the Headmaster murdered the Bursar, sir?'

'Certainly not.'

'Was Mr Masterton gay, sir? Is that why he had to leave? Are you a member of Jack Simmonds' party, sir? My father says he's a crook.'

'What did the Bursar actually die of, sir? Was it the booze?'

God! I was dreading parents' evenings with all these presumptions flying about. I just hoped some of them might be the imaginings of young and fertile minds. Where there's smoke, there's fire though, no doubt many parents would be thinking.

Towards the end of the autumn term, I had an unexpected letter from Sir John Glazebrook. It took the form of an invitation to lunch for both myself and Christine on the day after Bradchester broke up. Would we join him at his club in London at twelve thirty, and he hoped we wouldn't mind but he had taken the liberty of squaring it with Miss Walkham's employer that she could have the whole day off?

Speculation as to what it might be about was top of the agenda at the Fisherman's Creel that evening, and Richard and Christine were as perplexed as I was, as we laid bets as to the reason for this 'call from the top'.

'He's going to sack you himself,' suggested Richard, half joking. 'Or to ask you to be Headmaster.'

'Maybe he'll ask me if this Richard Pilcher should be sacked,' I was able to counter.

'It's probably to ask you if Alistair Norton has started fiddling the books yet,' he replied.

Christine was more serious. 'Shut up a minute, both of you,' she said. 'It's most probably to get a staff viewpoint of how the school is coping after the changes. He's a "hands-on" chairman I should imagine, and needs a report from the "sharp end" – that's what you said he called you teachers.'

'It maybe something like that,' said Richard, 'but – you'll forgive me, Chris – why should he ask you both up there? Why not just telephone Alan?'

She smiled. 'Maybe he wants his club minders to rough us up a bit before they throw us in the Thames.'

'Ah, right. Get his own back, you mean. Yes, that I should like to see.'

Somehow the idea of Sir John still taking an interest cheered us all up, even though we couldn't be certain the meeting would be all sweetness and light. There may be repercussions concerning Masterton to be ironed out, in which case it would not be an easy visit. Sir John, however, carried an aura of fair play with him as far as I was concerned, and even if it was to be unpleasant, I felt there would be a justifiable explanation.

We were late getting to St James's as we had decided to drive to London, and had got stuck in a traffic jam. When we found the club, it was twenty past twelve, but it was going to take me at least half an hour to park. I therefore left Christine in the car and nipped inside to leave a message for Sir John. When I said who I was, a commissionaire was immediately dispatched to park the car for me, and I escorted Christine into the club. As we went through the doors, she nudged me to look back at the amusing sight of my grotty yellow Fiesta being driven away, sandwiched between a Rolls-Royce and a huge Mercedes with three doors on each side.

Sir John was as charming as ever and took a particular interest in Christine's well-being. He was obviously very taken with the way she'd stood her ground at the yacht club on that depressing day back in the summer, and he said as much. He also hoped she and I had forgiven him. He asked how things were at school and how I felt the staff in general were settling down.

'Shouldn't you be asking Mr Norton, the Acting Head?' I enquired.

'Well, naturally I have,' he said. 'But you see, Alan, I will only get the answers he wants me to have. With the best will in the world, nobody likes being the bearer of bad news. So I thought I'd ask you as well. A second opinion, if you like. You don't mind, do you?'

'Of course not. In fact I think all in all, people have settled down very well. It's early days yet, but teachers are the sort who don't like extra hassle if they can avoid it. Most of us will be wanting to put the past few weeks behind us and get on with the job of teaching in a settled environment. There is uncertainty about who will be the new Head of course, and what type of person the board will appoint. That's only to be expected. What's happened to Masterton by the way? I suppose he'll fall on his feet, that sort always seem to. Why wasn't he sacked? I understand he resigned.'

'Jumped before he was pushed you mean,' put in Christine. 'That usually means a deal was done regarding a future position.'

'Believe me,' said Sir John, 'You're not the first to make that observation. But in this instance it is not the case. You see, a felony was committed and Masterton knew it. Although the misdemeanour is unproven, it probably could be so, and indeed Masterton might have come to us with a proposal that he would only resign if he was assisted in getting another post. Otherwise we would have to dismiss him. We were not approached, and for your ears only, I understand he now likes to be thought of as a gentleman farmer, but is in fact employed as a manager on his brother-in-law's estate in Scotland. I could not divulge more,' he continued, 'without contravening the privacy of my board's discussions.' He looked at me directly. 'And I would suggest, Alan, that you leave it at that and concentrate on your own future and not Masterton's.'

Christine took my hand in hers. 'That's the best piece of advice you'll ever get,' she said. 'That man is history as far as you're concerned, and,' she winked at Sir John, 'will never be included in any future school syllabus of yours.'

I raised my glass to both of them. 'I'll drink to that,' I said.

'And what about you,' continued Sir John. 'How are you settling down?'

'I'll survive,' I said, 'although I can't pretend it's been easy. Time will tell, no doubt.'

He looked at Christine. 'Is he telling me the truth? I'm not convinced.'

'It's true it's not been easy,' she said, 'but he'll have to survive. There's nowhere else to go.'

He paused while the wine waiter recharged our glasses. 'I'll come clean with you, Alan,' he continued. 'I wanted to see you to ask your opinion as to how things were going at the school, but that wasn't the only reason. No, the other reason was that I've got wind that you're not happy.'

He waved my protest away. 'Don't ask me how... It's my business to know these things. It's my belief that you're being held responsible for Masterton's resignation, and that while most people will agree that that in itself was a good thing, the manner in which it was instigated, namely by your revelations, does not make you an easy companion to have about the place.'

'There are only a very few people who feel that,' I said.

'That maybe so, but it still could make life difficult for

you, particularly if those people are senior and inclined to be nervous of you where promotion prospects are concerned. Because of your involvement in last term's affairs, about which others will know little but no doubt speculate a lot, you may feel you're being held back through no fault of your own. Am I right?'

'Well, I don't know. I...'

'Ah! I thought so. Now, listen to me.' He pulled his chair a little closer to the table. He addressed himself to me, but included Christine in his next remarks.

'As Chairman of the new Board of Governors, I speak for all its members, as well as all the other trustees of the School in saying that Bradchester owes you a great debt of gratitude for your part in what happened last term. It may not seem like it to some, but believe me, Alan, if the whole sordid business had not come to light when it did, things would have been a great deal worse. It's a terrible mess now and it will take the school a long time to recover, for the full damage is yet to be assessed in terms of pupil numbers for the future. The trend in registrations is already markedly down, and there are a serious number of cancellations being made for the next few years.

'We will struggle to stay alive in this uncertain economic climate with the recession still very much with us. Nonetheless, thanks to the stubborn attitude you both took, together with your friend Richard Pilcher, we have a chance to survive. Without your determination to retain your rightful position here, things would have turned out to be much worse, and the possibility of closure would be very real.'

Christine and I sat motionless, and I wondered how the hell he knew about Richard's part in the affair.

He took in some more wine and continued. 'In the aftermath of an event such as this, with all its sinister overtones, the innocent parts played by some can be misconstrued. Fingers of suspicion can be pointed unjustly at those who in fact should be praised. You, Alan, are in the unfortunate position of being one such suspect, and therefore I would like to make a proposal to you.'

I looked at Christine for some sort of recognition of what he might be about to say, but her expression was as mystified as my own.

Sir John went on. 'You may or may not know that I happen to be a member of the governing body of several other large schools. Not as well known, or should I say notorious, as Bradchester, and I have explained the whole chapter of events, including your part in it to my colleagues on the board and to the Headmaster of one of them, namely Denley College in Gloucestershire. Of similar size and beginning to go places. Indeed, if it wasn't for its geographical location, it would certainly have got some of the match fixtures Bradchester has lost. They are crying out for a young, go-ahead history graduate with teaching experience, who wants a career position. Your sporting qualifications and track record are just right for that sort of school, and you may take it from me that I've put them right about the "Bradchester Syndrome" as far as you're concerned. Actually it is generally expected that there maybe a bit of an exodus of teachers from Bradchester until things settle down again.'

Christine's impatience got the better of her. 'What exactly are you saying, Sir John?'

He held up one hand. 'Just this,' he said. 'That job is yours, Alan, if you wish. I understand how you might think you would have difficulty obtaining another post, but actually, I think you could be exaggerating the problems. If you wanted to leave, however, your field might be more limited just at the moment, and I would not expect you to take on something on an impulse, just to get away from Bradchester in a hurry. That would be a waste of good talent and something where I would feel it my duty to intervene.'

His face took on that boyish smile I had seen as he was leaving the yacht club. 'So you see, yet again I am meddling in your affairs for my own benefit. An unfortunate habit of mine, tending to get me thrown out of reputable establishments.' He winked at Christine.

'But you know, if you aren't happy where you are, that post would be perfect for you, as well as a great catch for Denley, which would be a feather in my cap, wouldn't it?' His grin reached from ear to ear.

'However,' he continued, 'and there's always a catch isn't there? For my sins, I do happen to be Chairman of Bradchester as well, and as such it is my duty to endeavour to hang on to talented young teachers and not to tempt them away for the benefit of other schools. Good heavens, I should soon be booted out, and I'm not sure Bradchester could stand another change of chairman so soon!' He was grinning again.

'However, as I say, Bradchester needs people like you more than ever, and don't forget there'll be a new Head in January and I've got just the man. I won't tell you who it is because he's not agreed yet, but he will and I think you'll approve. It's not an easy job to fill as you can imagine. People aren't exactly falling over themselves to join what could be a sinking ship. But he's a man who wouldn't take anything on unless there's a worthwhile challenge and I think you'll find the atmosphere he'll create will make teachers such as yourself feel you're all working for the same side. Anyway, enough about that. Let me just plead with you not to be hasty. Give this new Head a chance. I will entirely understand though if you do leave, and it will not diminish the debt Bradchester owes you, providing of course, you take the post at Denley.'

He sat back, grinning broadly, and polished off the remains of his wine. 'You've hardly touched your steak, and you your sole, my dear. Anything wrong with them?'

'I don't know what to say,' I stammered feebly. 'You're always about three steps ahead of me.'

'Well, don't think about it now. Just enjoy your meal. The chef gets agitated if things are not exactly right. Would you like that heated up again?'

'No, it's fine. I'm so dumbstruck by how you seem to know everything that's going on, eating seems to be of secondary importance.'

He turned to Christine. 'And you, my dear. How's the sailing going? Are you as fearless on the water as you are in the clubhouse? It's 470s you race, isn't it? I wouldn't like to duel with you at ten paces with racing dinghies.'

'Well, actually, Sir John,' said Christine, 'I've had a good year. So good in fact that subject to my office agreeing to a bit more time off, I'm looking for a suitable girl as crew next year to see if we can perform well enough to make the International events. 470s are an Olympic ladies class, you see, and I'm keen to give it a go.'

'Well, I wish you luck, young lady. I gather you've got a new hobby, Alan.'

'What do you mean?'

'Fly fishing.'

'What!' There's absolutely no way you could know...'

He was roaring with laughter at my complete amazement and tapping the side of his nose in a gesture of conspiracy. 'Ah, well, you see, Godfrey Baines-Fawcett just happens to be a chum of mine. We were at school together and he told me you helped him land a four-and–a-half-pounder down at Masterton's place. We were chatting about this and that, you know.'

'I'll bet,' said Christine. 'He rang you up just to talk about fishing, of course. Nothing to do with Masterton.'

'Well...a four-and-a-half pound brownie on the Test is certainly newsworthy to some people, and I'm a bit of a fisherman myself. But you're right, he did also impart a little piece of inside information obtained by his daughter-in-law, Joanna Calverton. Purely City press tongues wagging, you understand. Helpful to me though.'

'About Hedley, I suppose,' I said.

'Godfrey told me you showed great aptitude with a fly rod,' he said, steering the subject back to fishing. 'You should keep it up. Very helpful when under stress, I find.'

On the way home in the car, Christine and I discussed what he'd said about the post at Denley. It certainly sounded attractive and there was no doubt that I was unsettled at Bradchester.

'How the devil did he find out about me being unhappy?' I said to her.

'I should have thought it was obvious,' she said, giving me a superior look. 'Richard, of course.'

'What do you mean "Richard, of course"?'

'Well... his uncle's in the City, isn't he? Everybody knows

everybody else there, and Richard is very conscious of his part in putting you through all this aggravation. He feels responsible and is upset to see you so cut up about it. A simple call to his uncle would probably reach Sir John's ears in no time. They might even be fishing pals as well.' Her voice held a touch of sarcasm. 'Are you really going to take up the sport?'

'Don't know,' I said. 'Seems as though if you want to know what's going on in the world, you've got to be a fisherman, doesn't it? It is rather a compelling pastime, I must say.'

'More so than sailing, would you say?' She pouted at me.

'Both exciting, in different ways. What's all this about next year and a girl crew and international events? Are you serious?'

'I was thinking of having a crack at it, yes. Everyone I've talked to seems to think I'm good enough. I've nearly completed my legal executive exams and if my employers agree, and I could get a really good girl of the right weight and a good enough boat, I think it's possible.'

'What's wrong with your own boat?'

'Too old. Okay for club or maybe national racing, but you need the very latest hull, sails and high-tech equipment, and all the back-up to go international racing, and plenty of time off. It's a bit of a pipe dream. Pull up in this lay-by, would you, Alan?'

'What for?'

'Please, Alan.'

When we had stopped, she turned to look at me with her big, dark enquiring eyes that I could see were full of tears. 'Will you be taking that job in Gloucestershire?' she said.

'No, of course not,' I assured her. 'At any rate not until I've seen what a difference this new Head that Sir John has got up his sleeve makes. I'll have until April to make up my mind, anyway.'

She threw her arms around my neck and said that she was so glad as she thought she was going to lose me, she'd never get a job in Gloucestershire and she didn't want me to turn it down just for her sake. It all came flooding out how she'd been so upset to see me so unhappy, she'd discussed it with Richard, she hoped I wouldn't be cross and she was sure I was making the right decision.

I held her very tight and told her how much I loved her. She wiped her eyes and we set off again with me wondering what I'd done to deserve this girl with her incredible strength of feeling for me. When I asked her, she scolded me, and told me not to underestimate myself.

In my letter to Sir John thanking him for lunch, I told him how grateful I was for the offer of an alternative post and for his taking the trouble to arrange it for me. I would, however, be staying at Bradchester and would see how things turned out.

I bought a bottle of very expensive whisky for Richard, told him what a sod he was to rat on me, and thanked him profusely. He beamed expansively and said something about looking after our own, as he produced two tumblers. We polished off most of the bottle that night, our speech becoming more and more slurred as we elaborated on the brilliance of women and the ineptitude of fraudulent headmasters, finally being unable to understand what the other was saying.

Chapter 16

Sir John and his Board of Governors had their new headmaster in place by the beginning of the Lent term, and Colonel Trent's replacement had in fact taken up his post on 15th December. Richard and I had been slightly worried, in view of Sir John's comments at our lunch meeting, that the new Head might be a whirlwind type, prone to sweeping everything away regardless and commencing his reign with a clean slate. He would have to be a resilient person for sure, as he was taking on what Sir John had rightly described as a 'sinking ship'. Single-mindedness would also have to feature strongly in his make-up. We hoped he would be briefed by the board to take enough time to discover all Bradchester's good points, of which there were many, whilst uncovering and pruning away the bad. What we didn't need was a risk taker for a Head. The board, under the capable guidance of Sir John would, we hoped, take care of that side of things.

Our fears were proved groundless. Matthew Fairchild was a listener first and foremost, and an able delegator once he had gathered the right team around him. But, above all, he had the invaluable gift of getting the best out of those under him. He didn't bombard us with speeches about how he expected undying loyalty or how he looked forward to our total support. He was one who believed that loyalty, like respect, has to be earned and he wouldn't be stamping his theories on anything until he'd heard from those who had lived and breathed Bradchester long before he arrived on the scene.

He was a tall man of slightly advanced years for a newly appointed headmaster. Fifty-two to be exact, and his three children were all grown-up and either postgraduate or still at university. He had a slight limp, which gave him an apologetic air at a distance, but in conversation he would invite your point of view by inclining his head and fixing you with a shrewd and enquiring gaze. He made you want to express your views and opinions, and was skilful in sifting through them and discarding with logic and courtesy those that did not appeal.

At first, Richard and I were relieved rather than immediately impressed by his appointment. He was easy to talk to and always seemed to have time to chat. I suppose it was his skill as an administrator or maybe the fact that he couldn't walk very fast that gave one the feeling that everything was done at a stroll. As time went on, I did become impressed. Not only did I feel comfortable with him personally, but I began to see how his ideas and the way he handled people meant that if Bradchester was to survive, he would have a lot to do with it. I also began to understand what an astute choice Sir John Glazebrook and his board had made.

Unfortunately for all of us, the damage had been done to Bradchester just at the time when every public school, even without any self-inflicted wounds, was suffering from a decline in pupil numbers brought about by the economic recession. It was no secret that ours had fallen too far for us to survive unless they were somehow recouped. There had been some redundancies, mainly affecting the boarding services. Matrons and catering staff had been cut back, and some capital building projects, such as an AstroTurf pitch and a new athletics track had been deferred.

Despite this, I was finding life much less stressful in the classroom and common room, and although we were all looking over our shoulders at the pupil population, I found myself relaxed and more confident with my colleagues. The year had turned a full circle. The general election, eventually called in April, had come and gone and the summer term was once again with us. Cricket, swimming, GCSEs, A levels, pints at the Fisherman's Creel in the evenings, and weekends at the yacht club. There was some normality returning to my life.

The 1st XI had done well in its first few matches, due in no small measure to young Hedley's success with the bat. John Tanner, his Housemaster, had told me that following Masterton's departure, the boy had been put fully in the picture about the false accusations of homosexuality against him, and their connection with his father's unfortunate suspension as a commodity broker in the City. The new Board of Governors had agreed that, in the event of his father having difficulty paying school fees from now on, the boy himself should not suffer the consequences of others' actions and should be granted a bursary to enable him to complete his education at Bradchester. The youngster had regained his confidence and trust in others, and it was evident at the wicket at least, where he was currently averaging over 50.

Christine had found her new girl crew, and had really made an impression. With her old boat, the two of them had worked hard during the winter and spring and were now a fine team. They were encouraged by Christine's employer and supported by the club as much as possible and had travelled extensively to take part in the races that mattered. The word was, that with the right equipment they could go all the way, and work through national and world events, and even make the Olympics in 1996. Christine was philosophical about it, however, and kept reminding me that there were loads of 470 girl crews they would never be able to beat without a new boat.

'But you're doing so well,' I assured her. 'Everybody knows you're as quick as hell and have the potential.'

She looked at me sadly over her lager. 'I'm afraid potential and being quick isn't enough. Right at the very top in any sport that involves equipment these days, you've got the best people, and the not so good. Even the not so good are pretty talented. But they've all got two things in common, the latest equipment and the financial backup to go with it. Look at motor racing. There are loads of guys with stacks of talent in this country, but very few will make it to the very top. Remember that Italian girl who got a Grand Prix drive? Loads of money, but she couldn't even do the qualifying time to get on the grid. We're going to go on trying though. Somebody may notice us, but they certainly won't if we're not racing.' She smiled at me over the rim of her glass. 'It's fun, anyway. Wouldn't do it if it wasn't, would we?'

I desperately wanted to help her and had even been to the yacht club on my own to talk to some of the members, trying to establish how one went about looking for sponsors and financial backers for the sport. It seemed that everyone was after the same thing and it was the usual chicken and egg situation. Big sponsorship was hard to find unless you were already successful, and you couldn't be successful unless you had the finance to acquire and run the best equipment. Everybody agreed that Christine had the talent and the stickability to win at the highest level, but so far nobody had come up with the right kind of support.

I decided as a last resort to approach my 'man with friends in high places', only to find that as usual Richard had already thought of it.

'Bit of a long shot,' he said, 'but I've put the word out. Trouble is, the City isn't into small sponsorship of that sort, particularly at this time. The recession is biting hard and most companies are too busy just surviving or fighting off takeovers to be investing in chancy undertakings like that. Not much hope, I'm afraid.'

About the middle of May it became evident that something was up at school by way of planning for new buildings or that the sporting facilities were at last to be forthcoming. Surveyors and architects were to be seen wandering all over the school with Sir John's various new board members. They were poking about in corners of courtyards and at the far end of the playing fields, but nobody could get a word out of any of them as to what was afoot. Rumours began to spread. Perhaps another school was to join forces with us. Maybe we were to build conference facilities to host holiday conventions. Possibly a junior school was to be incorporated into the campus. Closure of the entire school might be imminent, and developers were assessing the value.

With such speculation rife throughout the staff, I knew it wouldn't be long before some sort of announcement would be made. It came in the form of a specially convened meeting of all staff at which Sir John and almost all his governors were present. There had clearly been an enormous amount of work done behind the scenes that had been kept a well-guarded secret for many months. As the Headmaster called the meeting to order and, without any preamble or beating about the bush, made his announcement, you could have heard a pin drop in the hall.

As from September the following year, Bradchester would be taking girls.

It was to be a last ditch effort to save the school, but not one that had been decided upon without an immense amount of thought and preparation. Things were looking so bad apparently that there was really no choice. Sir John and the new Headmaster and Bursar had come up with an extensive framework of proposals which would incorporate girls into the school at the age of eleven, and a stringent but manageable financial package had been arranged with a consortium of home and overseas financial institutions to underwrite them. Hence the planning, surveying and poking about in corners all related to the introduction of facilities for young ladies alongside and interwoven with those of the boys.

'Over my dead body,' was an expression commonly heard from the older staff during the next week or two, but realistically speaking, I thought it was a brilliant idea, and the most likely to keep Bradchester's teachers in full employment if it succeeded. It was a gamble, of course, but the alternative was unthinkable, and the majority of the staff were of the opinion that, in the circumstances and with the amount of adroit and professional thinking with which Sir John had surrounded the proposals, it was a gamble worth taking. Bradchester wouldn't be the first boys public school to break with tradition in this way. Girls in the sixth form had been the norm for some years in many cases, and full incorporation at a younger age was no longer the forbidden transgression of yesteryear.

There was to be a massive publicity campaign starting in the second half of the summer term that would launch the recruitment of girls in September of the following year. Building of additional facilities and modification of existing ones would commence immediately term ended, and these would include one new girls' boarding house, with another in the pipeline should registrations of the fair sex justify it.

The bombshell about Bradchester going co-ed was delivered to us just before half-term, and it coincided with the time that Richard had gone all uncommunicative on me and Christine. He knew something we didn't and it made me livid. All he would say was that it did have something to do with my resolve to stay on at Bradchester and was also connected indirectly with the decision to take girls.

'I can't say any more, Alan, so don't press me. It's not that I know any more than you could deduce, but simply that I've been asked not to confirm or deny any assumptions you might have as to what the future holds for any of us here.'

'That is the most pompous bit of ambiguity I've heard for years,' I said. 'What in God's name are you talking about?'

'Look, Alan,' he pleaded. 'It's not my fault I just happen to have influential relations. It's no big deal, honestly. People have been asking my opinion about things here, that's all. I just happen to be in the know about a couple of minor projects to do with the school which I can't talk about. Sorry, old chap, subject closed.'

'You're bloody infuriating, Richard Pilcher. If you won't

divulge any more than that, I'd appreciate it if you wouldn't hint that there was anything up in the first place.'

He gave me a supercilious grin. 'Be patient, young man. Have faith in your superiors.'

I stamped off in a fury.

Chapter 17

On the Saturday during half-term there was a barbecue at the yacht club in the evening. Christine and I had been very late getting there owing to the fact that on her way to the barbecue, a friend of hers had had a car accident some twenty miles away. Nothing serious, was the message, but could Christine please pick her up as she was stranded. I'd gone with her, but on reaching the place, it transpired that the car was hardly damaged and the girl had driven it to the yacht club after all.

Christine was a bit miffed as she was supposed to be organising a cadets' presentation at the club and we would now be a good hour late. When we arrived, she sensed something was amiss as there were some strangers' cars parked in front of the club and a lorry blocking the entrance to the dinghy park. As she ran towards the clubhouse, a couple of members told her there was a problem, and as sailing secretary would she please go in the back way and straight into the committee room. She ran ahead of me, and one of the members, who I recognised as Pete Matlock, took me aside.

'It's a surprise for Chris,' he said, 'and you for that matter. Now don't ask questions, just go into the committee room and do as you're told.'

I certainly had a shock as I entered that room. Richard was there, and Sir John Glazebrook, Matthew Fairchild, the new Bursar, two other School Governors who were both ladies, and two men I didn't recognise. Christine was sitting down opposite Sir John and wearing an expression of complete confusion.

'What's happened?' I said.

'Nothing. Just sit down and shut up,' said Richard with a huge grin. 'Sorry about the phoney accident, by the way. Didn't want you here earlier than this.'

They were all grinning.

'Now! I think we're all here,' said Sir John, 'and I'll be brief. You're wanting to get on with the party and so am I.'

I looked at Richard. He was gazing at the ceiling and his mouth formed a silent whistle. He looked as guilty as hell.

'Miss Walkham – Christine, if I may – we would like you to help us. These ladies and gentlemen form part of a finance and publicity committee set up to promote the inclusion of girls at Bradchester. We are determined to succeed in this venture and are prepared to back our judgement with hard business expertise and hard cash.'

He paused and turned to address the rest of us. 'We need an outstanding young lady to carry the female image that will, in fifteen months' time become an integral part of the school. Someone with whom our pupils, perhaps not only girls but boys also, will be able to identify. We are going all out to become the top co-educational independent school in the country. We have the determination, the financial backing, the ideas and the right people to carry them out. Now we need the best person to help convey that image of success to prospective parents. I would like to ask you to be that person, Christine.'

She was speechless. So was I.

'But I don't know how I can...' she stammered.

'Of course you do,' beamed Sir John. 'You want to have a crack at the 1996 Olympics, don't you? Well, I want you to win the gold medal.'

She stared at him without moving or making any sound. No-one said a word. It was the most deafening silence I had ever heard.

'I... I don't think you quite understand, Sir John.'

'And I want you to win lots of other medals along the way.'

'But I haven't got the right...'

'Of course you have, my dear. Show her, gentlemen, would you? Step this way, young lady.'

Christine was helped over to the window overlooking the waterfront and slipway. I peered over everyone's shoulder to see what it was.

Now I knew what the lorry was doing blocking the entrance to the dinghy park. It had disgorged its cargo, which was on a trailer at the top of the slipway. A brand new Ziegelmeyer 470, with the very latest and very expensive race-winning Ullman sails. Next to it was a long banner with the five Olympic rings and underneath in huge letters. CHRISTINE WALKHAM. GO FOR IT CHRIS!

'Oh my God! Oh my God! You can't mean it... You can't.'

Sir John reassured her. 'Now you know I'm not the sort of man to deal in false promises, my dear. Get her a brandy, somebody, would you? I'll explain the details later.'

Christine had slumped down in a chair. 'Tell me I'm not dreaming, someone.'

'We thought this was a good time to let you in on our little secret, and I do hope you can help us,' he said. 'Very simply... all we want you to do is to go sailing. It's our way of saying thank you to Alan and yourself for what you did for the school during a most unfortunate period a year ago. The board are determined to show their gratitude, and I'm told by Richard here that Alan won't mind if Christine seems to reap more benefit than himself. He would want it that way I'm informed. As usual however, there is a little self-interest in the arrangements the committee and I have made.

'You will be given every support to go all the way. This will include the provision of a new boat every year, subject to your success of course, and the latest equipment to make you competitive at the very top. You will have transport for yourself and your team, and I have made a part-time arrangement for you with the senior partners of your firm. You will run the team and it will be your baby and it will be in your name. We have to keep the thing as amateur as the regulations require, therefore we are not officially sponsoring you. It is, by way of a gift from a very grateful school, and an investment in the future of the feminine gender at Bradchester. You will be the school's adopted international sportswoman, and if you are successful, I want you to have the same facilities as anyone else racing in the women's 470 class at world level. I know you can make the Great Britain team and the Olympics in 1996 and can go all the way, and I want you to help me and Bradchester do the same.'

He broke off. 'Now, enough of this nonsense. Let's get on with the party.'

The door was thrown open and Christine was ushered through into the bar of the clubhouse. The strains of 'For she's a jolly good fellow' echoed across the estuary from the verandah doors as she was hoisted onto strong shoulders and carried down to the slipway to inspect her new charge. Sir John allowed her two minutes, before suggesting that he would not be a gentleman on this occasion, and would be delighted to encourage the throwing of Christine and me into the drink in the appropriate manner.

Next morning, being a Sunday, I persuaded Christine to accompany me over to the school as I had something I wanted to attend to. We drove from Thaxbury almost in silence, still smarting from the previous night's proceedings. As we entered the school gates, I could hear the sound I was hoping for. The chapel organ was being played, probably by one of the organ scholars who was putting half-term to good use. I took Christine by the hand and led her into the aisle until I reached my allotted pew. Placing her next to me I whispered that a year ago I'd sat here quietly on my own, desperately wanting to be able to say that this seat belonged to me but believing that I would never see Bradchester again.

'I believe it's yours now,' she said, as the soothing strains of that hypnotic instrument engulfed us with their peace and tranquillity. 'I have a feeling you're safe at last.'

The organ suddenly stopped, and as a ray of late spring sunlight moved over the deserted pews opposite, it began the first haunting bars of Parry's 'I was Glad'.

I turned to Christine as the music swelled into that first chorus opening, and where, twelve months ago I'd heard those voices willing me to 'go into the House of the Lord'.

'It's the same,' I said. 'It's the same as before.' I had tears in my eyes, and she did the very thing she'd done on the first night we'd met – she gently put her hand up to my mouth. 'Don't, Alan,' she whispered. 'Just listen.'